Also By T.E. Harkins

Egret's Loft Murder Mystery Series

Unnatural Causes

The Dead Men's Wife

Serial Seniors

Raven's Wing Murder Mystery Series

Strange Winds

This is a work of fiction. Names, characters, places, and incidents either are the product of the author's imagination or are used fictitiously. Any resemblance to actual persons, living or dead, events, or locales is entirely coincidental.

Copyright © 2022 by T.E. Harkins

All rights reserved. No part of this book may be reproduced or used in any manner without written permission of the copyright owner except for the use of quotations in a book review. For more information, address: teharkins.author@gmail.com.

Cover design by Joe Montgomery

THE DEAD MEN'S WIFE

An Egret's Loft Murder Mystery

T.E. HARKINS

CHARLES FORT PRESS

One

Gorgeous November day in the tropics? Check.

Multi-tiered, red velvet cake, frosted and delivered? Check.

White dress for a decidedly un-virginal and post-menopausal bride? Check.

The hot, steamy Florida air hums with excitement as the elderly residents of Egret's Loft, so recently rattled by the murders of two of their own, gather for the wedding of Helen Richards and Carl Hancock.

"At least we know it's not a shotgun wedding," my new friend, Gina, whispers to me, stepping out of the way of an anxious-looking young woman struggling under the weight of an enormous flower arrangement.

"True. It would be physically impossible for Helen to be

pregnant," I concede. "But Carl's got to be in his eighties. He can't be sure how much time he has left, so I suppose the same urgency applies."

The pace of the wedding planning had been nothing short of frenetic. The groom's niece, Tiffany—who also happens to be the activities director at Egret's Loft—has put the entire wedding together in less than a week.

The River Club banquet hall has been magically transformed into a kind of fairytale kingdom. On steroids. It's so over-the-top Disney themed, I can't help but wonder if I'll be charged $7 for a soda here too.

"I don't know that he should be quite so anxious to walk this particular bride down the aisle. The odds aren't exactly in his favor," Gina points out.

She's not wrong.

Helen's been married seven times already, but never divorced. All her husbands died, though I can't say whether the circumstances were suspicious or not. Given that I moved into the upscale retirement community less than two weeks ago, it seems a bit forward to ask the bride-to-be how all the past Mr. Richards met their ends.

Having already been on the receiving end of her temper, it's not a stretch to imagine her bumping off one, or even two, of them. But it's her wedding day. Not the right time to debate whether she's a homicidal lunatic. So I keep my mouth shut.

After bumping her head on a particularly low-hanging

balloon, Gina reaches up to adjust the royal blue, lace fascinator perched like an exotic bird on her shoulder-length gray hair. The hat perfectly matches her tailored skirt-suit, both of which pop against her umber-colored skin.

"Why did Holly want to see you before the ceremony anyway?" she asks, battling the string from the balloon that assaulted her.

"Helen! Her name is Helen. Can't you at least try to get it right today?"

Gina has a habit of forgetting the names of everyone she meets, including Leon, her own husband of forty years —whose name is actually Luis. She remembers *a* name, it's just never *that person's* name. In the short time I've known her, I've grown to accept that I will always be "Mandy" to her, even though my name is Madeline.

Still, a woman should be called by her own name on her wedding day.

"Helen. Holly. What's the big deal?" Gina waves off my concern. "What I don't understand is why she asked to see you before the ceremony. Less than two weeks ago, she wanted to skin you alive!"

"Well, to be fair, I did pop one of her breast implants," I remind Gina. It wasn't intentional, just an unfortunate golfing accident. Understandably, Helen hadn't taken too kindly to me after that first meeting. All was forgiven, though, when I saved her from dating a sociopath.

"She seems to think I'm the reason she and Carl ended

up together," I say, though I'm not particularly eager to claim credit. "She asked if she could borrow something blue for the day. That's why we're going to see her now. I need to give it to her."

Somewhere behind us, a musician runs through the scales, warming up on their harp.

"Something borrowed *and* something blue?" Gina scoffs. "That's kinda lazy, don't you think? Asking you for both."

"Not at all. I'm happy to help."

"You know your problem, Mandy? You're too nice. She's only asking you because she's not exactly spoiled for choice when it comes to friends."

"Shhhh!" I shoosh her. "You're not supposed to speak ill of the bride!"

"The dead."

My heart beats faster. "Who's dead?"

Gina rolls her eyes. "No. The saying is not to speak ill of the dead. Which, given her track record, would mean I shouldn't speak ill of the *groom*," Gina says, loud enough that one of the flower arrangers sends a disgusted frown in our direction.

I stop walking, partially because someone is relocating a large, balloon arch in front of us and partially for dramatic effect. "If you can't play nice, I'm going to have to leave you out here while I go in to see Helen."

"Fine, I'll behave." Gina pouts. "What are you going to loan her anyway?"

"That was a problem, since most of my things are still back at my house in DC. All I have here that's blue are my lisinopril pills."

"Oh, I used to take those. They made my tongue swell, so my doctor switched me to Lotensin," Gina says. "But really? Your something borrowed is blood pressure medication?"

"No, of course not! I had my son Ritchie go by the house in DC and pick something up for me. He sent it with that overnight delivery. The price was on the box. It's highway robbery what the post office charges these days!"

Gina shakes her head. "I remember when it cost six cents to send a letter."

"Here we are!" My hand rests on the handle of the door leading to Helen's makeshift dressing room. "Be good!"

Gina sticks her tongue out at me but quickly retracts it as I open the door.

Helen stands in front of a full-length mirror, turning this way and that, trying to get a view on all her angles. She's not alone. In the corner, a woman is packing up a makeup case, and a vibrantly dressed young man rolls up the cord of a curling iron. Both give me wan smiles as I enter.

"Madeline! Bless your heart, you're just in time!" Helen

gushes after spotting my reflection in the mirror. Turning around, she sees my companion and adds a curt, "Oh, hi there, Gina."

"Congratulations, Holl...en," Gina corrects herself mid-word.

"Oh, Helen! You look...beautiful!" I say.

And she does. Her long bleached-blond hair is curled and partially pulled back. Her gown is a vibrant white silk-and-lace creation that clings to her hourglass curves. It would all be so tasteful, if only the bodice wasn't so low-cut you can practically see the scars from her breast implants.

But, as my late husband Clint always used to say about women who opted for plastic surgery, if you've bought it, flaunt it.

"Thank you, sugar," she purrs in her thick Southern drawl. "Though I may be getting too mature for all this wedding nonsense. I've got a few more lines on my face this time around."

"Stop now. You don't look a day over forty-five," I exaggerate. Her numerous face lifts and Botox injections have certainly done wonders, but they're still no match for gravity. "How are you feeling?"

She picks up one of the wedding programs Carl's niece had printed for the occasion and starts fanning herself. "I'm so nervous, I'm sweatin' like a sinner in church!"

Gina opens her mouth to speak, but, afraid of what she

might say, I quickly cut her off. "There's no reason to be nervous! This is a happy day! Just try to relax and enjoy it. Oh! Doesn't Mitsy look precious!"

Helen's Pomeranian sits quietly at her feet. Mitsy has on her own silk-and-lace gown with a pillow perched on her back. Strings hang loose from the cushion, likely where the wedding rings will be attached for the ceremony.

"Doesn't she just?" Helen beams, then turns to the young woman in the corner. "Tanya, would you be a peach and pour me and my friends a glass of champagne?"

"Ummm...sure," Tanya replies, looking longingly at the makeup case she seems eager to depart with. "But if you want me to stay longer, we'll go into overtime."

"Fine, fine!" Helen waves a perfectly fake-tanned hand. "Not a problem. Now, Madeline. Do you have something for me? Nothing too fancy, though, I hope!" It's clear she means the opposite.

"I do! My Clint bought it for me ages ago to wear to a policeman's ball. I really hope you like it."

I reach into the little silk handbag I bought for this occasion and pull out a hair clip studded with blue and white sapphires. Clint had saved up for months to buy it for me. He loved my then-natural blond hair and said it deserved only the finest adornment.

"Well, butter my butt and call me a biscuit!" Helen exclaims. "It's gorgeous! Will you put it on for me?"

She turns around and I clip the barrette into her hair. By the time my arthritic fingers manage to secure the clasp, the woman named Tanya, who's clearly been waiting for me to finish my task, practically shoves a flute of champagne into my hand. Gina and Helen are already holding theirs.

"To you and Carl!" I announce, before Gina can congratulate the wrong couple.

"Yes, congrats!" Gina chimes in, her dark eyes glistening.

There are still a few sips left in our glasses when a knock comes on the door, and Carl's rotund niece pops her head in the door.

"Only me, only me!" Tiffany practically sings the words with theatrical enthusiasm. "It's nearly time! Are you ready to do this?"

Helen smiles. "Ready as I'll ever be!"

"Great! I'll go now and make sure the groom is in place. You don't have bridesmaids or groomsmen, so as soon as the theme song from *Beauty and the Beast* starts playing, you walk down the aisle. Walk slowly, though, because I want to sing the whole song before you get to the altar!"

When she pauses to catch her breath, Gina and I excuse ourselves to find our seats.

As we join the crowd of people now gathered in the banquet hall, Gina bumps her head on another balloon and whispers, "You know, for all the murders at Egret's Loft, someone could have done us a favor and killed the clown who turned this place into a Disney cartoon."

In the throes of celebratory fervor, neither Gina, nor any of the other guests assembling, would have ever imagined that, by the end of the day, another one of us would be dead.

Two

"I'm about to knock whoever did this so hard, they'll see tomorrow today!"

Newly married Helen, her face purple with rage, storms over to the DJ booth set up next to the outdoor swimming pool. Carl follows behind, trying to calm her down.

"I know you didn't marry me for my money," he pleads. "That's all that *really* matters."

Someone had put in a request for a song about a gold-digging female who won't give the time of day to "broke" men. The beat is pretty catchy. Marjorie Higginbottom is doing a slow-motion version of what, I'm told, kids these days call twerking. Whatever that means. Luckily, she has her walker to lean on for support as she enjoys the song.

But Helen is furious, thinking one of her guests is trying to humiliate her.

Sitting surprisingly close to the head table, I heard them talking as soon as the song came on over the big speakers. Carl said to let it go; it was just a bad joke. Helen, nearly tearing her hair out in rage, vowed to kick whoever requested it out of their reception.

"Uh-oh! Trouble in paradise already?" Roy Everhard's booming voice echoes from somewhere above my head.

I turn and have to tilt my head back to stare up at his balding head. He's a giant of a man, which he would have had to be in his younger days when he played quarterback for multiple NFL franchises.

"Nothing that won't blow over, I'm sure," I say, my tone defensive.

Every resident at Egret's Loft had accepted invitations to come to the wedding, but now that they're here, all they seem to want to do is badmouth the bride. I can't help feeling sympathy for Helen.

Roy, for all his thick-headedness, has the good grace to look chastened. "Of course, of course. Couldn't be happier for them. Quite the party they put together, too, in less than a week. Not really...my style, but it sure must have taken a fair bit of work."

"I couldn't agree more," I tell him with a conspiratorial smile.

It's hard to imagine whose style the wedding would have suited. The ceremony itself had been beyond excessive. As Helen walked painfully slowly down the aisle, Tiffany—or Bubbles, as I was told she likes to be called—belted out a rendition of "Tale as Old as Time" worthy of a cruise ship cabaret. Jinny Myrtle gave two readings, interlaced with some of her own folksy Canadian commentary. The vows between Carl and Helen were so heavily laced with double entendre, my face felt like it was on fire. And then, when it finally came time to exchange rings, Mitsy followed a trail of heart-shaped treats to the altar, stopping along the way to lift her leg on Stan Polotski's shoes.

Some guests laughed, some guests snored, and several of the guests had sneezing fits from all the flowers around the room.

"I would ask you to dance," Roy says, "but I got two right feet and I'm left-handed."

My feet, already sore from standing for most of the day, thank him for his awkwardness. "Just as well, I'm perfectly happy sitting down."

"I'll be heading out shortly anyway. Weddings aren't for me." Roy prides himself on being a lifelong bachelor. "We still on for a day out on the water tomorrow?"

"I'll be there." I smile, trying to pretend like I'm looking forward to it. I'd agreed to the outing in a moment of sentimental weakness and now can't find a graceful way out of the excursion.

"Great." He smiles back. "Pick you up at one o'clock. See you tomorrow."

He walks off and I find myself alone at the table.

Gina and her husband, Leon, are out on the dance floor. He's still in a wheelchair following double knee replacements, but it looks like they're having fun.

It's nearly eight o'clock, and after a day full of free drinks, everyone will likely be headed home soon. It's already past most of their bedtimes. I look around, trying to find Helen to congratulate her one last time, but I can't spot her anywhere.

It could take a while to get my golf cart out of the crowded parking lot, so I decide to make a quick stop in the ladies' room before taking one more stab at finding Helen. As I walk out into the foyer, where the fancier restrooms are located, I catch a glimpse of a tall, elegant woman with light gray hair and milk-pale skin on the other side of the main doors.

As she steps under the outdoor chandelier, I get a clearer image of her through the door's glass panels. She has large brown eyes, a dainty nose, and a high forehead. Her head is held aloft on a slender neck. Her movements are effortlessly graceful, almost as if she's floating on air.

I can't remember having ever seen her before, but the same could be said for most of the people inside at Helen's reception. It probably wouldn't hurt to start meeting people who don't live on Cypress Point Avenue, the circular street I now call home.

Deep in thought and staring out at the beautiful stranger, I nearly trip on the rug covering the marble-tiled floor. Despite having tried to pace myself with the champagne, I'm feeling a little tipsy as I enter the powder room —decorated with a few vanity tables, a loveseat, and very flattering lighting. It's empty as I pass through, pushing open the next door into a room full of stalls and sinks.

The older I get, the more I seem to find myself in rooms just like this one. In a way, I suppose, elderly people become almost connoisseurs of public toilets. You learn to find where all the best ones are. Which ones have the softest toilet paper, which ones are always out of hand soap, and which ones have those horrendous hand dryers that feel like they're about to rip the flesh from your bones, but never seem to actually dry your hands.

Fortunately, Egret's Loft still provides real towels.

By the time I make my way back into the powder room, it's no longer empty. Selena Fuentes, a.k.a. Selena Castillo, sits in front of one of the vanity table mirrors, applying lipstick. It looks like she might have lost a few pounds, though it's difficult to tell under the folds of her loose-fitting pastel caftan. It would make sense, though; she probably wasn't eating as well during her brief stint in prison the week before last.

"Selena, it's so nice to see you again!" I slowly

approach her. "I don't know if you remember me. I'm Madeline. I live three houses up from you on the other side of the street."

"I know," Selena says in a thick Colombian accent. She focuses her attention back on her lipstick.

"Are you enjoying the party?" I ask.

"Yes."

In my experience, Selena doesn't say much. But I suppose the ability to keep your mouth shut is a valuable trait for the wife of a Colombian drug lord. Not that they're still married! No, Alvaro Castillo was assassinated by a rival cartel ages ago.

Selena and Alvaro had a son, who was also a drug lord. But he died too. Just last year.

"I know it's not my place," I admit, "but I did want to say I'm really sorry about what happened to your son."

Her son, Jesus, was murdered in prison while serving time for money laundering. We only found all of this out because Selena was being investigated as the prime suspect in the murder of my next-door neighbor. Turned out, she didn't do it. But by that point, it was far too late to un-blow her cover.

At the mention of her son, Selena pauses and looks down at her hands. "*Gracias.*"

It's hard to tell, because the lighting really does make her eyes seem to sparkle, but I would swear Selena has tears in her eyes. How is her eyeliner not even smudging?

And, come to think of it, her face looks flawless. I wonder if she's using that foundation I love!

"This might not be the best time to ask," I acknowledge, "but I was curious, are you still selling Mary Kay cosmetics?"

When she was arrested, very publicly on our street, cops and the DEA had seized boxes of Mary Kay makeup from her garage. They thought she was using makeup as a cover to smuggle in illicit drugs. In reality, it was just makeup. The only cover it provided was for undereye bags and wrinkles.

"*Absolutamente, si!*" She turns to face me, suddenly seeming to come to life. "*Necesitas maquillaje?* Sorry. I try English. What makeup you need?"

"Well, I used to have this foundation that was wonderful. Now, I can't remember the name, because it was quite a while ago, but I know it was Mary Kay, and I was hoping they might still make it!"

Selena stares at me with vacant eyes. She has no idea what I just said. I try again. This time slower and much, much louder.

"I. Need. Foundation. I. Can't. Remember. The. Name. Do. You—" at this, I point at her, "—Still. Sell. It?"

"No need to scream. My hearing is okay," Selena says. "You want to buy foundation, *si?*"

"Yes! *Si!*"

"I going out of town. Meet Tuesday? My house? Morning time?"

"Wonderful, yes. I'll be there!"

With this, Selena puts her lipstick back in her purse and stands up. I follow her out of the powder room and back into the party. She curls her lips in what I assume is an attempt at a smile and walks off, toward the poolside dance floor.

I linger in the banquet hall, still decorated for the earlier ceremony. There's no one inside, so I follow Selena out toward the swimming pool, scanning for Helen so I can say goodbye.

After several minutes, I'm about to give up and head for my golf cart. The sun has gone down and, even with the outdoor fairy lights strung above the dance floor, it's hard to make out faces. There are too many people crowded together—most gathering up their things to leave—to even spot Helen's bright white wedding gown.

The DJ stops playing music and makes an announcement over the speakers, asking for the bride and groom to come forward for one final dance. Heads turn as partygoers search for the newlyweds. The DJ calls out for them once more. Silence ensues as everyone waits for the happy couple to appear.

The stillness is shattered by a piercing scream coming from inside. I walk quickly toward the sound. I think it's coming from the bride's dressing room.

"*No, no, no!*" Helen begins to wail.

With the sound of other feet hurrying up behind me, I look in through the open door and see Helen, kneeling over the prone body of her new husband. His eyes stare sightless at the ceiling, and his body is bent at impossible angles. A bottle of champagne drips onto the carpet, nearby.

The groom, Carl Hancock, is dead.

Three

"Can I have your attention, please? Someone will be with you shortly to take your statements. In the meantime, everyone please move aside so we can do our job," says a beautiful, young woman in white button-down shirt and gray slacks with a police badge clipped to the belt at her waist. She has jet black hair and her dark skin, a radiant bronze color, is flawless. She looks more like a model than a policewoman.

Behind her stands Detective Pete Fletcher, tall and balding with a deep cleft in his chin. We make eye contact. I look at her, then back at him. He shrugs his shoulders and shakes his head.

None of the shocked and voyeuristic wedding guests seem the least bit inclined to leave.

Bubbles, the dead man's niece, whistles loudly,

silencing the crowd's chatter. She stands by the door to the foyer, clipboard in hand. Mascara smeared across her cheeks, she still manages to command control of the situation. "Everyone needs to file through this door to the foyer. I'll take your names and cell phone numbers, while you wait to tell the police what you saw. Come on now. Hurry up!"

If Egret's Loft was a cruise ship, Bubbles would be the cruise director. Though displeased to be missing out on the action, the crowd follows the sound of her voice to the door, like Pavlovian dogs drawn to the promise of shuffleboard and bingo.

Before long, only five of us remain. I sit with Helen as she cries in the corner of her makeshift dressing room, unwilling to leave Carl's body. Dr. Frank Rosen, a resident of the community and guest of the groom, kneels next to the corpse, snapping off a pair of rubber gloves. Detective Fletcher and the as-yet-unidentified female police officer approach Dr. Rosen first.

"Sir, I'm going to have to ask you to step away from the body," the female detective curtly instructs.

Dr. Rosen stays put but tilts his bald head back to look at her. When he frowns, his large ears, which stick straight out at perpendicular angles to his head, inch higher. "Who are you and why should I follow your orders?" he asks, his already thin lips pursing.

Color rises to her cheeks. "I'm Detective Samantha

Baptiste, recently transferred from Miami PD. Who are *you* that you think you're above the police?"

I glance at Detective Fletcher. After I helped him solve my neighbor's murder, he trusts my investigative judgment. After he saved my life, I trust that he'll make sure I don't end up in an early grave. He doesn't look back at me now, though. He's too busy staring at his shoes.

"My name is Dr. Frank Rosen," the irritated elderly gentleman replies. "Up until I retired five years ago, I was the lead forensic pathologist for the NYPD."

Detective Baptiste's face falls. She wanted a pissing contest, but realizes she just got urine all over her shoes. "Well, then," she says, obviously looking for an avenue to save face, "You could prove useful in walking us through your theory on MOD."

Manner of death.

My husband Clint, a Washington DC police detective for nearly forty years, liked using acronyms too. We used to share everything, including details of his cases. Right up until he was killed in the line of duty six months ago. He'd been two weeks away from retirement.

"Really? I could be useful? Well, stop the presses while I call AARP. Someone my age might be worth talking to," Dr. Rosen deadpans.

"Sir, there's no need—"

"It's 'doctor' to you, young lady," Dr. Rosen interrupts, voice calm.

"And it's 'detective' to you, old man!" Detective Baptiste fires back, her voice rising in pitch.

Finally, Detective Fletcher looks up from his shoes. "Dr. Rosen, I'm Detective Pete Fletcher. We'd be grateful if you could give us the benefit of your expertise and tell us what you think might have happened here."

Detective Baptiste looks like she wants to say something, but her partner silences her with a look.

"I could make this highly technical," Dr. Rosen begins, "but I don't need to show off, and I only want to have to explain this once. There's a champagne cork lodged in his trachea. The force of the cork would have done some significant damage, but the cause of death is suffocation. He couldn't breathe."

"A champagne cork?" Detective Fletcher looks confused. He's not the only one.

"Oh, yes. Champagne bottles can be very dangerous," Dr. Rosen informs us. "Imagine, they can hold pressure as high as ninety pounds per square inch. Which means, when you open the bottle, and the cork launches, it can be traveling up to fifty miles an hour. Once it flew into Carl's mouth, he really didn't stand a chance."

Helen, who's been silently sobbing up until now, begins to loudly wail. Sitting right next to her, the sudden noise startles me. I don't know how many more surprises my heart can take tonight.

"Are you saying it was an accident?" Detective Baptiste

The Dead Men's Wife

asks before wheeling to face Helen. "Were you having a celebratory drink when it happened?"

Helen freezes, the air racing out of her lungs. "What?"

"Did you open the champagne bottle?"

"I most certainly did *not*!"

"It's hard to imagine he opened it himself," Detective Baptiste insists.

"I didn't do it!" Helen cries.

"If the cork was traveling that fast, is there any chance it could have ricocheted off the wall before it...killed Carl?" I ask, addressing Dr. Rosen.

He considers briefly before responding. "I suppose it's possible."

Detective Baptiste's eyes flash to me. "And who are you?"

"Madeline Delarouse." I extend my hand, but she chooses not to shake it. "I live across the street from Helen. I was the first person here—after we all heard Helen scream."

"Her late husband worked homicide in DC," Detective Fletcher tells his partner.

The blue line holds, because her attention shifts off me and back onto the doctor. "The coroner should be here soon, but is there anything else you can tell us before he arrives?"

"Not much without opening him up. There is some kind of sticky residue on his wrist, which could be from the champagne. You'll probably want to check that," Dr. Rosen says. "Also, there's some pre-mortem bruising around his mouth. It could be from the cork, but you'll want to confirm that."

Detective Fletcher looks up from notes he's been writing down in the little notebook he always carries with him. "Is there something there? In his left hand?"

Dr. Rosen moves to the other side of Carl's body, pulling a fresh pair of rubber gloves from his jacket pocket. I can't help but wonder why he thought he would need so many pairs of disposable gloves for a wedding.

"I only checked the right hand for a pulse," he admits. "Hmmm...this wrist has a bit of residue as well." He gently peels open the victim's left hand. "There is something here. It looks like a broach or barrette..."

"That's mine!" I say, before realizing the implications and quickly adding, "I loaned it to Helen for the wedding. You know...something borrowed, something blue."

"Why, Carl? Why?" Helen suddenly shrieks.

Her words are slightly slurred, likely by alcohol and the prodigious amount of mucus spewing out of her nose from all the crying. Poor thing, she really does have horrible luck with men.

Detective Fletcher walks over to me and puts his hand on my shoulder. "It's probably best if you take Helen out in the ballroom, while we finish up in here."

Nodding, I rise to my feet and help Helen up from her

chair. I rub her back as we walk out of the room. "Come on, dear, let's get you cleaned up."

We're just out of sight of the detectives and Dr. Rosen when Helen's knees seem to collapse under her. I struggle to hold her up, but it's a losing battle, and both of us begin to sink to the floor.

"You're okay," I assure her. "You're going to be okay."

"No," she cries, lost in her own suffering. "This is all my fault. All my fault."

I look around, checking to see if anyone else heard her admission. They didn't. "What do you mean it's your fault, Helen? Did you open the champagne bottle?"

She's not listening and doesn't respond. Even after I ask the same questions a second time. But there's no use pushing her for answers right now. She's not thinking clearly. She just lost her husband. And she's been drinking.

I'll ask her about it again after she's had some sleep. In the meantime, I should probably keep what she said to myself. She's already outlived seven husbands, and her eighth just died within hours of tying the knot.

How long before people start whispering about how the black widow of Egret's Loft just struck again?

Four

"I told you we should have gone with the retirement village in California!" Ritchie exclaims, far too enthusiastically for this early on a Sunday morning.

"Oh great, so if someone was murdered there, we'd both be on the other side of the country? At least here I'm within driving distance." Eliza heatedly replies.

"I thought the whole point was to have Mom in a place where no one gets murdered!"

Unbeknownst to me, my children had decided to hold an emergency family meeting over Skype. I heard the digital frame, the one Ritchie had given me for my birthday, start to ring as I was pouring my first cup of coffee.

It scared me half to death. I didn't even realize the frame was connected to the phone line.

"I never said it was murder this time!" Eliza rebuts. "If you remember, I very clearly called it a 'suspicious death.' That's the report I got. There's probably no need for alarm. But after what happened two weeks ago, I just thought it best to be a little cautious."

My gorgeous daughter, with her long blond hair and big turquoise eyes could have been a film star. Instead, she went to work for the Internal Revenue Service, or IRS, in Miami. At least, that's her job on paper. She's far too well-informed about matters of life, death, and national security to expect us to believe she's a mid-level government accountant.

"Mom, you were there, right?" Ritchie, my DC-based, brain surgeon son, asks. "Was it murder? If you're worried, I can jump on a plane and come stay with you for a little while. The hospital owes me some time off."

"That's not necessary. It's too soon to say what happened. It very well may have been a horrible accident." I try to calm them down.

"The guy choked on a champagne cork?" Ritchie's face reflects his skepticism.

"Not really choked," I clarify. "More like it flew out of the bottle and into the back of his throat."

"How is that even possible?" Eliza asks.

"I could probably get Curt to work out the physics, if you want," Ritchie offers. Curt is Ritchie's six-year-old son.

He has an IQ of 185, and a voracious appetite for sharing his knowledge with everyone he meets.

"Please, no!" Eliza groans. "Look, I called this meeting just to make sure everything was alright since *Mom* didn't even bother to tell us something had happened."

"Hey! Don't drag me into this. You're the ones who decided to move me here," I remind them.

The truth is, I refrained from telling them about the events of last night because of Helen. Her words had rattled me. But before I say anything to anyone, it only seems right that I give her a chance to explain herself.

"Oh, here we go again with the guilt." Eliza moans.

"No guilt, dear. I'm just saying, you two thought I'd be better off here after your dad died. You were worried about me being lonely, remember? You couldn't *possibly* have known my neighbor was going to be killed the night I moved in. How could you?"

"What's happening with your neighbor's place anyway?" Ritchie steers the conversation to more solid ground. "Do you think it'll just sit empty for a while?"

"Oh no! It's already been sold," I tell him.

"That fast?"

"Apparently, the waiting list to get into this place is a mile long. They had no trouble selling it."

"Do you know who bought it?"

"A woman. I hear she's Russian and used to live in Miami." At least, that's what Gina had told me. "I saw the moving trucks being unloaded a few days ago, but with all the excitement over Helen's wedding, I haven't had a chance to stop by and introduce myself."

"Do you know her name?" Eliza asks. "It wouldn't hurt to have her checked out."

I give her my sternest mom face. "You'll do no such thing. Unless they've been killed or might be killers themselves, my neighbors deserve their privacy! And so do I!"

"Is that Detective Fletcher at your front door?" This from Ritchie who's been glancing down at his phone while I admonished his sister.

"There's no one at my front door." The words are barely out of my mouth when my doorbell rings. "How on Earth...?"

Ritchie holds up his phone, and I can see he's watching video from the camera he installed in the doorbell.

My eyes narrow. "We're going to have a conversation about all this spying on me that you're both doing. But right now, I need to go talk to Detective Fletcher. Goodbye!"

I hit the button that I think will end the call, but it just changes the configurations of their video screens.

"Goodbye," I say for a second time.

I hit another button and little hearts start floating in front of their faces.

"You alright there, lady?" Ritchie asks, smirking.

"I don't know how to turn this darn thing off!"

He starts to laugh.

Eliza rolls her eyes. "Oh, for the love of…" she says and promptly hangs up the call. The picture frame reverts to a photo slideshow of my grandchildren.

I sigh deeply and walk to the front door. "Hello, Detective Fletcher," I greet him and then, seeing the weariness on his face, I ask, "Long night?"

"You could say that," he confirms, stepping into my foyer. "I don't suppose you have any coffee?"

"Of course!" I scan the front porch before closing the door. "Your new partner's not here with you?"

"Naw. I sent her into the office to start writing up her reports."

I walk into the kitchen, pour a cup of coffee, and hand Detective Fletcher the mug. "So, what do you think of her?"

He takes a sip. "She's alright. Just got promoted to detective before transferring here from Miami. She seems thorough. But a little too anxious to prove herself, if you know what I mean."

"I do." I'd seen it, too, last night. Like a little dog barking at the bigger ones so it won't get stepped on. "You were great, though! You did so well with questioning Dr. Rosen!"

"You think so?" He smiles. "Thanks. I was pretending to be one of the characters in my latest book!"

Prior to the recent murders at Egret's Loft, Detective Fletcher had never worked a homicide case. That didn't stop him from self-publishing a series of moderately successful crime novels, set in the Sunshine State. I'd even read one or two of them before we met.

"You're working on a new one? Excellent! I can't wait to read it!"

"You'll be the first, when it's done."

We drink our coffees in silence for several minutes. Detective Fletcher worries the cleft in his chin with his left thumb, as he thinks. I know there's a reason why he's here. Eventually, he'll get around to telling me what it is.

"Sorry to bother you so early in the morning," he finally begins. "But I was hoping I could run something past you."

"Absolutely! What's bothering you?"

"Well, the crime scene techs think it's unlikely that Carl could have opened the bottle *and* been killed by the cork. Much *more* likely, someone else opened the bottle, and his death was just a fluke accident."

"That makes sense," I agree. "So why the long face?"

"We interviewed everyone who was at the party last night, but no one admitted to having been in the room with Carl when he died. Someone is lying, right? But why would they lie about it, if it was just an accident?"

"Uh huh." I swallow the lump in my throat, Helen's words echoing in my head.

"And you know what else is weird?" he continues, oblivious to my discomfort. "That sticky stuff Dr. Rosen pointed out on Carl's wrist? Forensics are running some tests, but it looks like it might be residue from duct tape."

"Duct tape?" I echo.

"Weird, right? Almost like someone taped his wrists together at some point."

It might have been possible to assume someone was afraid to come forward about unintentionally and accidentally killing a man on his wedding day. If someone went to the trouble of taping Carl's hands together before opening the bottle, fear might not be why the culprit wants to remain anonymous.

Was Helen just drunk and emotional when she told me it was her fault? She had seemed genuinely shocked that he was dead. I don't want to judge what they did for fun in private, but if she'd taped his hands together and shot a cork into his open mouth on purpose, it wouldn't be quite such a big surprise that he died. Would it?

"What do you think?" Detective Fletcher presses.

I shake my head, thinking my kids will be back to babysit me when they get wind of this latest news. I should probably wash the sheets in their rooms.

When I look up, Detective Fletcher is looking at me expectantly. "I think you already know what I think," I tell him. "Do you want me to say it out loud?"

"You're probably right," he admits. "But yeah. Can you say it anyway?"

"Alright," I say, mentally preparing myself for the implications of what I'm about to say. "It's starting to look like Carl may have been murdered."

Five

"She's a real beauty, isn't she?" Roy asks excitedly, untying the ropes securing his large boat to his dock.

"She sure is," I agree, not really paying attention.

My mind is consumed by thoughts of murder.

I've been racking my brain since Detective Fletcher came by my house a few hours ago, trying to come up with a legitimate reason why Carl's hands would have been taped together before he died. So far, I haven't been able to come up with even one logical explanation.

"I just got her about a month ago," Roy says, starting the boat's engine and entering the cabin area to turn on the lights and refrigerator. "She's a Flyer 9. Same horsepower as my old boat, but she's got sleeping berths, so I can take her out for overnight trips." From under his fabric bucket hat, he winks at me, his body language suggestive.

Adjusting my own straw hat, I pretend not to notice. "Looks like your neighbor also thought it'd be a nice day for a boat ride," I say, watching a boat reverse into the dock just up the river from Roy's.

Roy looks perplexed. "My neighbor?"

His confusion is understandable. Just over a week ago, Gina and I had stumbled upon an alligator munching on the dead body of Roy's nearest neighbor.

"Not *that* neighbor," I explain. "Your neighbor on the other side."

"No, no, no!" Roy scowls, coming out from the cabin to join me on deck. "He's supposed to be in Italy!"

"I take it you're not friends, then?"

The veins on Roy's thick neck protrude, and I can see the muscles sausaged into his button-down navy-blue Hawaiian shirt tense. He's staring at the cabin cruiser as if willing his eyes to become lasers and blow it up.

Roy has what you might call an explosive temper, and as I've witnessed myself, you don't want to light the fuse.

"Friends?" He spits the word out like two-day-old chewing tobacco. "With that pompous blowhard? You've got to be joking!"

"Who is he?" And to keep Roy from flying into a rage, I quickly add, "So I know to avoid him in future, of course."

"His name's Andy Romano. Acts like he's the smartest guy in the room but he makes clothes for a living, for Pete's sake!"

"He's a fashion designer?" I try to quell my piqued curiosity. I do enjoy fashion, but I wonder why I've never heard the name before.

"Stuff for little guys. Overpriced European junk, if you ask me. What was the name…Sensulia? No, that's not it. Something that means…and pardon me for using this word in front of a lady…*sexual*. He's a man-whore! He even advertises it right there on the label!"

I shift uncomfortably. "It's clothing for little boys, and the brand name means sexual?"

Roy's blue eyes widen. "No, gosh no! He's not *that* bad. I mean men that are little, you know. Not real men with muscles and stuff. I tried on a pair of the pants once. The legs were so darn skinny, I couldn't even fit my calf in 'em!"

Relieved to have cleared that up, I think I know what he means now. "Oh! Sessuale? Is that the name of the brand?"

I'd looked at buying one of their sweaters for Clint once. The cashmere number would have set me back nearly a thousand dollars. Clint got a really nice bottle of whiskey instead.

"Yeah. Sounds about right," he says disdainfully. "But you wanna know the worst thing about that guy? He's a sports snob."

"A sports snob?"

"Yeah! When I told him I played professional football, he asked me what club I played for. A club! Can you believe it? I said I played for a *team*. And he just stuck his nose in the air and said, 'Oh, American football. Not the same.' Jerk." Roy shakes his head.

I frown and nod in what I hope is perceived as sympathy. Sports were never really my thing.

"Shall we get this show on the road?" Roy asks, forcing a smile.

"Yes, please! But first, can I have a life jacket?"

"You don't need one. The water's not that deep until you get out into the gulf," Roy assures me.

"All the same, I'd feel better with one on. It's been a while since I've gone swimming." I've always been terrified of drowning, though I can't trace any memories back to the source of my fear. I have been in the pool in my backyard, of course. But it's only two feet deep in most places. I've been in baths with more water.

"Your call. There should be a couple under your seat. Just lift the cushion."

As I search for the life vest, Roy walks up to the steering wheel and starts guiding his boat away from the dock. Passing by Andy Romano's house, Roy glares into the yard. There doesn't appear to be anyone there to witness his visual intimidation.

This part of the Caloosahatchee River is a no-wake

zone, so we sedately glide along the water. On the starboard side of the boat, we pass a few other houses on our street, then an open stretch of grass that I believe is the seventh hole on the golf course. The River Club is just up around the bend, beyond which the river widens before, eventually, emptying into the Gulf of Mexico.

On the port side of the boat, there is only mangrove swamp. The trees soar twenty feet into the sky with thick, leafy green canopies that blot out the robin's egg blue sky. Along the banks of the swamp, hundreds of brown roots, wide around as fire hoses, look like snakes coming up from out of the water. It gives me the shivers, despite the warmth of the day.

"You ever been fishin' before?" Roy shouts, turning his head to look at me, and almost losing his bucket hat to the wind.

"Not for a very long time," I admit. "All of my fish comes from the grocery store."

Roy laughs as we pull past the River Club. There are at least a dozen other boats spread out across the mouth of the bay. Roy waves at the other Egret's Loft residents as we motor by, just out to a spot before the bay becomes the Gulf of Mexico.

"Here we are! As good a spot as any. You ready?"

Shrugging, I tell him, "Why not?"

While Roy strolls into the main cabin to retrieve bait and beverages from the fridge, I quickly apply more sunblock. I can feel the sun's reflection off the water on my skin. My dermatologist back in DC, where I lived most of my life, was very concerned about me getting melanoma when I told her I was moving to Florida.

"If you like, I'll bait up the hook for you," Roy offers. I nod my acceptance, and he expertly threads the fishing hook through a wriggling worm.

I stare at it a bit too long, and Roy starts to chuckle.

"Don't worry. There's nothin' to it, really. Just start out by positionin' your rod behind your head at two o'clock, like so." He demonstrates. "And then swing it through to ten o'clock, sendin' the line out in front of you. Got it?"

"Alright. Here goes nothing." I take a deep breath and mimic Roy's movements. The lure sails smoothly past, overhead, and plops in the water a safe distance from the boat.

"Great job! See, I told you there was nothin' to it!"

As we wait for something to bite, I can't help but bring up the subject forefront in my mind. "Such a shame about Carl."

Roy's smile disappears. "A helluva thing, that."

"You'd already headed home when it happened?"

"Yeah. That detective and his new partner turned up at my door late last night, askin' if I'd seen anything."

"What did you tell them?" I ask, staring out at the water.

"Only that the last time I saw Carl was during that

dustup about the song. Never saw him again after that. Never saw Helen again, either."

I turn to look at Roy. "Did they ask you about Helen?"

"Yeah. They were curious about where she was. I guess it makes sense. A bunch of dead husbands under her belt already, and the new groom winds up dead."

My heart sinks, Helen's words replaying in my head. "You don't think they actually suspect Helen of killing any of her husbands. Do you?"

"There was talk. Back when Donald died." Then, remembering I haven't lived at Egret's Loft long, he adds, "Helen's last husband. I mean...before Carl."

I remember a conversation I'd had once with Gina. "I thought Donald died of kidney failure."

"Yeah. I think that's right. But some people thought—"

Just then, something tugs on my line, nearly ripping the fishing rod out of my hands.

"You've got a bite!" Roy sounds excited. "Start reeling it in, nice and slow."

My heart beats wildly, and the rod shakes in my hand. The wooden handle digs into the flesh of my stomach as I try to pull in what feels like a forty-pound fish.

"Almost there!" Roy encourages.

"I see it! I see it!" I exclaim. "Now what do I do?"

"Swing it up on the boat!" Roy instructs. Which is exactly what I do.

Belatedly, Roy realizes two things. One, that the fish I

caught is a bottom-feeding catfish, not worth the effort. Two, that he was standing too close to me when I swung the fish onboard. The sharp dorsal fin of the frantically struggling fish pierces the flesh of Roy's upper thigh.

He starts screaming. I start screaming. The fish continues fighting for its life.

Eventually, Roy is able to extricate the fish from his leg, blood trailing down his calf onto the deck.

My face burns hotter than an oven set to broil. "Roy! I am so, so sorry!"

"It's alright," he says through clenched teeth. "But that hit pretty close to my babymakers. I think I need to call my doctor."

"Oh, Roy, of course. What can I do?"

"You want to examine the wound for me?" He shoots me a pained smile.

I take a step backward. "Anything but that."

"I guessed as much. Look, sorry, but we should probably pack it in for the day."

"Yes, yes! Do you want me to drive the boat? I don't really know how, but how hard can it be?"

"No, no! I got it," he says, returning to the captain's chair. I rush over to put a towel down before he sits. The seat is white vinyl, and he *is* bleeding a lot.

The trip back seems to go much quicker, probably because Roy pretends not to see the "no wake" signs.

As we're approaching his dock, we pass by Andy's

house. A man, who I presume is Andy, stands next to his boat and watches us pass. He doesn't say hello. He doesn't wave. He just watches.

It's rapidly becoming clear to me why Roy took such a dislike to the man. He was jealous. Andy is a tanned, gracefully aging Adonis.

Six

This is it. This is what death feels like.

My legs refuse to cooperate, and I can no longer move my arms.

"I know you can do it! Just one more leg raise!" Molly encourages, her teeth radiantly white against her dark skin. "These really are so much better for your spine than sit ups!"

Gina had warned me that spending a day with Molly could physically break me, and while no bones have fractured, my will to live has definitely been broken.

"I can't," I tell her from my position, lying on the floor. "I've had a good life. I think I'll just spend the rest of my days right here."

My son, Ritchie, had signed me up for a day-long wellness evaluation with Molly Bitty, the physical fitness instructor. It was supposed to happen during my first week here, but two murders got in the way. Now it seems Carl may have been murdered, as well, but I couldn't put Molly off any longer. So here I am, on my third Monday as a resident of Egret's Loft, being tortured to death myself.

"It's not that bad. You're super fit for your age. You've got this!" Molly kneels beside me.

I vaguely remember when I used to be able to kneel. When you're young you don't realize how hard it can be on the knees.

After an aborted afternoon out on the water, I'd gone to bed early last night to be refreshed for today. But it's barely noon, which means we're only three hours into an eight-hour evaluation. More than ever, I'm convinced, my son wants to kill me.

"No. I really, really don't got this," I assure her.

The morning had begun comfortably enough, with a tour of the gym and the ladies' dressing room, followed by questions about my normal exercise routine. At first, I admit to being intimidated by Molly's physique, which can only be described as glorious. I think her abs and her behind could literally cut glass. But she was very nice and respectful.

Up until she hooked me up to a heart monitor and stuck me on the treadmill. Every minute or so she'd reach over and either increase the speed or the incline. After twenty minutes of this, my manners deserted me, and I swatted her hand away. She looked at me like I used to look at my children when they misbehaved. Then she made me walk even faster.

It only got worse from there, as she dragged me around to every machine in the place. Under the guise of teaching me how to use the equipment, she made me do twenty reps of each exercise until my arms and legs had the rigidity of overcooked noodles.

Despite the abuse, when Molly smiles at me I can't help but smile back. Which turns out to be a bad idea. Even the muscles in my face hurt.

"Can I let you in on a little secret?" Molly asks.

Using the word "secret" is almost enough to get me to sit up. Almost. "Of course, dear!"

"You've heard the rumors? About me being a total workout tyrant?"

Of course, I have! Literally everyone I told about this session seemed downright scared for me. But, aside from making me feel like I'm several feet closer to the grave, Molly seems nice, and I don't want to be rude. So, I say, "You? No, I don't believe it."

She squints her eyes. She knows I'm lying. Probably because I'm a terrible liar.

"Alright, yes," I confess. "Everyone here is absolutely terrified of you."

She laughs. "It's all an act. An inside joke, if you will, with my clients."

She's completely lost me. "I don't understand. Why would you do that?"

"Honestly, I found that a lot of the people, like you, who come to me, feel like nobody takes them seriously anymore. Like they've lost their edge. They've just become harmless *active elders*, you know?"

One of the rules of Egret's Loft is that no one is supposed to use the words "old" or "elderly." "Active elders" is acceptable, but every time I hear it used, it has the opposite of its intended effect. It just reminds me that my back seems to go out more these days than I do.

"You make yourself appear tougher than you really are —" I try to piece it together out loud, "—just so your clients can find their...what did you call it...edge?"

"Exactly!" Molly nods animatedly. "It gives them street cred. Like, 'Wow, did you hear that so and so did a whole day with Molly? They must be super tough. I don't want to face off against them in pickleball!' You see?"

"And that actually works?"

"A thousand percent! My clients get a lot of confidence from it. So, I started doing the evaluation days. Everyone who lasts until lunch, gets let in on the secret. Anyone who leaves early thinks I was too hard on them, so the messaging is consistent."

"Does this mean I passed?"

"With flying colors!" Molly praises. "The rest of the day is just paperwork and goal setting. If you do just one more leg lift—just raise your legs to the sky and lower them back to the ground one more time—we can break for lunch, and it'll be an easy afternoon. What do you say?"

I think about it for a minute. "I really don't think I can."

"I know you can!"

"I probably could—" I drop my voice to a whisper, "—but I really need to use the ladies' room first. You've had me drinking an awful lot of water, dear."

Molly blushes a little. "Oh gosh, yeah! Sorry about that. Here, let me help you up!" She holds her hand on my elbow for support as she walks me toward the dressing area. "I'll see you after lunch. And remember," she winks, "it's our little secret."

"Of course, dear!"

Walking into the dressing room, I collapse onto a cushioned bench next to the lockers. I didn't actually have to use the ladies' room. I just couldn't manage another leg lift. If my kids can tease me about having a tiny bladder, it only seems fair to use that to my advantage every now and again.

I'm trying to massage the feeling back into my thighs when the door opens and Helen walks in, looking down at the floor tiles and carrying an exercise mat under her arm.

"Helen!" I try to stand up, but quickly decide to remain seated. "I came by your house yesterday, but there was no answer. How are you?"

Helen looks up at me, but it takes her eyes several seconds for recognition to dawn.

"Bless your heart, sugar. That's real decent of you to come by. I just couldn't face anybody, being so out of sorts and all. Ya know?"

"I do," I tell her, remembering how lost I felt in the days and weeks after my Clint died. The way I still feel. "You came here to turn off your brain for a little while?"

She nods. "Yoga, mainly. I was gonna do the treadmill, but I'm too weak to whip a gnat."

That makes two of us, though for very different reasons.

"Have you heard anything?" I ask, swallowing distaste for myself. "About what happened to Carl?"

"Not yet." She slumps down onto the bench next to me. "Those detectives want to come 'round later to talk to me. I don't know what to tell them. It was an accident! Just an awful accident, right?"

"Helen..." I'm trying to find a polite way to ask her if she killed her husband. She *had* said it was her fault. "Were you maybe in the room? When Carl died?"

Her eyes open wide. "No, I told you I wasn't there. I found him like that."

I don't say anything.

"You don't believe me?" Vulnerability punctuates her words.

"No, I do believe you!" I try to reassure her. "It's just that, well, you kind of confessed."

Her exercise mat slides out from under her arm and falls to the floor. "What?"

I try to meet her gaze, but the intensity in her eyes makes me a little uneasy. As I've learned from personal experience, she has a fierce temper, and sitting right beside each other, I'm easily within slapping distance.

"I came by yesterday to check on you, yes. But also, to ask you what you meant on Saturday night," I admit. "You were crying, and you'd had a lot to drink. But you said it was all your fault. Do you remember that?"

Her eyes scan the room, like a deer sensing a hunter is nearby.

"Not here," she whispers. "Come to my place. We can talk in private."

I hesitate to respond. If she did kill Carl, and she thinks I know, what's to stop her from trying to silence me? Permanently. Then again, if she didn't kill Carl, she might genuinely need my help.

"Alright," I finally agree. "But I have to meet Molly in an hour. She's expecting me back."

"Sure thing, sugar. Come on, my golf cart's out front."

As the door to the ladies' room shuts behind us, I could swear I hear one of the toilets flushing.

Seven

A heart attack sits staring back at me from my plate.

After returning to Helen's house, she insisted on cooking me a mouthwatering selection of fried chicken, mashed potatoes, gravy, and cornbread. She made the entire meal in less than half an hour, never once looking at a recipe.

"Do you eat like this often?" I ask, wondering if her doctor has her on a high dose of statins.

"Oh golly, no!" She chuckles. "Gravity bein' what it is, a girl's got to be careful. But, as my mama always said, there's nothin' like good ole fashioned home cookin' when you're feelin' blue."

I wink at her. "I think your mother was on to something."

Mitsy, Helen's preternaturally silent Pomeranian, looks up at me from the floor. She's not begging, exactly, but she's licked her chops enough in the past few minutes to let me know she's not above accepting table scraps.

Fork and knife in hand, I attack my lunch. The morning workout must have given me some appetite, because no further words are exchanged until my plate is clean, save a few morsels of chicken for the adorable ball of fur at my feet.

"That was absolutely delicious, Helen. You should have been a chef!" I praise.

"Ain't nothin' to it, really." She blushes, her plate still half full. "My mama made me learn to cook. The best way to a man's heart is through his stomach, she'd say."

"Well, you've certainly done her proud."

"Thanks, sugar," Helen says, clearing the plates. When she sits back down, her hands are fidgety and her leg bounces under the table. "I can whip us up a pecan pie, if you like. It won't take no time at all!"

"I couldn't possibly eat another bite," I assure her. "And I'll have to be heading back to meet up with Molly soon."

"Right." Helen takes a long sip of her sweet tea. "I guess you'll be wantin' to know what I meant about Carl's death being my fault. Am I right?"

"You're not wrong."

Helen looks down at her perfectly manicured fingernails, her leg still bouncing. When she finally speaks, the words trickle out slowly. "If I tell you what I think is goin' on, you're going to think I'm nuttier than a porta potty at a peanut festival."

I frown. "I can't say I've ever been to a peanut festival..."

"That's not really the point, sugar."

"No, of course it's not." I try to refocus. "But whatever you tell me, I promise I won't think you're insane. Deal?"

"I suppose." Helen doesn't sound convinced, but after a brief pause, she looks straight into my eyes and continues. "Alright, well, I did say it was my fault. And it is. Somehow."

"Somehow? You don't know how?"

"Not really. I mean, I must have made someone madder than a hornet to do all this. That's the only thing that makes any sense."

"You think someone killed all of your husbands to get back at you for something?"

"Not...exactly."

My head is starting to hurt. "Helen, just spit it out, would you?"

"I'm cursed," she blurts out.

"Well, that's just crazy!" I can't help the words slipping out of my mouth.

Helen's face flames. "You promised you wouldn't go sayin' I was bonkers!"

"No! Wait a second now, I wasn't saying *you* were crazy. Just that being cursed would be a bit...unlikely. Why on Earth would you think you're cursed?"

She tilts her head to the side. "Having eight husbands die on you isn't enough?"

I hate to admit, she has a point.

"But there has to be a more...logical explanation, right?" I ask her. "I don't mean to be rude, but do you mind me asking how your other husbands died?"

Her shoulders tense up slightly, her discomfort obvious. "Well, now, Donald—he was my seventh husband. He died of kidney failure. He was eighty-five when he passed on, and he'd been feeling poorly for weeks. So, it wasn't a total shock," she says. "Before Donald there was Jeff. We lived in Colorado. Our outdoor cooker killed him."

I'm not sure I heard her properly. "I'm sorry, you said your outdoor cooker?"

She looks out her glass patio doors, remembering. "Yeah. Jeff really loved to grill. And he was mighty good at it. He'd been goin' on about this fancy gas grill he wanted, so I went and surprised him with it. First time he was fixin' to use it, the gas canister exploded. The coroner said he coulda survived the burns, but the cooking grate flew clean off, and went straight into his chest. Bless his heart, he died right there in my arms."

"Oh, Helen, I'm so sorry." The fried chicken isn't sitting so well in my stomach anymore. "But that sounds like it was just a terrible, freak accident. Not a curse, just devastatingly bad luck. What about the husband before Jeff?"

"That'd be Herbie. Poor Herbie." Helen sighs deeply.

The Dead Men's Wife

Dare I ask? "What happened to Herbie?"

"He was a rancher. Had the most beautiful farm out in Montana with all his horses. He was richer'n Croesus, but was so cheap he wouldn't give a nickel to see Jesus ridin' a bicycle. So, when he needed to clear out some trees to build a bullpen to train up his stallions, he said he'd do it hisself. One evenin' he didn't show up for supper, so I went lookin', you know? I found him alright. In a manner of speakin'." The color drains from her face. "You've never seen so much blood."

"How did he..." I can't bring myself to finish the sentence.

She glances up at the ceiling, trying to hold in her tears. "Somehow, he'd fallen into the wood chipper he'd got to get rid of the trees. Didn't want to pay good money to have someone else do it for him. There was nothing left of him."

Gagging, I can taste the acidic remains of my lunch at the back of my throat. "Good Lord, that's just awful!"

The visual she described easily springs to mind. Clint dragged me to a film set in North Dakota years and years ago. I'd covered my eyes, and he'd laughed as a very pregnant lady sheriff walked up to a fugitive as he was wood chipping his partner in crime. If Clint were still alive, I'd have another go at him for taking me to see that film. I had nightmares for weeks.

"Derek, at least, was all in one piece when I found him," Helen continues, her voice shaky.

"Derek was before…" It's getting difficult to keep all their names straight.

"Before Herbie. Derek and I lived in Los Angeles. He was a screenwriter. Couldn't get that man outta the pool. Lord, did he love to swim." The tears are freely flowing down her cheeks now.

I cough to cover the growing feeling of being a rubbernecker to her grief. "We can stop if this is getting too much for you."

Lost in memory, it's as if she doesn't even hear me. "He was practically a fish. I never woulda thought he could drown, especially not in our little pool. And Jimmy. He could run faster than the wind. But he couldn't outrun the car that hit him, and then drove off like he was nothin'. He was almost home too. I found him next to our driveway."

The only things these stories seem to have in common are that, with the exception of Donald, all her husbands died in bizarre accidents, and Helen found their bodies. Oh, and the men were all married to Helen when they died, of course.

"You see? I *am* cursed!" she cries. "Do you believe in voodoo? I read all about it when Jimmy and me were livin' in New Orleans. Do you think maybe someone is makin' all this happen to me? I've turned down a fair number of suitors in my day. Maybe one of them is tryin' to get back at me?"

Her eyes beg me for an answer. Any answer. Unfortunately for her, all I have are more questions. "Do you have any reason to believe that any of those 'accidents' weren't really accidental?" I ask.

"What do you mean?"

"Were there investigations? Autopsies?"

She shakes her head, and I think she's trying to frown, but hundreds of dollars' worth of Botox make that impossible. "No. Why would there be? It was clear how they all died."

"Did the police talk to witnesses, at least?"

"There weren't any. Only me findin' their bodies."

I'm desperately trying to resist falling into the trap of suspecting what so many others in Egret's Loft already believe, that Helen is a black widow. But she's not making it easy. Her dead husbands all suffered strange accidents, their cases received no real police attention, and there were no witnesses to cast doubts on her version of events. Not to mention, from what she's said, most of the deaths happened in different states, which means different police jurisdictions. No wonder she's been able to elude suspicion for so long.

"Madeline? Are you alright?" Helen asks, a flicker of annoyance in her voice. "You're not thinking I had anything to do with their deaths. Are you?"

"No, of course not," I stretch the truth slightly. "But I do think the police are going to have a lot of questions when they come by later."

It crosses my mind that, as a woman, I probably don't have to worry about Helen being a danger to me. Then again, if what she's said is true, she's never come under suspicion before. Who knows what could happen if things started to get ugly for the resident Southern belle?

I need to know more about Helen. There's one person I know I can count on for all the gossip, I'll just need a bag full of diabetic sweets and a truckload of patience.

Eight

"Can I tempt you with a little more macaroni and cheese?" I offer.

George Myrtle nods his balding head enthusiastically as he makes room on his plate for more processed cheese pasta, which, I've been told, is his favorite food group. It was also convenient for me, since I'd extended them a last-minute invitation after I'd spent the entire afternoon at the gym with Molly.

"Not too much more now, George," Jinny scolds her husband before sending a pink-lipped smile in my direction. "It was so nice of you to invite us over for dinner! We've been in such a tizzy the past few days, don't you know. What with Carl dying at his own wedding and our grandson Paul coming down from the Peg to visit us for a few weeks. George and me have just been all aflutter.

Barely have the time to sit down, let alone make a nice, homemade meal."

Jinny and George officially live in Winnipeg, Canada—or, as they call it, the Peg. But over the years, George developed SAD, Seasonal Affective Disorder. As a result, the couple bought a second home in Egret's Loft so they could spend their winters, which typically last eight months in Canada, in the sunshine.

"It's my pleasure," I assure her. "When does your grandson arrive?"

Jinny's only mentioned that he's coming about six times since they arrived less than an hour ago. Reading between the lines, it sounds like Paul has run afoul of his father's good graces. Rebellious teenage boys tend to do that. So, he's being temporarily relocated to his grandparents' house in an apparent bid to put some manners on him.

"He gets in Tuesday, which would be…tomorrow! Goodness me, where do the days go?" Jinny adjusts the arms of the pink tracksuit top draped over her shoulders. "We haven't seen him since last summer, don't you know. I bet he's grown so much since then. Tall as a maple tree, I'd wager. He's a good boy. And a tremendous singer. Always polite to us, too, isn't he, George? But now, his parents' divorce has been rough on him, and he's been acting up." She leans toward me and lowers her voice. "Why, just last week, he was caught cow tipping in a neighbor's farm! Luckily, the farmer decided not to press charges, eh. But our son is at his wit's end with the boy, so we said we'd take him in for a while. My George won't tolerate any back talk or misbehaving, so a little visit should be good for Paul."

I nod, not picturing George as much of a disciplinarian. In the few weeks I've known him, he's barely said ten words, and most of them have been "yes, dear" or "no, dear" in response to something Jinny said.

"Listen to me, going on about people you haven't met yet." Jinny lightly taps the palm of her hand to her forehead. "But we'll pick him up at the airport in the afternoon, and you'll be sure to meet him soon after, won't you? I hope he still likes playing Scrabble. He used to love playing board games and the like with me and George when he was a wisp of a thing, but now he's growing up you never know what he'll like from one day to the next, don't you know." Jinny pauses and sighs deeply. "And there I go, doing it again. You better get me talking about something else, or I'll ramble on all evening."

She laughs and gazes adoringly across the table at George, who is still tucked into his macaroni and cheese.

I seize the opportunity.

"It's so sad about Carl. Helen and I spoke earlier today. She was mentioning her last husband dying as well. Donald? I think you'd said before that you knew him pretty well."

In a conversation after my neighbor Carlota's death, Jinny had told me Donald had died last year of kidney failure. George had apparently been chosen by Helen to dispose of her dead husband's things. As if reading the intention behind my words, George looks up from his plate at Jinny and shakes his head. I notice it, Jinny does not.

"Oh, Donald! He was such a lovely man," she gushes. "I think he and Helen met somewhere out west. Arizona? Or New Mexico maybe? Never mind about that. He was quite a bit older than Helen, don't you know. And he'd had a real successful career. What did he do again now, George?" George opens his mouth, but Jinny, snapping her fingers, doesn't give him time to speak. "He consulted on hostile takeovers! Right you are, George. That's what he did alright. A whirlwind courtship from what I hear. They hadn't been married long when they bought their place here in Egret's Loft. He died about three years after they moved in. No family to speak of, save Helen. He *was* quite a bit older, as I said. Bad kidneys, or so they *say*."

I stop her monologue. "You don't sound so sure. Did something happen?"

George's head shakes more frantically at his wife. She either doesn't see him or doesn't care. "I hate to speak out of turn. My daddy always used to tell me that what Susie said about Sally said more about Susie than it did Sally, don't you know."

I'm confused. "Who are Susie and Sally? Do they live on Cypress Point Avenue too? Did they know Donald?"

Jinny looks confused now as well. "Do Susie and Sally live here?"

"That's what I was asking you."

George puts his head in his hand. "No, it was just somethin' her dad used to say. We went to school with Susie and Sally as kids. They were twins. But Jinny, I really don't think—"

It's the most I've ever heard George say at one time, but Jinny abruptly silences him.

"They *were* twins, weren't they? I'd plum forgotten about that. But, no, they don't know anything about Donald dying. Carlota had some thoughts on it, though. May she rest in peace. Why, did you know that she tried to get the police to test Donald's body for antifreeze after he died? She said she'd seen a bunch of empty bottles of the stuff in the garage. Which is mighty curious when you think about it, because nothing freezes here…except the lemonade if you leave it in the back of the fridge. Have you ever noticed things get a lot colder back there?"

I have noticed that, actually. But if I allow myself to get sidelined, I'll never get any useful information. "Did they end up doing a toxicology panel on him?" I ask instead, remembering the lingo Clint used to use when poisoning was suspected in his homicide cases.

"I'm sure I don't know what that is. But they never did test for anything. The coroner chalked his death up to natural causes, don't you know. Helen had a little service in the church a few miles away, then she had him cremated and scattered the ashes out in the ocean. Poor thing, she was heartbroken. Always walking around in sunglasses after he passed. I imagine her eyes were a sight from all the crying."

Another strike mark against Helen on the suspect checklist in my mind. By having her dead husband cremated it ensured those tests could never be performed.

"Did Helen know Carlota asked to test Donald's body for poison?" I ask.

George pushes his plate away from him, even though quite a few elbows of macaroni remain.

"Oh goodness, no," Jinny says. "I don't think so, anyway. Carlota kept that quiet, not wanting to make any fuss in the neighborhood, eh. Helen would have been fit to be tied, too, if she'd found out. No. She didn't know. And it was for the best, what with her being so sad and all. She was just holding on, best she could. But people can be mean spirited, don't you know. Lots of folks started snickerin' behind her back about being a gold digger and a black widow. As for me and George, well, we just helped out with food and the like whenever we could."

"Poor Helen," I sympathize, but my mind is racing. "Now Carl's gone too. His niece, Tiffany, is the activities director here, isn't she?"

Jinny and George look confused, but then realization dawns on them both at once. "You mean Bubbles," Jinny says, chuckling. "She makes us all call her Bubbles, so that's the only name we know her by. Yeah, she came to work here not long after Carl moved in. She used to sing on one of those cruise ships out of Fort Lauderdale, don't you know. Her parents are gone, I think. Only family she had left was Carl, and now he's gone too. Of course, she tells us all we're like family to her now, but I guess the proof'll be in the pudding with Carl dead."

For the first time, it occurs to me someone else might have had a motive for killing Carl. If Bubbles was the only family he had left, she probably stood to benefit in the event of his death. When Carl got married, her chance of inheriting his money may have dropped. Or, since he was killed so soon after his wedding, did he even have time to change his will in Helen's favor?

Jinny has once again proved to be a valuable source of information, even if the nuggets of usefulness are tucked away like needles at the bottom of a pile of porcupine quills. I make a mental note to ask Detective Fletcher to look into it as I begin clearing the dishes from the table.

All that's left is to make it through the rest of the evening without developing a migraine.

I give Jinny and George a big smile. "Anyone for sugar-free ice cream?"

Nine

The woman staring back at me from the mirror looks surprised, horrified, and completely unrecognizable.

"You like?" Selena asks after wheeling my chair around so that I'm facing the mirror.

When I'd arrived, as arranged, on Tuesday morning, to look at her Mary Kay selections, we'd had a bit of trouble communicating. Her English is a bit rusty, and my Spanish is nonexistent. So, when she had pantomimed giving me a makeover, I'd enthusiastically agreed. What woman doesn't enjoy a little pampering every now and again?

That was before I saw the results.

Selena is smiling. Something that, I sense, doesn't happen often. I don't want to hurt her feelings.

"It's definitely...something!" I try to smile back at her

from underneath several layers of bright red lipstick and shiny gloss.

While it does appear she has the foundation that I love so much in stock, she used that as a literal base coat before painting heavy layers of blush, bronzer, and eyeshadow on my face. It would not surprise me to learn she used every single one of her products in the demonstration.

"You want buy everything I use?" she asks, pointing to a line of nearly a dozen jars, compacts, and tubes, all laid out on the portable vanity table she has set up in her living room.

"Oh. Um. I definitely want the foundation!"

She rests her hands on her ample hips, her smile disappearing. "That's it? What about eyeshadow or blush? All best quality."

Confrontation isn't my area of expertise. And even though Selena was cleared in the recent murder of my neighbor, I'm still a bit terrified of her. "Of course! I'll take everything!"

She claps her hands, arm flab jiggling, and starts bagging up my purchases in little pink bags with black writing. I'll have to cut back on groceries for the next few weeks to cover the cost, but I don't see another tactful way out of the situation.

Selena probably assumes that, like everyone else at Egret's Loft, money is not an issue for me. She couldn't know that, were it not for my children paying for me to live here, I would never be able to afford the place.

Given that I'm now her client, I don't see any reason not to try and get a little information out of her. "Such a shame about Carl. You were out of town, but I assume you heard that he died?"

"*Si.*" She smiles for the second time in our acquaintance, revealing dazzling white teeth.

I frown, wondering if she misunderstood what I said. "Carl is dead."

"*Si,*" she repeats, still smiling.

I try to remember the Spanish equivalent. "*Muerdo.*"

The smile turns into a frown, and she takes a step back. "You want bite me?"

"What? No! Doesn't *muerdo* mean dead?"

"Ahhh, *entiendo.*" She seems to relax. "*Muerto*, with 't.' This means dead, *si!*"

She did understand me. "You don't seem that upset about it."

She makes a tsking sound with her mouth. "Carl was a good salesman, but he lie. He try to sell me fancy, old car. Big problems. It was a lime."

"Lime? Oh, you mean he tried to sell you a lemon?"

Her hands are back on her hips. Her large breasts leaning menacingly toward me. "That's what I say."

"Yes, of course it was!" I inadvertently put up my hands to block her attack, but quickly realize how silly that must look. I try to cover by running my hands through my shoulder-length white-blond hair. "Carl wasn't a very ethical used car salesman, then?"

"No." She laughs, her brightly colored caftan quaking, then abruptly stops and narrows her brown eyes. "But no one cheat Selena Castillo."

I swallow the lump in my throat. "How much do I owe you? For the makeup."

She waves a meaty hand, diamonds from her Rolex watch catching the late morning light. "You pay me later. In two weeks. If you not like, I not charge."

I wonder if this is a tactic her husband and son used when selling drugs. Get people hooked, then start driving up the price. Hopefully, none of the products she's selling me are as addictive as meth.

"Thank you so much," I tell her as she hands me my purchases and walks me to the front door. "I'll be back soon to pay for everything. I'm sure I'll love it all."

"*Vayase por la sombrita.*" She smiles, points up at the sun, and then closes the door in my uncomprehending face.

Being in Florida now, I should probably start learning Spanish.

During the short walk back to my house, I think about Carl. Gina mentioned that he'd made his money as a used car salesman, but I hadn't thought much about it at the time. It strikes me now that, if Carl was willing to sell dodgy cars to his neighbors, he'd have no compunction about selling lemons to perfect strangers. It seems like a stretch to think that could be a reason someone would want him dead but, having been married to a homicide detective for nearly forty years, I know people have killed for a lot less.

As I approach my house, I turn and wave to Phyllis Dipner. She lives in the house across the street. The eighty-eight-year-old rarely leaves her house, but when she does, she moves with the stealth of a ninja. The curtains flutter, and I see the kitchen light in the back flash on and off. It's her way of saying hello.

Just then, I see movement out of the corner of my eye. A petite woman wearing a large hat and a loose white shirt is kneeling in the front yard of the house next door to mine. Thinking she must be my new neighbor, I walk quickly into my own house and grab the welcome basket I'd prepared for her but hadn't yet had the time to carry over.

"Welcome to Egret's Loft!" I announce loudly as I advance up the woman's driveway, not wanting to surprise her. As you get older, you start thinking about things like this. That something that would once send your heart racing, can now stop it altogether.

I see the woman's back stiffen, then she rises as if there's a string on her head pulling her toward heaven. In her movement is an effortless grace that seems vaguely familiar. When she turns to face me, removing large-framed sunglasses, I understand why. I saw her, outside the clubhouse, the night of Carl and Helen's wedding.

She stares at me, a puzzled expression on her face. Then I remember, I never took off the makeup Selena applied on my face. I must look like a clown.

"My name is Madeline. I live next door." I get the preliminaries out of the way. "Forgive my appearance, I just had a makeover that didn't go quite as planned."

Her delicate lips tilt upward politely, revealing the slenderest veins of crow's feet at the corners of her eyes. She pulls off a heavy rubber gardening glove to shake my hand.

"It's pleasure to meet you," she says, all her vowels heavily stressed. With her thick Russian accent, *it's* sounds like *eats*. "My name is Natasha Boriskya."

It takes some effort not to giggle. Her name brings back childhood memories of a cartoon featuring a pair of Russian spies called Boris and Natasha. Somehow, she ended up with both of their names. I almost want to ask her to quote the show, *"You're so bad, you're good."*

Instead, I say, "I brought this for you," and hand her the basket filled with wine, cheeses, and gourmet crackers. "Please excuse me for not calling around sooner. I'd meant to bring it by when you first moved in, but things have been a bit chaotic lately."

She nods, her back ramrod straight as she accepts my offering. "Yes, I was very sorry to hear that man die here."

"Yes. Carl. Did you know him?" I ask.

One perfectly groomed eyebrow raises slightly. "How would I know this man? I only just move here."

"Oh, my mistake. I thought I saw you at the wedding on Saturday."

She smiles accommodatingly but says nothing. She sets the basket down on the ground and removes her other gardening glove. Even her fingers are long and elegant.

"What brings you to Egret's Loft?" I ask. "It's quite a bit different from Miami. That's where you moved from, right? My daughter lives there, so I've visited a few times."

The muscles between her eyebrows clench briefly, creating a slight furrow above her delicate nose before her face softens once again. She breaks eye contact to look at the gloves in her hands. "My husband die last month after very long and painful struggle. There were many memories. I needed change of scenery."

"I'm very sorry for your loss." My heart aches for her. "My own husband passed away recently also. If there is anything you need, anything at all, I'm just next door."

She glances up at me. There's a dewiness, like you'd find in a field on a misty morning, in her eyes. "Thank you for your kindness. It has been very hard time."

"I mean it. Anything you need," I feel the need to add before switching to a lighter topic. "Those are gorgeous flowers you're planting. What are they?"

She's lining the front of her house with basil-colored

shrubs that boast dainty, yellow blossoms. Each flower has five fragile petals in the formation of a star. I move closer, reaching out to touch one of them.

She puts her hand over mine. The pads of her fingers are cold despite the heat. "They are oleander plants. Safe to look. Not meant to touch."

"They're poisonous, aren't they?"

She lifts her hand from mine to wipe away a stray lock of light gray hair that's come loose from under her large sun hat. "Only when eaten. But touching can also create... discomfort. Better to admire at distance or wear strong gloves."

A car pulls onto our street and turns into my driveway, drawing our attention away from the potentially deadly shrubs. I recognize the car.

"It was very nice to meet you, Natasha," I tell her, suddenly eager to leave. "I look forward to getting to know you better."

She bends her slender neck in acknowledgment. "As do I."

With a quick smile, I take my leave, careful to walk the long way around on the sidewalk rather than traipse through the bushes and palm trees that separate our properties.

Detective Fletcher is waiting for me by my front door, his face grim. When he sees me approaching, the expectant look in my eyes, he simply shakes his head. It can only mean one thing. Confirmation.

Another killer is loose in Egret's Loft.

Ten

"I don't have much time," Detective Fletcher says, full of wary energy. "Got to get back to the station. I just figured I'd stop by to let you know."

"The coroner ruled Carl's death a homicide," I guess.

"How can this be happening again? So soon?" he laments, shifting his weight from foot to foot. "And who would kill a man by taping him to a chair and shooting a champagne cork into his mouth?"

"It is rather...imaginative," I agree.

Standing under the beating sun outside of my front door, caught up in our own thoughts, neither of us notice Jinny and a handsome young man pausing on the sidewalk.

"Hi, Madeline! Oh, Detective Fletcher, hello to you too!" Jinny calls out. "This is my grandson, Paul. Paul, say hello to the nice people." Paul opens his mouth, but Jinny doesn't give him the time to speak. "He's just arrived, so I thought I would show him around a bit. He's very interested in singing, so I was taking him over to meet Bubbles. She used to sing on a cruise ship, don't you know."

Out of the corner of my eye, I see Detective Fletcher checking his watch.

"Welcome, Paul!" I pause, waiting for him to reply. He glances at his grandmother to see if she'll let him speak but, in the end, he decides to say nothing. He must be taking his cues from George. I continue, "I'm sure we'll be seeing a lot of each other. But right now, I need to get out of this heat. Have a wonderful day!"

Before Jinny can embark on a long-winded soliloquy about the near triple-digit temperature, I open the door and pull Detective Fletcher into the house. Jinny is a lovely woman, and she's a great resource for learning about the neighbors, but the detective is clearly pressed for time, and I'm eager to hear what he has to say.

"I have to leave in a minute. Sammy will be looking for me, wanting to know our next move." He rolls his eyes.

I frown. "Sammy?"

"You know her as Junior Detective Samantha Baptiste. My new partner. She's the most by-the-book cop I've ever met. It's good. I mean, I appreciate it. I do."

"But...?"

He lets out his breath in a long exhale. "It's so exhausting."

I can't help but laugh. Clint used to have a partner like that. Detective Jeffries. He was a tall, handsome black man, who looked tough, but anyone who knew him longer than five minutes could see his insides were made of jelly. It drove Clint to distraction, the way Jeffries would spend hours on his incident reports. He wrote down everything, even the most seemingly inconsequential details. Then, after the first time it saved their case in court, Clint converted to Jeffries's way of thinking.

"You'll appreciate it someday," I tell him, but by the look on his face it's obvious that time is not now.

"Anyway," he changes the subject. "I can't tell you anything about who our main suspect is just yet—"

"Helen, you mean?" I interrupt.

"Not necessarily. We're looking at other people as well!" he insists.

"Such as?"

He opens his mouth, then closes it. "Alright, fine. Helen is our main suspect. But I promise to keep an open mind until we have more evidence against her."

Once he hears the circumstances of her other husbands' deaths, I'm pretty sure his mind will slam shut. Since I haven't known Helen long, or well enough, to say whether she's just supremely unlucky or a full-blown psychopath, I don't try to defend her to Detective Fletcher.

"Were you able to get any new information out of her yesterday?"

Detective Fletcher looks at me like I'm a magician who refuses to reveal the nature of my tricks. "Is there anything happening on this street you don't know about?"

"Plenty!" I assure him.

"Just between us, we didn't talk to Helen for long. She confirmed some witness testimony concerning her whereabouts before the murder, but stuck to her story that, when she found Carl, he was already dead."

"You don't believe her?"

Detective Fletcher rubs at a small mole on the top of his tanned, bald head. "I don't know. She seemed pretty broken up about the whole thing, but this was her eighth husband. I mean, what are the odds they'd all be dead?"

"Did she talk to you about how they died?"

He shakes his head. "We tried, but that's when she told us to get lost. She said, if we wanted to talk about her past, she'd need to have a lawyer present."

"So now you *really* think she did it?"

"Heck yeah! In my experience, you only need a lawyer if you've got something to hide."

There have been plenty of proven cases of wrongful convictions, enough to know that even the innocent can benefit from decent attorneys. But Detective Fletcher is looking at his watch again, and I remember I'd made a mental note to ask him who stands to benefit most from Carl's passing.

"You don't happen to have a copy of Carl's will, do you?" I ask. "I was just wondering who was named as his beneficiary."

"Yeah, as a matter of fact, I do. Hang on a second," he says, pulling a notebook out of his back pocket. A pair of handcuffs seems to get caught up in the reach-around, but he doesn't notice them until we hear the heavy metal bracelets slamming against the floor tiles in my foyer.

"Gosh darn it! I'm always dropping those blasted things!" he complains.

In my experience, Detective Fletcher isn't the most squared away with his police-issued equipment. He'd once left his gun sitting on my sofa cushion after it had fallen, unbeknownst to him, out of its holster.

I watch as he shoves the handcuffs back into his pocket forcefully. He glances around momentarily, trying to think back to what he was doing before the handcuffs got in his way, then, remembering, he opens his little police notebook.

"Carl's will. You wanted to know who the beneficiary was. I have it down here as a Ms. Tiffany Hancock, niece of the deceased. Does that name mean anything to you?"

I try raising just one of my eyebrows, but I can feel both lifting at the same time. I've never been able to master those facial muscles. "Umm, yes. It means something to you too."

He looks up from his notebook. "It does?"

"Bubbles? The singing Egret's Loft activities director. The one who got everyone away from the crime scene the night of the murder. Remember her?"

"No way! That's his niece? She's about to become one lucky lady."

I know it's gauche to ask, but I can't stop myself. "How much does she get?"

"Says in my notes she'll get at least fifteen million greenbacks. Not counting property and stock and all that."

I whistle. "That's a pretty strong motive for murder. Was Helen in the will at all?"

"No. Not on paper anyway. Carl's attorney told me she could contest it, since she was legally his wife. Even if the marriage only lasted a few hours."

"Did the attorney say how much luck she might have if she contested the will?"

"He wasn't sure." Detective Fletcher closes his notebook. "He'd never had a client die within his first few hours of wedded bliss. But he did tell me something interesting."

I wait for him to continue, but he seems content to torture me by withholding.

"Honestly, Pete," I call the detective by his given name for the first time, "my blood pressure can't take much more of the suspense."

"Alright, alright," he capitulates. "Apparently, Carl was scheduled to go into the lawyer's office on Monday."

"The first business day after the wedding," I point out. "Did the attorney say what this meeting was about?"

"Carl said he wanted the attorney to draw up a new will. And he was planning to bring Helen along to the meeting."

"And there was no prenup?" I ask.

Detective Fletcher shakes his head. "Not that I've seen."

I take a minute to process the information. We've been standing this whole time in the entryway, and my knees are starting to lock up. I begin to pace.

It would seem Carl had every intention of putting Helen in his will. He just didn't live long enough to go through with it. If Bubbles knew her uncle planned to redo his will, she stood to lose a lot of money by the end of the weekend.

"It seems to me," I finally say, "you have yourself another suspect. Have you questioned Bubbles yet?"

"We took her statement after the murder, but that's it." Detective Fletcher's phone starts to ring. He looks at the caller ID and sighs. "Anything more will have to wait for now. I've got to get back to the office."

I open the door for him, saying, "You go ahead. We'll speak again soon."

After shuffling him out the door, I head straight for the

events calendar on my refrigerator's touchpad screen. I'm in luck.

It's time to get better acquainted with Bubbles.

Eleven

"You told me we'd be investigating a murder," Gina whispers. "Why in the heck am I holding sheet music for *Cats*?"

We're standing a little apart from the crowd, mostly women, who've assembled in a side room of the main clubhouse for Bubbles's daily chorus practice. A half-moon of chairs is set up facing a large flat screen television and a portable conductor stand that's bright pink and covered in glitter.

I'd have thought Jinny would love it, but she doesn't seem to notice it from where she's standing across the room next to the refreshment table. She's accepting a cookie from Marjorie Higginbottom, who has a tray of treats affixed to the front of her walker.

"What is a Jellicle cat anyway? Is it like a calico?" Gina continues.

"No, they're not real. T.S. Eliot created them for a poem," I tell her.

"T.S. Eliot?" Gina shakes her head. "Never heard of him."

"He won a Nobel Prize."

"For writing poems about make-believe cats?" she asks, incredulous.

"Never mind. Can we just focus on why we're here?"

"Sure," Gina agrees. "Care to fill me in on why we *are* here, in a room full of people about to start singing about some fictional felines?"

"Bubbles," I tell her.

Gina frowns. "What now?"

"You know, Carl Hancock's niece." I tilt my head toward Bubbles, who is currently excitedly waving her arms around, deep in conversation with Jinny's handsome grandson. She seems in high spirits for someone who just lost her uncle, but perhaps they weren't particularly close. Or she knows how much he was worth.

"Why the sudden interest in her?" Gina asks, then grabs my upper arm as delight twinkles in her eyes. "Oh, oh! Is she a suspect in Carl's murder?"

"Shhh. Keep your voice down!" I whisper, even though there's no one around to hear us. All the other choral participants are selecting their seats in the semicircle or snacking at the refreshment table. Only Gina and I are standing in the corner like two shy teenage girls at their first boy-girl dance.

"Give it a rest, hun." Gina waves off my concern. "No one can hear us over here. Besides, they've probably all turned their hearing aids down before the singing starts. Is that why we're here?" she continues. "To get the 411 on our new murder suspect?"

"Does 411 still work?" I ask, realizing we're being sidetracked, but also wanting an answer. "I tried calling it a while back, wanting to find an old friend, and somehow ended up ordering a pizza."

Gina thinks about it. "Does your friend make pizza?"

"No."

"Then you could be right. 411 might not work anymore," she agrees. "What are we trying to find out about Bunny?"

"*Bubbles.*" I look over at the round, perky woman, my eyes squinted. "I don't know. Not yet anyway. What do you know about her?"

"She hasn't been here long," Gina says. "Maybe six months or so. She used to work for one of those big cruise ship outfits. Singing in the shows and stuff like that."

"So how did she end up at Egret's Loft?"

"The way Carl made it sound when he asked the board to hire her, she got replaced for a younger model. At work and at home. So, she was out of work and in the middle of a divorce. The board put her on a trial period, and here we are."

"Did she and Carl get along?"

"Sure, as far as I could tell," Gina says.

I'm about to ask about Bubbles's finances but am interrupted by a loud clap from behind the fancy pink conductor stand.

"Seats everyone. It's time to start singing," Bubbles croons, stretching out the last syllable.

She claps her hands a few more times to get everyone in their chairs. Marjorie is taking a little while to maneuver her walker with all the treats attached to the front. She hands out fresh baked cookies to everyone she passes on the way to her own seat. Gina and I are on the other side of the semicircle so, sadly, we don't get a cookie. They smell delicious.

"Everybody ready for some *fun*? No video recordings, please. I don't have rights to the songs, and the last thing I need is Andrew Lloyd Webber coming after me for royalties!" She laughs, a big theatrical laugh that shakes the rolls under her linen top. "Today, we're just going to sing along to karaoke as you get familiar with the lyrics. Doesn't that sound nice?"

Out of the corner of my eye, I see Marjorie and Jinny smiling and nodding.

"Here we go then!" Bubbles twirls around on the balls of her feet and sets the television to play our first song.

Over the next hour and a half, Bubbles runs us through nearly all the songs in her *Cats* karaoke playlist. Three things become glaringly obvious. One, Egret's Loft has a lot of tone-deaf residents. Two, Gina has an incredibly glorious voice, and when she sings, she completely loses her Bronx accent. And three, that Jinny's grandson, Paul, might have a career in musical theater.

At one point, during a song about two cats called Mungojerrie and Rumpleteazer, Paul got up and started dancing. Bubbles joined him, singing the other part of the duet, and doing the same dance. Gina and I looked at each other, confused.

When my parents took me to my first musical, *The Music Man*, I'd been very perplexed by the dancing. If it was supposed to be spontaneous, how did they all seem to know the same dance? I have the same feeling now, only this is real life.

Still, when the song ended, and Paul took a bow, I couldn't help clapping for the kid. His smile was so wide I could practically see his molars.

After what feels like an eternity, Bubbles pauses her playlist, and my aching throat rejoices.

"Did everyone have an amazing time?" Bubbles asks, slightly out of breath. The murmur of enthusiasm from the crowd is less than she'd been hoping for. "I can't hear you! Did you have *fun?*"

Gina clears her throat to speak, but my hand on her arm, and the roar of Paul's clapping hands stops her.

"I'm so glad you all came today! Before you go, I do want to invite you all to the River Club tonight." Bubbles's face transforms, like those theater masks where one is smiling, and the other is crying. She just put on the other mask. "We're having a little memorial for my Uncle Carl. Some songs, some stories. Things like that. I hope you'll all be there."

Jinny rises first from her seat to rush over to Bubbles, offering her condolences. Other choral members follow suit until Bubbles is surrounded by well-wishers. Gina and I saunter over to the refreshment table in an attempt to wait out all the people wanting to talk to Bubbles.

Forty-five minutes later, the water pitchers empty and the last of the crudités consumed, Jinny and Paul are still deep in conversation with Bubbles. Gina looks at her watch and shoots me a look that tells me it's time to leave.

Reluctantly, I set down my empty water glass and start moving with Gina toward the door.

"Talk it over with George," I can hear Bubbles saying to Jinny. "I'd love to do some private lessons with your grandson. He has so much talent. We can work out a price you're comfortable with. It doesn't have to be much. But I do think he would benefit from daily instruction."

Paul looks anxiously at his grandmother, his hands folded in silent prayer. From the look on Jinny's face, it's obvious she'll agree to whatever Bubbles wants to charge for the lessons.

I can't help wondering if Bubbles needs some extra income as she waits for her uncle's inheritance.

Twelve

"Mrs. Delarouse, we have a few questions we'd like to ask you."

Looking up from my golf cart's power cord, which I was just about to plug in, I see a woman's trim body silhouetted by the late afternoon sun flooding into my garage. I've only just returned from choral practice and haven't even made it inside yet for a sip of water to ease my sore vocal cords.

"Who's there? I can't see you in this light," I tell the unknown and unfamiliar figure.

Accommodatingly, she steps to the side, and I recognize Detective Samantha Baptiste from our initial meeting the night Carl was killed.

"Hello, Detective Baptiste," I greet her as Detective

Fletcher walks up. Behind his partner's back, he shakes his head, and I know not to mention our earlier meeting. "It's rather warm this afternoon. Would you like to come inside to ask your questions?"

"We can either do that," the beautiful, young female detective informs me, "or we can do this down at the station."

Surprised by the escalation in what I'd assumed would be a friendly follow-up, I turn to Detective Fletcher for guidance. Detective Baptiste follows my line of sight and frowns.

"There's no reason we can't handle this here," Detective Fletcher assures me. "Let's just go inside so we can get to the bottom of things, yes?"

While I do feel proud of him for taking the initiative to speak up to his new, junior partner, I am confused about what things they think I'll be able to help them get to the bottom of. After offering them water or iced tea, both of which were soundly rejected, we take our seats at the kitchen table.

"I'm just going to come right out with it, Mrs. Delarouse," Detective Baptiste begins. "We think you were having an affair with the groom, Carl Hancock. We also think you haven't been honest with us about where you were at the time of his murder."

She leans back in her chair, forcing a look of relaxation

that's betrayed by the rapidly pulsing artery in her slender neck.

I'm tempted to laugh but that would probably just make her angry. "First of all, I've never even been alone in a room with Carl Hancock, let alone for any kind of sordid tryst!" The thought alone turns my stomach in loops. "Second, I told you exactly where I was from the time Carl went to the DJ booth to the time Helen found his body. There were witnesses. Now, would you care to tell me why I'm getting the third-degree for no apparent reason?"

Detective Fletcher coughs to cover a laugh; he's probably relieved someone else is on the other end of my no-nonsense attitude. His partner looks like she wants to take me down a peg.

"Oh really?" She shoots her eyebrows up toward her hairline. "Do you want to explain to me then why your fingerprints were on the hair thingy clutched in our victim's hand?"

I tilt my head slightly. "Hair *thingy*?"

"Yes, it's like a barrette," she says, in a manner that can only be described as patronizing. She pulls out a picture of my hair clip, labeled now as evidence, from her purse. "Maybe this will help jog your memory."

"You may be an officer of the law, young lady," I tell her, "but that's no excuse for being rude. While I may shuffle a little slower these days, I do still possess a full deck."

Detective Fletcher doesn't even attempt to cover his laugh this time, which makes his partner even angrier.

"Now," I continue, "there was a lot of confusion the night of the murder, so I will forgive you for forgetting what I have already told you. The hair clip found in Carl's hand was mine. It's not surprising that you found my fingerprints on it. Helen borrowed it for the wedding."

Belatedly, I realize, by saying that, I might be throwing Helen under the proverbial prison bus. My lips snap shut.

"So, Helen was wearing it that night?" Detective Fletcher asks, opening his notebook for the first time since they'd arrived.

"I put it in her hair before the wedding. To be honest, I didn't notice if she still had it on at the end of the night," I quickly add, for Helen's sake. "If it had fallen out, anyone could have picked it up. Were mine the only fingerprints you found?"

Detective Fletcher nods. "Well, yours and Carl's. Obviously."

"Did you dust the champagne bottle?" I ask, using my peripheral vision to assess whether Detective Baptiste objects to me asking them questions about the case. Unsurprisingly, she does.

"We'll be asking the questions, thank you." She smiles through bared teeth. "How close is your relationship with Helen Richards?"

"She lives down the street." I point out the obvious. "I

haven't been here long. I only got to know her because my neighbor was murdered, and I was looking for suspects. We're not that close." I bend the truth slightly. There is a special kind of bond that grows when you've falsely accused your neighbor of murder.

"You were close enough to loan her a very expensive, jeweled hair clip," Detective Baptiste points out. "Are you covering for her now?"

Her eyes bore into mine, and I swallow the lump in my throat that's threatening to suffocate me.

I'm a terrible liar. If I say I'm not covering for Helen, the young detective's predator-like eyes will seize on my dishonesty. Then again, if I tell them what I'm hiding—that Helen told me Carl's death was all her fault—I might as well be telling them she's guilty.

"I loaned her something blue because I felt sorry for her." I try to stick as closely to the truth as possible. "She doesn't have any family or many friends. I just wanted her day to be special." All true. "Oh, and I did feel responsible for popping her breast implant. And for having the guy she used to like arrested for murder. So, there might have been a little guilt at play as well."

Detective Baptiste, jaw hanging slightly open, turns to look at her partner for a translation.

Detective Fletcher closes his notebook. "As far as I am concerned, you're in the clear," he says. Detective Baptiste opens her mouth, likely to challenge him, but he silences her by holding up his hand and shaking his head. "Madeline, thank you for your time. We appreciate your assistance."

Detective Baptiste turns to me, a fake smile painted on her face. "Will you please give us a moment?" she asks me.

I look around, wondering if she realizes she's in my kitchen. She's asking me to get lost in my own house? Children just aren't raised with the same respect for their elders that they were in my day.

Then, I remember the app Ritchie had installed on my iPad. He'd linked it to a portable security camera that's on my kitchen counter. If I open the app, I'll have video and audio of everything that happens in my living room and kitchen.

"Of course," I graciously acquiesce. "Take all the time you need."

I walk slowly to the bedroom, the detectives' silence shadowing my every step. Once I close the door, I race to my nightstand, pick up my iPad and open the app. An image of the two detectives, still seated at the kitchen table, fills the screen.

"I think she's lying," I hear Detective Baptiste say from behind closed doors in the other room. Unfortunately, I had the volume up high on my iPad, so she hears herself too.

"Did you hear that?" she says, turning her head toward my bedroom door.

I grab a pair of headphones off the nightstand and quickly plug them in, just in time to hear Detective Fletcher say, "I didn't hear anything."

"There's something she's not telling us," Detective Baptiste says. "I think she's involved somehow."

"Madeline? No way! She's the one who caught the last murderer here at Egret's Loft. She's a bit nosy, sure. But she means well, and she's good at solving crimes."

The comment about being nosy stings a bit, but I suppose it's an accurate assessment.

"You're just sweet on her because she's helping you with your books," Detective Baptiste accuses her partner. "As cops, we have to check our emotions at the door."

Detective Fletcher sits up straighter in his chair. "You might want to watch your tone, detective. I'm still your senior officer," he reminds her. I want to cheer him on for being so assertive on the job. I don't because that would give me away, but I really want to.

"Plus, we have nothing on her," he continues. "If we'd found her prints on the champagne bottle that would be one thing. But the bottle had been wiped clean, as you know. If she did kill Carl, why would she wipe the bottle and not the hair clip? It doesn't make any sense."

With that, Detective Fletcher stands up and puts his notebook back in his pocket.

"So, what? We're just going to leave now? I have a few

more questions about her relationship with Helen." Detective Baptiste pouts.

"No, you don't," he says, then in a louder voice, "Madeline, we're heading out."

I drop the iPad and headphones on my bed and walk as quickly as I can to the bedroom door, pulling it shut behind me.

"Off so soon?" I ask the detectives, my face flush from the ignominy of eavesdropping.

"We can see ourselves out. Thank you for your time," Detective Fletcher says.

His partner just stares at me, the way you'd stare at a dog you suspect might be rabid.

"One quick thing, detective. When can I get my hair clip back? My late husband gave it to me. It has a lot of sentimental value."

Detective Fletcher frowns apologetically. "Oh, I'm sorry. As long as this is an open case, I'm afraid we'll have to hang on to it."

"But it's not evidence! Not really. Only my prints were on it. And Carl's, of course, but that's to be expected since the clip was in his hand. I really would like it back, detective."

He shakes his head, but says in a low voice, "I'll see what I can do."

Detective Fletcher is the first out the front door and halfway to his car, when Detective Baptiste stops before stepping out onto my welcome mat. She turns around and looks me square in the eye. "You're hiding something," she whispers. "But know this, I will find out what it is."

As soon as she's across the threshold, I close and lock the door.

I should probably call Ritchie and Eliza to tell them Carl's death has been ruled a murder. Especially since it's quite clear Detective Baptiste thinks I'm a suspect.

Thirteen

Dozens of helium balloons shaped like classic cars float by in the twilight overhead as I curse my kids for making me late to Carl's memorial service.

Ritchie and Eliza had spent the vast majority of the past hour and a half bickering with each other over the phone about whether I should remain at Egret's Loft and which one of them should come down to stay with me until the case was solved.

In theory, it was a group call for the family. In reality, they didn't once ask me for my opinion.

And now I'm late paying my respects, not to mention I've missed a prime opportunity to assess the pool of potential suspects in Carl's murder.

Clint always used to attend the funerals for the victims

in his cases. He said killers often have an irrepressible desire to relive their crimes by witnessing the hurt they left behind. Of course, that was before shows like *CSI* and *Criminal Minds* clued prospective criminals in on ways to outwit the law. Maybe times have changed.

Walking up to join the candle-wielding mourners next to the pool at the River Club, I can't help but notice that the crowd is even larger than the one that assembled a mere three days ago, in this same location, to celebrate Carl's wedding. All the staff and residents of Egret's Loft seem to have turned out for his memorial.

I suppose, at our age, it's only practical to put more faith in death than weddings.

"Pardon me, but it looks like you're in need of a candle." A husky male voice draws my attention.

Turning, I see the man Roy had identified as his neighbor, Andy Romano. His cheekbones sit high on his face, under piercing brown eyes with impossibly long lashes. Jowls haven't gained any ground on his strong jawline. He still has a full head of dark hair, though the sides have begun to turn white, almost as if he dipped his hands in white paint and then ran them through the hair on either side of his head. A patch of skin behind his left ear is white and pitted, likely a scar from a very old burn, but the minor deformity only seems to add to his appeal.

"I'm afraid I arrived late," I admit, admiring the pattern on the silk scarf that sits loosely around his neck. I wonder if it's one of his own design. "You wouldn't happen to know where I could get one, do you?"

"My dear lady, all the candles have been handed out already," he says regretfully. "Please, take mine."

I look down at the unlit, white taper candle in his hand. "Thank you, but I couldn't possibly."

"It would be my honor to give it to you," he insists. "Also, since I didn't know the man very well, it will make me feel less like an impostor if you carry his flame, so to speak."

"In that case, I accept. Thank you." Taking the candle in my left hand, I blush. I've always been a sucker for good manners.

"We haven't been introduced. My name is Andy Romano." He takes my right hand in his and kisses the top of it. His eyes angled up, he watches me as his lips brush against my skin.

While I'd be blind not to find the suave continental man attractive, I have no interest in dating anyone. Clint has been gone for six months, but I don't think I'll ever feel like we're not still married.

"I'm Madeline Delarouse. I think we're on the same street. You live next door to Roy, don't you?"

"Ah yes, the delightful Mr. Everhard." He smiles, though his aquiline nose twitches disdainfully. His hand continues to gently clasp mine.

"What are you flappin' your lips about?" Roy must have

heard his name, because suddenly he's limping over to me, breathing heavily, and looking territorially down at my hand, which Andy hasn't yet released. "I don't have a spiteful bone in my body. I told you, I didn't mean for that football to break your window. It was an accident!"

Andy calmly looks on, unruffled by the much larger former football star trying to intimidate him.

"Roy. He said *delightful*, not *spiteful*," I clarify what I perceive to have been a misunderstanding.

Roy looks at Andy, who just nods.

"I see," Roy says, relaxing his fists. "My bad. Just feeling a bit tense, I guess. What with Carl dyin'. What were you two talkin' about?"

Roy tries to put his arm around my shoulder. I purposefully drop my candle and lean to pick it up, effectively outmaneuvering Roy's attempt at possessiveness.

Andy smiles. I get the sense that little slips past his notice. "I was about to extend an invitation to a small get-together at my house this Friday," he says. "Consider it my reintroduction to Egret's Loft, after having spent a fair bit of time away in Italy working on my new clothing line. Anyone who lives on Cypress Point Avenue is welcome to attend."

Roy's silence sits heavily on the humid night air. He grimaces as he shifts his weight. It seems his right leg, the one that took a direct hit from my fish, is still giving him a little discomfort.

"That sounds lovely!" I break the standoff. "I'm sure it will be a nice distraction for Helen too."

Realizing I haven't seen Carl's widow since my arrival, I search the crowd for her long blond hair. I spot her, dressed in a tasteful knee-length black dress, in conversation with Serenity Karma, Egret's Loft's resident artist and art teacher. Helen looks angry. Serenity strokes the small yellow flowers woven into her loose braid.

"I don't suppose any of you has a match?" Dr. Frank Rosen joins our conversation. "They want everyone to light their candles."

Roy and I shrug our shoulders, unable to be of assistance. Andy reaches into the back of his khaki-colored linen pants and pulls out a sterling silver refillable lighter.

"Allow me," he says, proceeding to light all our candles.

"Oh, can you get mine too?" Gina asks, sidling up next to me in the group. After Andy has lit her candle, she examines his face. "You're the guy that lives two houses down from me. The fashion designer. It's Antonio, right?"

Andy's jaw clenches and his nostrils flare slightly. "My name is Andy. Not Antonio."

"That's the one," Gina says, oblivious to the irritation she causes by constantly misidentifying people. "Thanks a million. I'm Gina. My husband, Leon, is around here somewhere. Probably hiding, in case Bunny starts to sing again."

"Andy was just inviting us all to a party at his house on Friday," I tell Gina. "Everyone on our street is invited."

"It's been some time since anyone's arranged a block party," Dr. Rosen chimes in, his eyeglasses looking misty from the humidity. "What can we bring? Beer? Burgers for the grill?"

Andy's mouth falls open, only for a moment, before he regains his composure. "That's a kind offer, but unnecessary. I'll be having the event catered. Some Italian favorites of mine and, of course, plenty of wine."

Roy snorts, sophistication likely being another reason he thinks Andy is a snob.

"I'm more of a beer aficionado, myself," Dr. Rosen says. "The Italians do have some nice breweries. Peroni makes a wonderful lager, Menabrea a good blonde. Moretti's nice, as well, though I think Heineken owns them now—so, I'm not sure if that still classifies as Italian. What do you say, Andy?"

"You must excuse me," Andy demurs, "I'm afraid I never drink beer. As a result, I cannot contribute anything worthwhile to the discussion. But I will make sure to have a few options for you at the party."

"Good man!" Dr. Rosen says, removing his glasses and wiping them on a cloth from his shirt pocket. "A party will do wonders to lift our spirits after what happened to Carl."

"What party?" Bubbles sounds simultaneously upbeat and put out. She's wearing a black dress that looks like it would be better suited to a high school prom.

Paul, trailing behind her in slacks and a tie, looks like he wants to be anywhere else.

We fill her in on Andy's plan, with Gina clarifying it's only for residents of our street, lest Bubbles announce it to everyone at the end of tonight's event.

"I guess that means I can come!" Bubbles claps her large hands. "I'm moving into Uncle Carl's house tomorrow! Not permanently, only until it can be sold. Someone has to clean out his things, and Helen didn't want to do it, so..."

"You poor thing," I sympathize, remembering all the bittersweet tears I shed when going through Clint's papers. "That won't be easy. If you need any help at all, I live just up the street."

"No, it won't be easy." She looks away in a manner that seems overly dramatic. It's hard to tell whether she's been in cabarets so long that even her honest expressions seem staged, or if she's faking her grief now. "But I've already been learning a lot I didn't know about Uncle Carl."

"Nothing dirty, I hope!" Gina chuckles. I elbow her into silence.

"Lordy, no!" a reanimated Bubbles exclaims. "Nothing like that! Things like...oh...did any of you know that Uncle Carl went to medical school?"

Gina frowns. "I thought he was a used car salesman."

"My uncle had many dealerships. Only a few sold used

cars. And those were all classics." Bubbles defends her dead relative.

"How do ya go from med school to selling cars?" Roy wants to know.

"I have no idea!" Bubbles admits, holding her stomach as she laughs. "All I know is I found some of his old things from college. Apparently, he was pre-med. I even found a picture of him, dissecting a dead body. I can't believe he never *told* me."

Bubbles, still smiling, locks eyes with Dr. Rosen.

"Very interesting," he says, before breaking eye contact to stare at his shoes. Seconds later, he glances back at Bubbles and, noticing that she hasn't averted her gaze, he shoots a stern frown in her direction.

I'm finding the awkward moment between them very interesting, indeed, though no one else seems to notice. Is Bubbles trying to insinuate something about dead bodies? Maybe that Dr. Rosen did something to her uncle's?

"I guess it's all about repairs in the end," Roy continues, oblivious to the unspoken communication. "Whether it's a body or a car, both are gonna need a service every now and again, am I right?"

"Right you are!" Bubbles says, finally taking her eyes off the doctor. "Anyway, I just came over to make sure you all had your candles lit. I'm about to sing a few more songs."

"Really?" Gina blurts. When I glare at her, she adds, "I

mean, your voice must be tired from all the singing you did earlier."

"My uncle deserved a little discomfort. And like Neil Diamond said, everybody knows a song sung blue. Excuse me."

As Bubbles marches away, Gina leans toward me and says, "I don't know how Carl would feel, but I gotta tell you, we don't deserve any more discomfort. I'm outta here before she opens her hole again. See you later."

As Gina disappears into the crowd, I see Bubbles mounting an impromptu stage next to the pool. Out of the corner of my eye, I spy Helen sneaking around by the back fence, making an escape from her own husband's memorial service.

Microphone feedback causes everyone in the crowd to cover their ears, giving me a perfect opportunity to slip away.

If I hustle, I just may be able to catch up with Helen before she gets to her golf cart.

Fourteen

"Goodness gracious, sugar!" Helen exclaims, clutching her chest.

"Sorry! I didn't mean to scare you," I assure her.

"It's a bit late for that!" she complains, her hand still resting above her left breast. "My heart's fixin' to fall outta my knickers! What are you doing out here anyway? The memorial service isn't over."

"I could ask the same of you," I remind her.

"You have me there," she admits, leaning back against the frame of her golf cart. Shadows, cast by a nearby streetlamp, lend a sinister edge to her unnaturally smooth face. "Bless her heart, Bubbles really wanted to have that memorial. But all that singin' was a bit much for me."

She lifts her hands to cover her ears in an attempt to block out Bubbles's rendition of "Wind Beneath My Wings," which chases us into the empty parking lot on the breeze from the nearby river.

I find myself torn.

On the one hand, I want to get her away from everyone else so I can pump her for information about Bubbles. On the other hand, there's a chance Helen's already killed at least eight people. I may be old, but I'm not dead yet, and I have no desire to hasten along my end. But a sour note—more of a high-pitched screech—wafting from the stage at the River Club makes my decision.

"Would you like to take a walk with me? We can leave our golf carts here," I say.

"It's hotter than a goat's butt in a pepper patch," she grumbles. "But I suppose a walk would do me some good."

Giving the River Club a wide berth, we circle around to the river path and head southwest, toward Cypress Point Avenue. Not much light reaches the path, just the reflection of the moon on the languid waters of the Caloosahatchee River and randomly placed solar safety lights.

The rustling of leaves alerts us to movement in the mangrove forest on the other side of the river, but I try to shut out the sound. Alligators do love their swamps, and I'd prefer not to think too much about becoming their next meal.

Every few feet, Helen takes a deep breath and lets out an extended sigh. She seems to want to talk but can't find the words.

"How are you holding up?" I finally ask.

She kicks at some packed dirt with her open-toed, designer sandals. "Truth be told, I'm not sure I am. But I think I'm beginnin' to know how Dorothy must have felt—when she was halfway between Kansas and Oz. Like everything's spinnin' round and round, and I got no power to stop any of it. I feel about as useful as a screen door on a submarine."

I know how she feels. When Clint died, the smallest things sent me spiraling into confusion and self-doubt. Who would help me when I couldn't reach things on the top shelf of the pantry cupboard? Was the mechanic going to start telling me a myriad of things were wrong with my car, just so he could charge me more for repairs, thinking I didn't know any better? Would I be able to sleep at night in our now half-empty bed?

"You don't need to be useful right now," I assure her. "You're still in mourning."

She stops, halting our slow stroll toward Cypress Point Avenue. I want to ask her if we can keep walking. I can't say for certain, but I would assume moving targets would be harder for alligators to catch.

"Can I let you in on a little secret?" Helen asks and any thoughts of alligators instantly retreat.

"Of course, you can, dear!"

"I'm sad about what happened to Carl. I really am..."

"But?"

There's a moment of silence as she searches for the right words. "It's not like Carl and me had known each other—in a biblical kind of way—for very long. Our whole engagement went by quicker than a knife fight in a phone booth. Catch my drift?"

I think I'm starting to. "You're wondering why you don't feel worse about Carl's death."

She nods. "I know that makes me sound like a bad person. But when you've been through eight husbands, you get a little numb to one of 'em dying. I bet some fancy Yankee doctor would tell me it was some kinda defense mechanism or somethin'. All I know is, I don't feel as bad as I think I should be feelin'."

I swallow a twinge of doubt about Helen's capacity for remorse. Instead, I do my best to make sense of her emotions. "Like you said, you and Carl hadn't been together for very long." Another thought occurs to me. "And Jinny told me about what happened when Donald died. She said you wore sunglasses for over a month because your eyes were so red from crying. So, you can feel sadness, right?"

A strangled sob escapes her throat. "It wasn't because I was cryin', though I did miss Donald somethin' fierce."

"What do you mean? Why else would you be wearing sunglasses for a month?"

"I mean, I did cry for a coupla days," she corrects herself, but still looks forlorn and something else—something that looks a lot like guilt. "But then I started noticin' my eyes were lookin' a little worn out. From being sad and all, ya know? I went and had blepharoplasty."

"Blepha-what?"

"You know," she lowers her voice conspiratorially. "A little nip, tuck on the old eyelids."

"You had surgery on your eyelids? That's why you needed the sunglasses?"

A scowl forms on her face. "Don't you go tellin' anyone about any of this, will you? I got enough problems—what with the cops coming around, things goin' missin' from my house, and now Bubbles promisin' to make sure I don't see a dime of her uncle's money."

"Bubbles expects to inherit all of Carl's money? She told you that?"

"She sure enough did. I'd always tried avoidin' the woman. She just butters my bread the wrong way. All that drama and carryin' on. Always wantin' to be the center of attention. It all feels a little...desperate."

In some ways, Helen just described herself—at least that's how many of her neighbors see her. I wonder if she makes the connection.

"Not to mention," Helen adds, "she's so ugly she'd make a freight train take a dirt road."

I hadn't thought it was possible to choke on thin air, but my reaction to Helen's comment proves me wrong. She's patting my back as I continue to cough, physically unable to come to Bubbles's defense.

"I know, I know. My mama always said, if you can't say somethin' nice, keep your big ole trap shut," Helen admits and resumes walking toward our street. "But I can't help it. The woman is meaner than a wet panther! Goin' round and tellin' folks that I was only after her uncle for his money and that the only way I knew how to make money was on my back or at the altar."

"That wasn't very nice of her," I feel compelled to concede.

"I'm thinkin' she's the one who asked for that song to be played at the weddin' too. The one about the gold digger. But she's the one askin' for a quick payout on Carl's estate, sayin' she needs at least some of the money now!"

That's very interesting indeed. Not only is Bubbles a natural suspect as the beneficiary of Carl's will, but it also now appears she *needs* that money in a hurry. I'll have to let Detective Fletcher know about this latest development. Unless Helen already has.

"The police were at your house the other day. Did you tell them Bubbles is desperate to get her hands on the inheritance?" I ask.

Helen grunts, dainty but disdainful. "As if they'd listen to me. That lady cop has her nose so high in the air she could drown in a rainstorm. She thinks I'm guilty as sin. And Detective Fletcher? Well, that man's about as confused as a fart in a fan factory, as my daddy used to say."

"He's not so bad," I defend Detective Fletcher, believing he really is trying to do better.

And, quite frankly, it's no surprise she's at the top of their suspect list. Spouses usually are the first port of call in the stormy aftermath of a murder. Throw in the fact that her previous husbands died under bizarre circumstances, and most prosecutors would see the case against her as a slam dunk. Even though I've tried to steer the investigation in Bubbles's direction, it'll be difficult to shift the pall of suspicion off Helen. Especially since Detective Baptiste already thinks I'm trying to cover for her.

We turn left away from the river, onto a path between Selena and Marjorie's houses, which drops us back onto our street. Moments later, we're standing in front of Helen's home. Its pale gray exterior is similar to most of the other domiciles in Egret's Loft—with a pitched slate-colored roof, large front door, and four sets of floor-to-ceiling paneled windows—but Helen's also sports a smaller, extra garage for her luxury golf cart.

Before she disappears inside, I remember something she said earlier.

"You mentioned that things were going missing from your house? What kinds of things?" I ask.

"You name it! A diamond tennis bracelet, a Honma Beres eighteen-karat gold nine iron, a Romero Britto sculpture..."

"Sometimes I forget where I put things," I point out. "It's happening more and more these days. Are you sure you didn't just misplace them?"

Helen's forehead shifts slightly into what I assume would be a frown, if her face wasn't frozen with Botox. "You sayin' I'm going senile?"

"No, not at all!" I backpedal. "I'm not senile, but just last week I thought I'd lost my phone, until I went to the fridge for milk and found it next to the carrots. And with the wedding and all, you probably just had a lot on your mind."

"Why would I put a sculpture in the fridge?"

"Well, I suppose not a sculpture or a golf club. Not in the fridge anyway," I have to agree. "Maybe the maid moved them while you were out?"

"Trust me, sugar. They're gone," Helen confidently asserts. "My maid didn't move 'em, and she swears she didn't take 'em. I gotta believe her, on account of the sculpture goin' missin' since her last cleaning day."

"Did you report it to the police?"

"You mean the ones that are fixin' to stitch me up for

murder?" She vehemently shakes her head. "No way. And they wouldn't like what I had to say regardless."

She's lost me. "Why wouldn't they like you reporting a theft?"

Her eyes narrow and she leans in close. "Cause the only people in my house around the time the sculpture went missing *were* the cops."

Fifteen

Standing at the kitchen counter, a mug of steaming coffee in my hand, I can't get over the feeling that something isn't right.

I'd woken up just before my alarm went off and went through my normal routine of using the washroom, then washed down half a dozen prescription pills with water from the bathroom sink. Nothing out of the ordinary so far.

A trip into the kitchen followed, where I cut an English muffin in half and deposited the two pieces in the toaster. My doctor had advised me to always eat something with my morning medications or I might start to feel nauseated. The coffee maker—which my grandson, Curt, had programmed to activate at my normal wake-up time—is already steaming and sputtering away.

Everything is just as it should be. But something feels different.

My cell phone, nestled in the pocket of my thick, chenille robe, begins to ring. Before I can remove the device, the speakers on the smart refrigerator tell me it's my son Ritchie calling.

"Hello, lady. Is there something you want to say to me?" he asks when I answer the phone.

"Umm…" I stall, trying to think of what I might have done that's upset him. "I did walk alone with a suspected murdered last night on the river path. But I'm sure she would never hurt me, even if it turns out she did kill her husband. Or husbands."

At least, I think she wouldn't hurt me.

"What are you on about?" Ritchie asks. "What killers are you walking around with?"

I'm confused. "You mean that's not what you're upset about?"

"How could I be upset about something I didn't even know about?" he asks, then says, "Hold on a second."

My phone beeps. "Hang on a second, Ritchie. I think I'm getting another call." I look down at the screen. Ritchie's name comes up again. I press connect and raise the phone back to my ear. "Did you hang up? Or did I just miss another call?"

Ritchie chuckles. "Hey, lady, can you move the phone? All I can see is your ear."

"How can you see my ear?" I ask, moving the phone so I can look at the display. I see Ritchie's handsome face—blond hair, bright blue eyes, and expertly groomed stubble. "Oh, have we been on a video call the whole time?"

"Yes. I've been getting a glimpse of what's between your ears. By the way, are you having trouble finding Q-tips down there?" He's trying not to smile, but I can hear the amusement in his voice.

"What?" I ask, slightly insulted. "I'll have you know I clean my ears every day!"

"Calm down!" Ritchie laughs. "I was teasing. I just switched over to video. That beep you heard was me switching to video."

"Oh," I say, slightly mollified, but now feeling a bit silly. "Why are you calling anyway?"

"Look." He sighs. "I know you're upset with us for spying on you, but did you have to turn off the camera? Now? When there's another murderer potentially on the loose?"

"Camera? I didn't turn off any camera," I tell him.

"Don't be coy with me, lady. The camera we set up on the counter between the kitchen and the living room? There's no live stream coming from it anymore. If Eliza finds out that you turned it off, she'll go through the roof."

"I do hate that you both are spying on me, but I didn't turn it off. Look, it's still..." I pause mid-sentence, the little robot-looking security camera that has been sitting on the counter since Ritchie installed it a few weeks ago is gone.

"If you're looking at something, I can't see it," Ritchie informs me. "You have to turn the camera around for me to see what you're looking at."

"It's gone!"

"What's gone?"

"The camera. It's not there anymore." I circle around the counter, wondering if it got knocked over somehow. But it's not on the floor either. "Maybe the maid moved it?"

"Why would she do that?" Ritchie asks.

"I don't know. Helen was just saying things had gone missing from her house. Do you think someone could have broken in and taken it?" I blurt out before thinking about the implications.

"Someone's been breaking into houses and taking things? Why didn't you say anything?" His normal witty charm has been replaced by a kind of frightened anger.

"I didn't know until just now. How could I have told you?"

"Craig, can you book me and Curt plane tickets to Mom's place?" Ritchie calls offscreen to his husband. "Mom, I was planning to come this weekend, but I'll try to be down there later today."

"Don't be silly! This weekend is fine. But not Friday night. I'm going to a party."

"A party? Someone just died! Who's throwing a party?"

"You wouldn't know him, dear."

"Him?" Ritchie asks, probably thinking back to the last time I went to a relative stranger's house and nearly got my head bashed in with a statue.

The doorbell rings. It must be Gina coming to pick me up for our art class. Glancing down at my robe, it occurs to me I'm not even dressed yet!

"Can we finish this conversation later, dear?" I ask, hurriedly taking a bite of my English muffin so I won't feel sick later. "There's somewhere I need to be."

Astonishment washes over Ritchie's face. "But...what about the camera?"

"We can figure that out later, can't we?" I say as the doorbell rings again. "I really must go now. Talk soon, dear. Love you."

Hitting the red button that will end the call, I rush in my slippered feet to open the front door. Gina gives me a once over, before planting her hands on her hips.

"You made me get out of bed for this art class. I'm not letting you back out on me now," she huffs.

"I'm coming, I'm coming!" I assure her. "Give me five minutes to get dressed."

"Fine, I'll wait out here," she says. "I think I saw your new neighbor when I drove up. Maybe I'll go say hello."

After promising to hurry, I rush into the walk-in closet in the master bedroom and pull out a simple wrap dress and some low-heeled mules. Then, a little Mary Kay foundation magic on my face, followed by blush and a little mascara. It'll have to do.

When I shut the front door behind me, Gina is seated behind the wheel of her golf cart.

"Are you finally ready?" she asks.

"Yes, let's go!" I wait until she's pulling out of the driveway to mention, "I thought you were going to go say hello to the new neighbor."

"Ohhhh, I said hello to Nadia alright." She scrunches up one side of her mouth.

"Her name is Natasha," I tell Gina, wondering why I even bother.

"That's the one. She's a bit of a strange one."

"Really? Why do you say that?" If I'm honest with myself, I'd been slightly awed by Natasha. She's stunning, effortlessly graceful, and has an aura of elegance, even in the depths of her own personal grief.

"She was losing her mind over a mailbox. Someone knocked hers over last night."

"Phyllis?"

Gina nods. "Who else?"

Catching sight of Phyllis is a bit like coming face to face with the Loch Ness monster. Both are tough as dragons, but a little shy when it comes to public appearance. Phyllis does, however, have a tendency to run over mailboxes with her car on the rare occasions when she sneaks out of her house. Maintenance ordered a bunch of replacements to have on hand, just in case.

"I didn't see her at the memorial service last night, did you?" I ask.

"No. But then you wouldn't, would you? The way she broke into your house that one time still sends shivers up my back."

"Broke in" sounds a little harsh. True, Phyllis did enter, uninvited, into my house. But she only trespassed in order to pass along information about who had left a dead bird at my doorstep. Then, when I stepped away for less than a minute, she was gone. The house was empty. All the doors and windows were locked.

I still have no idea how she did it or how to prevent her from doing it again in the future. Which means she could, theoretically, get into my house anytime she likes. Would she have had a reason to take my security camera? I wonder.

"Anyway," Gina continues. "Back to Nadia..."

"Natasha."

"Yeah, yeah. I introduced myself and she launched into how someone in Egret's Loft was obviously trying to harass her because she's Russian. She thinks the mailbox was a threat. Like someone is trying to warn her to leave."

That kind of panicked behavior isn't in keeping with the woman I'd met. Then again, I've only spoken to her once. "Did you explain to her that hers isn't the first mailbox to have a run-in with Phyllis's car?"

"I tried, but she was having none of it," Gina says. "What can you do? Some people look for the worst-case scenario, even when a rational explanation is staring them in the face."

While I don't know that a woman close to ninety, driving around knocking over people's mailboxes, technically qualifies as a "rational explanation," Gina's comment does get me thinking about my security camera.

"Have you had anything go missing from your house?" I ask.

She takes her eyes off the road to glance at me. "Now that you mention it, Leon can't find one of our Le Creuset casserole dishes. I never would have noticed. Leon does all the cooking. But he's been asking me if maybe the maid put it in a different spot. Why?"

At our age, we could be forgiven for misplacing things every now and again. Keys, a phone, Helen's diamond tennis bracelet. They're all smaller things that can easily be hidden. But misplacing a statue, a tabletop security camera, and an expensive casserole dish?

"It's probably nothing," I lie, needing more time to think about what it could mean. "I had something go missing too. But like you said, the maid probably just moved it."

"Right," Gina says turning her cart into a parking space

in front of the Golf Club. "Before we go in, you want to tell me why you texted me last night that you wanted me to come with you to Serenity's art class?"

"No reason," I say, getting ready to climb out of the golf cart.

Gina puts her hand on my arm. "Spill it."

"Fine." I settle back into my seat. "I saw Serenity chatting with Helen last night at the memorial service. There was something weird about it. Helen looked upset. I want to try to find out what they were talking about."

Gina shakes her head, grumbling, "First chorus practice, now an art class!" She stands up and stares at me, still seated in the cart. "Honestly, Mandy, the way you're going about trying to catch this killer is going to be the death of *me*."

Sixteen

"**E**veryone, gather round!" Serenity Karma calls us all over to a table that's been set up in the back of the room with a Japanese-style clay teapot, little cups bearing Chinese characters, and a statue of the Indian goddess Kali. A Tibetan prayer flag serves as a runner for the table.

Serenity radiates peaceful superiority—as if she alone is at home with her higher self. I don't have the heart to point out that her table is a nonsensical hodgepodge of Shinto, Buddhism, Hindu, and Communism—the last of which leaves little room for the rest.

"I have a little surprise for our class today, which I hope you'll find exciting. But before we get started, I thought we'd have a little tea ceremony in honor of Carl."

She pours bright green tea into the little cups, then

hands them around to Gina, myself, Selena Castillo, Marjorie Higginbottom, Jinny Myrtle, and four other women I haven't yet had the pleasure of meeting—though I'm pretty sure I recognize their faces from Carl's wedding. And, of course, his memorial service.

"Carl has entered the next dimension of existence." Serenity concentrates as she holds up her mug, a fine beading of sweat appearing on her forehead. "He is now at peace, but we will miss him in this earthly realm."

Serenity lowers her cup and drinks the tea in one long gulp. The rest of us, somewhat skeptical of drinking anything that's the color of a tree python, opt for tiny sips. The bitterness hits my tongue first, followed by an earthy kind of savory flavor. It's not something I would ever make for myself, but it's pleasant enough.

Judging by the look on Gina's face, she disagrees. She looks like she's about to retch, then spits the contents of her mouth back in the cup. "What was *that*? It tastes like grass, after a dog lifted its leg on it."

Serenity, looking almost as green as the tea, acts taken aback. She probably put a lot of thought into trying to do something nice for Carl, however culturally misguided. "It's matcha tea. It's meant to improve your mood and help you to lose weight."

"Yuck!" Gina sputters. "My mood and my weight are fine. Keep that junk away from me."

"Alright." Serenity sounds resigned. "Everybody, pick a

workstation, and we'll get started with the class. I think you're all going to really enjoy today's activity!"

Everyone sets down their cups and walks off to pick an easel. Hanging back a bit from the rest of the group, I notice Serenity resting her hand against the table, as if for support.

"Is everything alright?" I ask her. "You look a little peaked."

"I'm fine. Everything's fine," Serenity assures me. "Just a little lightheaded. Must have spent too much time nude sunbathing lately. Now off you go. Your easel awaits."

When we're all suited up in aprons and seated in a circle around the room—with easels in front of us and tubes of paint nearby—Serenity clears her throat and walks to the center of the room.

"As you know, we normally paint inanimate objects in this class," she says. "Today, in honor of our dear friend and neighbor, I thought we should do something a little different."

Gina glares at me, not liking the sound of where this painting class is going and preparing to blame me for any potential negative outcome.

"When I was a young artist," Serenity continues, "I got my break painting the beauty of the naked human body. So that's what we're going to do today!"

Titillated murmurs echo around the room. Not one woman in this room is under sixty-five, but you'd think we

The Dead Men's Wife

were all teenagers again. Giggling and blushing. Except for Gina. Her scowl has been transformed into the slightly manic grin of a repressed 1950s housewife.

"Well, not quite nude," Serenity clarifies. "Everyone remembers Carl's favorite American flag Speedo?"

"How could we forget?" Gina calls out, and the class responds with laughter.

"Alright, settle down, ladies," Serenity says, grimacing as if in pain, as she waits for the amusement to fade away. "I think you've guessed that we'll be painting a man wearing an American flag Speedo. But did you all guess there would be a male model posing for us?"

Applause breaks out in the room. Gina tries to catch my eye, but I'm too embarrassed to look at anyone. My paint brushes are suddenly the most interesting things in the room.

"Will our model please take his position?" Serenity calls out to the mystery exhibitionist in the adjoining room.

The women are still clapping their hands as the door to the classroom opens, and Roy Everhard enters, dressed in a white cotton robe. Smiling broadly so that all his veneers are on display, he doesn't seem to notice the applause becoming less enthusiastic. I think we'd all been expecting a professional male model. A *younger*, professional model.

"Roy has graciously agreed to pose for us today!" Serenity says. I notice the beads of sweat at her hairline have turned into rivulets that now run down the sides of her face.

Winking in my direction, Roy says, "My pleasure. I'm gonna warn you all, though, this Speedo's a little snug."

With that, he unties his belt and lets the robe slide to the floor. He's facing me, so I get the first glimpse of the American flag—stretched in places Betsy Ross, hopefully, never had the misfortune to contemplate.

Since all of us are speechless at the sight of a near-naked Roy, with a bandage on his upper thigh from the fishing incident in his boat, nobody notices Serenity doubling over in pain until we hear her vomit splashing against the wooden floor.

Roy's face turns bright red. "I've never had that reaction before!"

I jump out of my seat and race over to Serenity. Heat emits from her clammy skin, and her wild eyes beg me for an explanation for what's happening to her. With one hand on her elbow and the other resting gently on her back, I try to help her into a nearby chair. Halfway there, she grabs my arm.

"I think," she mutters, "something might be wrong with me." Before I can catch her, Serenity slumps down to the ground, unconscious.

"Somebody call 911!" I instruct, checking to make sure she still has a pulse.

"Already done. I also called our own medics. They'll get

here faster," Gina says, moving to gingerly kneel beside Serenity. "What do you think is wrong with her?"

"I have no idea," I say. "Maybe that tea disagreed with her?"

"The tea didn't agree with me either," Gina points out, "but you don't see me emptying the contents of *my* stomach on the floor."

Roy, now redressed in his robe, joins us on the floor next to Serenity.

"Is she still breathing?" he asks.

"Yes," I confirm. "She seems to have fainted."

"Hopefully, she didn't break her hip when she fell over!" Marjorie, leaning against her walker, hovers above us.

"She didn't fall so much as slump, don't you know," Jinny chimes in. "Her hips should be fine. I'd be more worried she'll choke on her own vomit. George and me like to watch this show from back home in Canada about paramedics saving lives. We can't get it on any of the local channels here, though, so we have to watch it on YouTube. It's really interesting, even if some of the scenes are a little too graphic for my taste. I get a little queasy at the sight of blood. Why, when the kids were little, George had to—"

"Jinny!" Roy nearly shouts. "Can we skip the play-by-play? Just tell us what your show said we should do!"

Jinny looks a bit stunned, but quickly recovers. "Right, well, first, you have to turn her on her side. I don't think it matters which side you turn her on...or did it?" She thinks for a minute as Roy kneels next to Serenity, ready to turn her. "No, I don't think it did. Roll her to her right, though, just in case."

"Just in case of what?" I ask, standing up as quickly as my aching joints will allow to make room to move the prone woman.

"I don't know," Jinny admits, her right eye twitching. "So her heart is elevated, maybe. I'm not a doctor. I just watched a show!"

"You're doing great," Gina reassures the suddenly pale Jinny. "What did the show say to do next?"

Jinny wipes her hand across her forehead. "Take the top leg and bend it at a ninety-degree angle. Not the bottom leg," she corrects Roy as he positions Serenity's limbs. "The bottom leg stays straight, eh. Now what was next, something about the arms? Yes, that's it. Her bottom arm shoots out straight ahead and the top arm bends, with the hand just under her head."

Roy follows Jinny's instructions, and we all stand back to consider the results. It looks like Serenity is in a game of Twister with herself.

"Oh good, someone put her in the recovery position. Well done." Jimmy, Egret's Loft's overworked medic, says as he's rushing into the room. He's gangly, but strong, and soon has Serenity hooked up to a blood pressure cuff and an oxygen mask.

The paramedics arrive soon after. Serenity is strapped to a gurney and wheeled out to a waiting ambulance.

The entire class follows her out and down the hallway. Along the way, a door flies open, nearly hitting me in the face. Bubbles storms out. She closes the door behind her, but not before I catch a glimpse of young Paul sitting in her office.

"What's all this commotion about?" Bubbles cheerfully demands. There's a smile on her face—the kind of smile that hides its rage behind Broadway show tunes and Disney princess costumes. "It's hard for a girl to think with all this racket going on!"

The rest of the crowd moves along with Serenity and the paramedics. I see it as an opportunity to pump Bubbles for a little information.

"Serenity fainted during art class," I explain. "Probably the stress of everything that's been happening is catching up with all of us. How are you holding up? Are you getting settled alright into Carl's house?"

Bubbles waits until everyone else is out of earshot, then turns to me with narrowed eyes. "I've seen you lurking around, searching for an opportunity to talk to me," Bubbles says, the usual singsong timbre of her voice replaced by something deeper, darker. "But I'll tell you now, it's not going to happen. I saw you slinking away from the memorial service with Helen last night, and I have no interest in speaking to someone who's dead set on defending my uncle's killer."

With that, Bubbles pivots on her chunky heels and strides back into her office, slamming the door behind her.

Helen was right. Bubbles does appear to be out to get her—either because she truly believes Helen is guilty or because she wants a clear shot to inherit all of Carl's money. Either way, Carl's niece has just shot straight to the top of my suspect list.

Now I just have to convince Detective Fletcher to give her a second look.

Seventeen

Driving home from the community's tiny grocery store on deserted streets, past empty golf courses and abandoned pickleball courts, it almost feels like I've stepped into one of those post-apocalyptic films the kids these days like so much—cities emptied of their residents as the result of a zombie outbreak, plague, or lawyers who don't know the devil is their father.

The reason my golf cart is the only one on the road, after picking up some bread and sandwich meat for lunch, is far less sinister. It's the middle of another scorching hot day, and people with advanced life experience don't do well in the heat. I can feel the sun burning the top of my scalp through my sun hat and the plastic canopy of my buggy.

I'm glad my dermatologist convinced me to get the fabric hat with an extra 65 SPF protection.

Turning off Augusta Boulevard, I make a left onto Cypress Point Avenue. Not that it matters which direction I turn. I could go either way and still end up at my house.

All the residential streets within the retirement community were designed in large circles around a central lake. The thinking was, even if a forgetful active elder decided to take a stroll through their neighborhood, they'd always be able to find their way home.

Expecting my street to be as barren as the rest of the community, I'm surprised to find a large crowd gathered along the sidewalk near my house. Pulling into my driveway, I catch a glimpse through the press of bodies and walkers and see several police cars parked in front of Helen's house. Yellow crime scene tape flutters in the breeze from her front lawn.

Following all the morning's excitement in art class, I'm not prepared for any more drama today. At least not for a few more hours, in any case.

Taking a deep breath, I stroll over to join the crowd.

Upon closer inspection, I spot Helen in the back of one of the cruisers, hiding her face from the nosy neighbors.

"What's going on?" I ask Marjorie Higginbottom, who's leaning on her walker with one hand and holding a bag of cookies in the other.

"Oh hi, Madeline. Would you like an oatmeal raisin

cookie? I'd just taken them out of the oven when I heard all the hubbub out here. Try one! I use that new-fangled sugar substitute in them, so you don't have to worry about the diabetes."

"I don't have diabetes," I tell her.

"And you won't get it either from my cookies." She shoves the bag toward me.

Suddenly not hungry in the least, I take a cookie anyway to appease Marjorie. She waits, staring at me expectantly. I'm forced to take a bite if I want to get her talking. The center is still warm and gooey. Before I know it, I've devoured the whole thing.

"Absolutely delicious," I compliment her.

She beams with pride. "Have another!"

I hold my hands up in front of me. "Thank you, but I couldn't possibly. What's been happening here? Has Helen been arrested?"

Marjorie shakes her head in disapproval. "I always knew there was something off about Helen. First Donald, and now Carl. How she thought she'd get away with it is beyond me."

"You think she killed Carl?" I ask, trying not to be disappointed that everyone seemed so willing to accept the worst about their neighbors.

"Of course, she did!" Marjorie emphatically states, then leans in closer to me conspiratorially. She's so close I can smell denture cream and raisins on her breath. "Apparently, someone overheard her in the ladies' room admitting as much!"

My mind flashes back to my conversation with Helen in the gym locker room on Monday, when I'd confronted her about her admission that Carl's death was her fault. As we walked out, I'd thought I'd heard a toilet flush. It seems like there was someone in the room with us, after all. Someone who knows I was aware of Helen's alleged confession but said nothing to the police. Detective Baptiste has already accused me of holding out on her. Now she'll know I did.

"Do you know who overheard her?" I press Marjorie for more details.

She shrugs her shoulders, the plastic bag of cookies crinkling in her hand. "No one seems to know. From what I've heard, it was one of those anonymous tips to the police."

My eyes scan the crowd, wondering if whoever reported Helen is now a spectator to her arrest and humiliation. It seems likely, given the entire block has assembled for the spectacle.

Carl's niece, Bubbles, is up front, trying to talk to the police officers as she wipes tears from her eyes. Paul, her young acolyte, stands by her side, his hands in his pockets and staring down at his shoes. To my left, Dr. Rosen surreptitiously eyes my lovely neighbor, Natasha. To my right, Stan Polotski is having an animated conversation with Roy Everhard, who's too busy glaring at Andy Romano to hear a word Stan says. Jinny and George sit on folding chairs in their driveway, sipping glasses of what looks like lemonade.

Selena Castillo is further up the block, watching from a safe distance. I can't blame her, really. It wasn't that long ago the police were coming to arrest *her* for a murder she didn't commit.

"Looks like the gang's all here," Gina observes, sneaking up behind me.

I whirl around, clutching my chest. "Gina, you startled me!"

"Oh no!" She takes hold of my arm, a devilish glint in her eyes. "Are you having chest pains? Has your arm gone numb?"

I shake off her hand. "Very funny. I'm not having a heart attack. Though you should be more careful sneaking up on people. Especially around here these days."

"True." Gina nods. "Three people arrested for murder on this one street in less than a month. That's got to be some kind of record."

"Only one of them confessed to being a killer," I point out. But after glancing at Helen in the back of the cop car, I add, "So far."

"Do you still think Holly is innocent?" Gina asks.

"Helen," I correct her. "To be honest, I'm not sure."

Spouses who kill are usually motivated by love or money. That's what Clint always used to say.

This couple had seemed happy enough on their

wedding day, aside from the drama with the gold digger song. There'd been no evidence of a pollution to their affection in the brief time they were husband and wife. As for money, all of that was currently earmarked for Bubbles. If Helen had killed Carl for his wealth, surely, she would have waited until after he had amended his will in her favor.

Then again, I can't ignore the fact that Helen has now survived eight husbands. It's not surprising people would start whispering about her being a black widow, like the infamous spider that sometimes devours its mate after, or even during, sexual encounters. Same story with the female praying mantis.

For both species, it's not a malicious or psychopathic act, just a biologically motivated survival technique. They're hungry. It really should be a lesson to men to always take their dates to dinner if they're even thinking about trying to get lucky.

"Don't be ridiculous!" Marjorie, who had been listening to my conversation with Gina, interrupts my thoughts. "You don't admit to doing something if you didn't do it! She killed Carl. Just you wait and see."

Gina cocks her head at me, wondering if I'll rebut Marjorie's assertion. Just then, Detective Fletcher storms out of Helen's house, his eyes surveying the crowd. When he spots me, his shoulders tense. He lifts his left hand, curling the fingers toward him. I'm being summoned.

Gina and Marjorie must have seen the detective's gesture, too, because they both take a step back, away from me. Walking toward the police tape, I can feel the heat from my neighbors' eyes burning a hole into my back.

"You've been busy," I say to Detective Fletcher once we're standing, facing each other.

"And you've been lying to me," he says, hurt reflected in the furrow of his eyebrows. Whoever reported the anonymous tip must have also mentioned I was the other party in the ladies' room conversation.

"I never lied," I defend myself. "I just didn't tell you what Helen said that night. She'd just lost her husband. She was talking nonsense."

Detective Fletcher shakes his head. "I can't believe you didn't tell me."

"I was going to. Eventually," I say, believing it's the truth. "Look, all she said was that Carl's death was her fault—"

"Oh! Is that all?" Facetiousness drips from Detective Fletcher's tongue.

"No, no." I try to calm him down. "She didn't say she tied him to the chair and shot a champagne cork in his mouth! Please, if she'd said that, I would have told you. You know I would. She thinks it's her fault because she thinks she's cursed."

His eyebrows shoot up. "Like some voodoo kind of thing?"

"Something like that," I confirm. "I mean, eight dead

husbands. At some point, you'd have to wonder where you're going wrong. Right?"

Detective Fletcher squints as he looks up at the sky. I can see the muscles in his shoulders beginning to relax. "So, it wasn't like a real confession or anything?" He doubles back on my perceived deception.

"Not at all," I assure him. "I'm not saying I know for sure she didn't kill Carl. I don't think she did, but that's just my opinion."

"Well, we're taking her in for questioning anyway," Detective Fletcher says, granting me access back into his good graces. "The anonymous caller also mentioned something about a fight she had with another one of your neighbors last night at the memorial service. Can you point out which one of these people is—" he glances down at his notebook, his tone slightly incredulous as he reads out the name, "—Serenity Karma."

Perspiration runs down the small of my back. "Serenity? You don't say," I stall. "What was the fight about, supposedly?"

Detective Fletcher shrugs. "Something about Serenity wanting to paint Helen."

I frown. "Why would that make Helen angry?" After all, she loves attention.

"She wanted to paint Helen...surrounded by all her dead husbands. Apparently."

"Oh…" I hold the vowel until my facial muscles settle into a grimace. "Not the most tasteful suggestion."

"Maybe not," Detective Fletcher concedes, "but our tipster said Helen threatened her. So, Sammy and I will want to have a word. Jeez, your whole street turned out for this. Which one is Serenity?"

"She's not here," I tell him without turning around.

His eyes narrow as he wipes sweat off his bald head. "Can you check again?"

"I know she's not *here*," I tell him, unable to meet his gaze, "because I know where she is."

I can feel frustration building inside him. "Which would be where?"

Exhaling deeply, I tell him, "She's in the hospital. The paramedics took her off about an hour ago."

"What happened?" Detective Fletcher demands. "Was she hurt somehow?"

"Not hurt, per se. She vomited, passed out, and then was having trouble breathing."

Detective Fletcher writes something in his notebook, then looks back up at me. "Was she poisoned?"

The thought had been crossing my mind all morning. Every time I became aware of it, I shoved the notion harshly aside. Hearing him ask about it directly meant I could no longer avoid the possible reality.

"Maybe," I admit.

After a long moment of acknowledgment, Detective Fletcher sighs and shoves his notebook inside his back pocket. I notice something metal falling onto the grass behind him.

"I got to tell you, Madeline. Things aren't looking so good for your friend. You might want to start reconsidering your allegiances."

He turns and is about to make a dramatic exit. It seems a shame to stop him, but I have to.

"Detective Fletcher," I say as softly as I can, so none of his colleagues will overhear, "you appear to have dropped your handcuffs again."

Eighteen

Coming in from the heat, after all the excitement across the street, I find myself needing to rest my eyes. Removing my sun hat and slipping off my shoes, I settle onto the large sofa in the middle of my living room. Before long, my whole body relaxes, melting into the velvety softness of the cushions.

Nothing can come between me and a quick snooze.

My left big toe begins to tingle. *Poor circulation*, I think, sighing and wiggling the toe to get the blood flowing again. Shifting positions slightly, I prepare to let unconsciousness claim me.

A few seconds later, I feel it again—that tingling. Only now, it's moved higher. I feel it on the top side of my left foot. Annoyed now, I lift my left leg and, with my eyes still closed, I shake the whole thing. But the more I shake, the faster the tingling comes, moving higher, from my ankle to the base of my calf.

"Oh, for Pete's sake," I say to myself, lifting my torso off the couch and opening my eyes. That's when I see it. A spider the size of a cockroach, sitting on my knee. I can feel its eight eyes all watching me. Its bulbous, black abdomen rises and falls, giving me glimpses of a red hourglass on the underside of its belly. A black widow!

A whimper escapes my lips as I try to find a way to get the spider off me before it can bite. The spider seems to read my mind because it suddenly buries its fangs deep into the tender flesh of my lower thigh.

I scream and scream and scream…

"Hey, lady, wake up!" A disembodied voice calls to me.

"Help me! I've been poisoned by a spider!" I cry out. "Where are you? I can't see you! Why can't I see you?"

"Because your eyes are closed," the voice says.

I open my eyes. My son, Ritchie, hovers above me. His six-year-old son, Curt, stands behind him looking decidedly uncomfortable.

"Ritchie? Be careful! There's a black widow in the house. It just bit me!"

"A black widow?" Curt screeches, shaking off his pants and climbing onto the coffee table. "Its venom has neurotoxic proteins that attack your nervous system! Kill it, Daddy, kill it!"

"Calm down, buddy," Ritchie says.

Curt is having none of it. "Easy for you to say! You're an adult! The young and the old are far more sensitive to adverse reactions to venomous bites. Please kill it. I'm too young to die!"

Ritchie rests his hands on his son's small shoulders. "I can't kill the spider, because there is no spider. Your grandmother was just having a nightmare. Weren't you, lady?"

Ritchie's eyes beg me to agree with him, and now, seeing that the sun has set outside, it occurs to me that it's much later than I thought. Which means I must have fallen asleep on the sofa and had only been dreaming that I was still awake.

"You're right. It must have been a nightmare," I admit. "What time is it?"

"Ten past seven," Ritchie says while helping Curt down from the glass top of my coffee table. "We let ourselves in. I hope you don't mind."

There are no keys at Egret's Loft. Everyone has a personal code for the keypads on our front and garage doors. Ritchie had set mine, picking a numerical date he said I would never forget. His birthday.

"Why are you here?" I ask. "I thought I told you not to come until this weekend."

"After you misplaced the security camera, Eliza and I thought someone should check in on you. You know, make sure you're not starting to lose your marbles." He winks at me.

I give him my sternest look. "I'm not losing anything—"

"Except your security camera," Curt interjects.

I take a deep breath. "Don't you start with me, too, young man. Heaven help me if you turn into your father."

"If only you could be so lucky!" Ritchie smiles.

"Are you boys hungry?" I rub my eyes to get the sleep out of them. "Or did you eat something on the plane?"

"Relax, lady. We already ate," Ritchie says, flopping down into the loveseat across from me. Curt perches on the arm, next to his father, his eyes still on the lookout for a runaway spider. "I see there's some activity across the street. Looks like you have some new neighbors."

"Across the street? You mean Helen's place?" I ask. "She was arrested this afternoon. There's already someone else moving into her house?"

Using both hands for leverage, I push myself off the sofa and walk gently to the window in the front sitting room. From here, I have a clear view of Helen's house. Sure enough, there's a woman in the driveway, roughly the same age as Helen and me, with curly black hair and a slim build. She's lifting a suitcase out of the trunk of a blue Ford Taurus and handing it to a younger woman with fiery red hair.

"Well now, who are *they*?" I ask no one in particular.

"Jolene and Savannah," Ritchie confidently replies, still sitting in the other room.

I turn to glare at him, thinking he's teasing me again. "Yeah, right. How would you know their names?"

"They told me. I introduced myself and offered to help them carry their things inside," he says. "They seem nice."

"I'm sure they are. But what are they doing at Helen's house? She didn't mention anything about visitors."

"You probably didn't mention that Curt and I were visiting, but here we are!"

I wave his comment away. "Yes, but you're family."

"So are they," Ritchie says.

I don't understand. "Whose family?"

He chuckles. "Helen's family. That's her sister, Jolene, and her niece, Savannah. Apparently, they decided to come down to Florida to support Helen through everything that's been happening."

"But Helen never mentioned having a sister." I scratch my head, still fuzzy from sleep, as I walk back into the living room. "You'd think her sister would have been there for the wedding."

Ritchie holds up his hands in surrender. "I have no idea, lady. You want me to invite her over so I can pump her full of sodium thiopental and you can ask her all your questions?"

"Sodium thiopental?"

"You know, the *truth serum drug*." He makes air quotes with his fingers.

"I know what it is." I mimic his air quotes. "I just don't understand why you'd be carrying any around."

"True. Eliza would be far more likely to have it," Ritchie says, only half-joking. "Speaking of Eliza, she said she tried calling you earlier but couldn't reach you."

Sinking back onto the sofa, I pull my phone out of my purse. "She didn't leave a message on my answering machine."

"This is the twenty-first century, Mom. It's called a voicemail," Ritchie teases.

I stick my tongue out at him before asking, "Do you know what she wanted?"

"She'll be so mad if I steal her thunder." Richie's grin widens. "So, of course, I'm going to tell you! She's been doing some digging into your neighbors' backgrounds."

My mouth falls open. "I told her not to do that! It's not polite to investigate people behind their backs!"

"Uh huh." Ritchie tilts his head down and looks at me through his thick, dark eyelashes. "Meaning, you don't want to know what she found out?"

I look over at Curt, peeking under furniture for signs of the imaginary spider. He's not paying any attention to us, so I feel comfortable that I won't be setting a bad example. "Alright, yes. Tell me what she found out."

Ritchie's eyes gleam as he leans forward, elbows resting on his knees. "Eliza was able to pull police reports on the deaths of six of Helen's husbands."

"Six?" I ask, mentally adding up the husbands she told me about in reverse order—Carl, Donald, Jeff, Herbie, Derek, and Jimmy. That's six. Helen had told me that Carl was her eighth husband. *So what happened to the other two?* I wonder.

"Exactly, only six," Ritchie continues. "Eliza traced Helen back thirty-odd years to when she was married to a guy named Jimmy Sanders. He died in a hit-and-run accident. It sounded horrible."

"Not as bad as husband number five. Herbie. He fell into a wood chipper!"

Ritchie's face contorts in shock. "Yikes! Eliza didn't mention anything about that!"

"I bet she didn't." I smile, enjoying knowing something Ritchie doesn't. "Why didn't Eliza go back further? She found six police reports. What happened to the other two?"

"Eliza couldn't find Helen's other husbands because Eliza couldn't find any information on Helen at all before she was in her forties."

I frown. "What do you mean?"

"I mean—" Ritchie leans in closer, "—Helen *Roberts*—that was the name she used on the earliest marriage license Eliza could find—didn't exist until she married Jimmy Sanders."

"Didn't exist? That doesn't make any sense. Maybe Roberts was her married name? With eight husbands, she's probably gone by a lot of last names," I reason.

"That's true," Ritchie concedes. "But Eliza found all the others. So, why couldn't she find anything about Helen Roberts? No driver's license, credit cards...heck, she couldn't even find a library card for her prior to the 1990s. I'm telling you, Helen's like a ghost. She could be a criminal mastermind who's been on the run for decades!"

"You've always had a very vivid imagination," I say, patting Ritchie's knee.

"Really? Is it so far-fetched? What about Selena Castillo, down the street? Huh? She was living here under an assumed name for years, hiding the fact that she'd been married to a drug lord. It's not impossible."

"What *would* be impossible is having two criminals living under false identities on the same street in Egret's Loft." I shake my head. "Statistically, it's not realistic."

"This is Florida, Mom! You want to talk stats? The Federal Trade Commission routinely ranks Florida as having the highest rate of fraud in the country. This whole state is scam central."

I raise my eyebrows, still unable to get the hang of lifting one at a time. "Did you know those stats when you and your sister decided to move me into a retirement village here?"

Ritchie, not often at a loss for words, takes a second too long to respond. "That's irrelevant. What is important is that Helen is lying about who she is. Which means, you really can't trust her."

The Dead Men's Wife

I wouldn't say I trust Helen, but then I wouldn't say I distrust her either. Overall, she strikes me as a genuine person, some might say genuinely annoying. But I don't get the sense that she has the temperament to hide her true nature—after all, I've seen her lose her ferocious temper.

"Thank you for the warning," I say to Ritchie. "Was there anything else, dear?"

"Not about Helen." Ritchie looks off to the side. He always stares into space when he's trying to remember things. He's done it since he was a child. "But there was something about your other neighbor, the Russian one."

"Natasha?"

"Right, Natasha," Ritchie snaps his fingers, annoyed that he'd forgotten some of the details while in the process of stealing Eliza's thunder. "It seems like she recently became a widow. According to the records Eliza found, Natasha's husband, Nikolai, *officially* died last month."

"What do you mean *officially*?"

"Meaning his heart recently stopped, but he'd been brain dead for over ten years," Ritchie says, his tone sympathetic. "He'd gotten into a nasty car accident and never recovered. Natasha's been caring for him all this time."

"How sad," I sympathize.

As I'm thinking of all the suffering Natasha must have gone through, my phone alerts that I have a new text message. It's from Detective Fletcher.

Lab work just came in. Serenity Karma was poisoned. Watch your back.

Nineteen

"Poisoned?" Molly's hand freezes, midair, on its path to the buttons on the elliptical machine. "But how?"

I'd timed the revelation perfectly, knowing there would come a point in our Thursday morning workout session where she would want to push me further than my body would allow me to go. After fifteen minutes on the elliptical, with Molly consistently increasing the speed and elevation, I'd arrived at that point.

"All I know is that she was poisoned." My speech is slowed by heavy panting. "I don't know what was used or when."

"But who would want to hurt Serenity?" Molly asks, completely forgetting all about my workout regimen. "I don't know her that well. She only comes in here to do yoga when it's too hot outside. She's a little...eccentric for my taste, but she seems completely harmless."

"I was hoping you might have heard something—" I have to pause to catch my breath before finishing my sentence, "—from one of your other clients."

Molly's left lip rises skeptically. "I don't think there's much crossover between my clients and Serenity's art students. Present company excluded, of course," she acknowledges. "And with all the aura cleansing and spiritual vibrations stuff she's always going on about, I can't see her doing anything that would make anyone upset enough to want to kill her."

Muscles I didn't even know I had are beginning to cramp. "Uh, isn't it about time for me to get off the elliptical, dear?"

"Oh gosh, yes!" Molly exclaims. "Sorry, I lost track of time. Just a cool down now and then you're done on here."

As she adjusts the buttons on the machine, I can feel the resistance against my legs fade away. Moving now at a comfortable pace, my heart slows down, and I'm able to breathe again.

"What about Helen? Do you see her here very often?" I ask.

There's a quizzical expression on Molly's face when she asks, "Why? Do you think she had something to do with Serenity being poisoned?"

Not wanting to be the one to spread rumors about the

women's fight at Carl's memorial, I quickly resolve to shift focus. "No, nothing like that. I was just wondering how well you know her. You must have heard by now that she was arrested yesterday for Carl's murder."

"I did hear about that," Molly confirms, her expression unreadable. "Helen's a lot tougher than she looks. A while back, there was some punk snatching women's handbags over at the supermarket. So, I offered a special class on self-defense. Brought in a male trainer from a gym nearby. I thought it would make the exercise more realistic, you know?"

"That must have been some class," I say.

"Yeah, it was great. Right up to the point where Helen fractured the guy's arm when she judo tossed him onto the mat! Laid him out flat, then dropped all her weight on him."

My eyes widen. "How big was the guy?"

"Easily twice her size! The whole room went dead silent, until the guy started screaming that he needed a medic. It was insane!"

"Did you teach her how to do that?" I want to know, partially because, if it's a skill that's easily learned, it wouldn't hurt to ask Molly to teach me. After all, three people have been murdered here since I moved in. Self-defense could come in handy.

"No way! We were teaching the old 'handbag to the groin maneuver.' It's effective, and there's not a lot of strength required. What Helen did, she didn't learn from me. It's not that difficult, but it can be dangerous."

Helen stays in shape. You can tell she takes pride in her body just by looking at her. Up until now, I thought her time in the gym was all about personal aesthetics. Now, I wonder if there was more to it. If she'd taken self-defense classes, learning how to flip grown men, she must have feared for her personal safety at some point. "Did Helen ever mention she was afraid of anyone or anything?"

"Not to me," Molly says. "And she's in here working out all the time. Not that there's much to be afraid of at Egret's Loft. Or at least, there didn't used to be. There was always some drama, sure. But it was your standard *Days of Our Lives* variety. Now, it feels like we're harboring *America's Most Wanted*."

"How long have you worked here?"

"Going on five years now."

"Do you like it?" I wonder, hoping she won't notice that the elliptical has slowed to a crawl.

"I do. I mean, it gives me plenty of time to train for weightlifting competitions. And the people I work with are great." She winks and then gives me a bittersweet smile. "But it's tough to lose clients. I had a woman die last year. Emphysema. And then Carl. That one hit me pretty hard."

"Carl was one of your clients?"

"Oh yeah! He was here three times a week, religiously. I joked with him that he had to earn the right to walk around the place in his Speedos!" She smiles, lost in the memory. "He was so happy the last time I saw him. It was the day before the wedding. He was so excited that Helen had finally said yes."

"Everything was good between the two of them?"

"As far as I could tell. He was over the moon about getting married! Even if he did get some pushback from that niece of his."

"Bubbles?"

"Yeah. He said she was trying to talk him out of it for some reason." Molly stops talking, suddenly realizing that the elliptical has shut itself off. "You know, Madeline. I think you've been distracting me on purpose to get me to go easier on you today!"

"I wouldn't dream of it," I say.

We both know I'm lying.

Molly chuckles. "Alright, we'll take a quick break. I've been dying to try out this new body composition analyzer I got. I need a guinea pig. What do you say?"

"That depends," I tell her. "What do I have to do?"

"Lie down and let me drape a special mat on top of you."

"That's it?"

"That's it," she confirms.

When I nod my assent, she leads me to one of the treatment rooms off the main gym, and types in a code to unlock the door. Machines to check vital signs line the walls, and there's a defibrillator hanging by the door. In the middle of the room, there's what looks like a massage table.

"Just climb on top of the table and relax while I get everything set up," she instructs.

"What exactly does this machine do?" I ask as I follow her instructions and hear her opening cupboards around the room.

"It measures muscle mass, body fat, and water content. Another tool that helps me to know where my clients are with their physical health. It was a bit pricey, so it took some convincing to get it cleared by the board." She pauses as I hear more cupboards opening and closing. "I know it's in here somewhere. I could have sworn I put it in this cupboard."

I sit up on the table. "Do you need some help? What does it look like?"

She frowns. "It's relatively small—just a monitor and a rollup mat. It can't have gone far."

Molly and I search through all the cupboards, double checking each other's work. We go through everything, but there's no sign of Molly's expensive new equipment. We can't even find the box that it came in.

"This is not good," Molly says, her hands shaking. "The board is going to *kill* me when they find out the new four-thousand-dollar machine they bought is missing!"

First, items went missing from Helen's house. Then, the security camera disappeared from my own kitchen counter.

Now, Molly can't find her body monitoring device. On the one hand, I want to believe all the items are just misplaced and it's a coincidence that it's happened to multiple people at the same time. On the other hand, I don't believe in coincidences. Clint always used to say there was no such thing.

"Have you had anything else go missing lately?" I ask Molly. "Anything portable but expensive?"

"You think someone stole my machine?" she demands. "But this room is always locked. I'm the only person with the code!"

"Do employees have access to all the codes in Egret's Loft?" I ask. "Maybe a cleaning person moved it by accident?"

She tilts her head, thinking. "Only board members have access to all the codes. Security can remotely open doors, but they can't actually see the codes."

"So how do the cleaners get in?"

"Security opens the door for them. But it's documented every time and it has to be pre-scheduled with authorization. Except in emergencies."

That is a complication. If I am to assume that someone has broken into Helen's house, my house, and Molly's treatment room—and I do—how could they have gotten all our codes? Security guards wouldn't be foolish enough to leave a digital trail, and I can't imagine a board member resorting to grand larceny.

"I'm so sorry," Molly apologizes. "This isn't your problem. I'll get to the bottom of this, don't you worry." She takes a deep breath and forces a smile. "Anyway, we have thirty minutes left. What would you like to do? Do you want to work on arms? Abs?"

I take a minute to think. Carl is dead. Serenity has been poisoned. And now, it seems pretty clear that someone broke into my home, probably while I was sleeping, to steal my security camera. There's only one reasonable response to Molly's request.

"That move Helen used in the self-defense class," I say. "I want you to teach me how to do that."

Twenty

"Come on, buddy," Ritchie implores, his elbows resting on the side of the swimming pool. "You're always saying you want to increase your chances of survivability. Learning how to swim greatly improves your odds."

Curt, looking pale and gangly in his swim trunks, has his thin arms crossed in front of his chest. "Not if I restrict myself to only entering bodies of water in which I can safely sit or walk."

The active elders' Water Zumba class has just wrapped up, which means the pool area is empty except for Ritchie, Curt, and I. After I returned from the gym, Ritchie had insisted we all get out in the sunshine and enjoy the fresh air. I'm enjoying my sunshine from under a very large umbrella.

"Go ahead, Curt," I encourage him, trying not to feel like a hypocrite. "You might have fun!"

He whirls around to stare at me, a shocked expression on his face. "You think it would be fun jumping into a potentially hazardous biological cesspool? I haven't tested the pH levels of the water, not to mention the chlorine levels or alkalinity! As you know, my skin is remarkably sensitive."

"Just try it for a few minutes. It'll be fine." My voice sounds less than confident. I'm sure I'm not helping the cause, though my concerns about the water have nothing to do with germs.

Ritchie opens his mouth to speak but is interrupted by a voice yelling, "Cannonball!" and a large splash.

"Please be careful, Paul," Jinny says, her sun hat nearly flying off her head as she rushes out onto the patio. "You don't want to get another ear infection like you had last summer, eh?"

After adjusting her hat, made of bubblegum pink fabric that perfectly matches her pants, Jinny spots me reclining in a shaded sunchair.

"Madeline! Fancy meeting you here!" She strides over to where I'm sitting. "Do you come out to the pool often? Not that I would see you if you did, as I'm never out here myself. I've only just come now because I wanted Paul to get a little sunshine and exercise. Why, he'd spend all his time in his room singing or playing games or talking to his little friends if I let him, don't you know. But that's not good for a growing boy. They need to be running around or swimming or playing sports. I see you've brought your grandson out here, as well, eh? He doesn't seem too keen on getting into the water though. Do they do a lot of swimming in Washington, DC? We do up in Canada, but usually only in the summer. Except for the polar bear plunges, don't you know."

I glance over at Ritchie. He's floating along the edge of the pool, watching me with a smirk on his face. Paul has swum over to the side of the pool and is currently chatting with Curt. He seems to be trying to convince the younger boy that water doesn't have to be terrifying, that it can actually be quite fun. Being intensely afraid of drowning myself, I'm secretly hoping Curt holds his ground.

"I'm not much of a swimmer." I seriously understate my expertise. "Hey, have you heard anything about Serenity? Is she still in the hospital?"

Jinny settles her petite frame purposefully on the recliner next to me. "That was an awful business yesterday, eh? I went straight home and told George aboot it, yes, I did. He thought it would probably give me nightmares, but I think I slept alright last night. At first, I was thinking it must have been something in the tea, don't you know. But then none of the rest of us fell ill, so it couldn't have been that, now, could it? I heard she had to have her stomach pumped, so it must have been something she ate or drank that she shouldn't have. But her kind...now, I don't mean it in a bad way, but she is a bit of a hippy...they do seem more careful aboot what they put in their bodies. Unless, of course, she didn't know she was putting it in her body."

That's the closest thing to an accusation I've ever heard from Jinny. "Are you suggesting someone might have poisoned her?" I wonder if anyone else knows about the toxicology reports.

"Golly gee, I sure don't have any idea of who would do a thing like that!" She shakes her head, pausing. Jinny never hesitates mid-speech. I lean closer to her, more interested than ever in what she'll say next. "Then again, it *does* make you wonder. Seeing Helen arrested yesterday and all. If the police think she killed Carl, maybe she tried to bump off Serenity too. I mean, you'd hate to think there were *two* people running around the place trying to murder people, don't you know."

"Do you know of any reason Helen would have to want Serenity dead?" I ask.

"I'm sure I don't know anything aboot that. They never struck me as being friendly, but then they didn't strike me as unfriendly either. I always assumed they just ran in different circles. You know, they have different interests. Except for men. They both seem to enjoy the men." Jinny blushes, her cheeks turning the same pink as her hat and pants. "But now, thinking aboot it, I can't think of anyone who had a problem with Serenity—not one big enough to try to kill her anyway. Except that one fight I saw her get into, but that was a while ago, and I'm sure that's just water under the Esplanade Riel now." She sees my look of confusion and adds, "That's the most famous bridge in the Peg."

"I'm sure it's lovely." And I'm sure it is, but I don't care much about Canadian bridges at the moment. "That fight you saw Serenity having? Who was it with?"

"Oh, don't be paying any attention to me aboot that. I'm sure it was more of a kind of professional rivalry, don't you know. Why, I never worked myself, but—"

"She got in a fight with someone over art?" I interrupt. When it comes to the arts, everyone's a critic when they don't like something. But having a professional rivalry would seem to necessitate the presence of another artist in Egret's Loft, and I don't know of any.

"Goodness me!" Jinny chuckles. "No, it wasn't aboot art. It was aboot medicine."

Clapping captures my attention poolside and I smile. It seems Jinny's grandson just convinced my grandson to give swimming a go. Paul looks triumphant, Ritchie looks thrilled, and Curt looks like he probably just accidentally altered the pH in the pool water.

Applauding briefly for Curt, I then turn my attention back to Jinny. "Medicine? What does Serenity know about medicine?"

"Oh, she's big into that...oh now, what do you call it? I think she said alternate medicine. Alternative, maybe?

Anyway, she described it as healing people with her hands. Apparently, she went to some famous healer-type person in Japan to learn how to do it. She wanted to try it on George, when he was suffering with the sciatica, but he said he didn't want any woman—other than me, of course—touching him. He's such a prude, my George. Always likes having men for doctors. Maybe he's worried I'd get too jealous if he had a nice-looking lady doctor. Course, there was no such thing when we were growing up, don't you know."

I think Jinny is describing Reiki healing. Clint came across it in one of his cases, years ago, so he did some research. We never tried it though. Our insurance didn't cover it.

"She fought with someone about alternative medicine?" I ask. "Who? Why?"

"Well now, she thought Marjorie should try energy healing, rather than insulin, for her diabetes," Jinny says. I nod, finding it ironic that the cookie lady of Egret's Loft has to watch her own sugar intake. "That put a real bee in Dr. Rosen's bonnet, don't you know. When he found out Serenity was convincing Marjorie to stop taking her insulin shots, Dr. Rosen stormed on over to Serenity's house. You could hear the two of them screaming across the lake, you could."

"How long ago was this?"

Jinny tilts her head, as if looking at the underside of the

umbrella will give her the answer. "I want to say it was right before you moved in, which would make that, what? Aboot a month ago?"

That argument seems to have happened too long ago to have been related to Serenity's poisoning. Also, I've never heard of an argument over medical treatment options leading to murder. Not that it couldn't happen, it just seems far more likely that Serenity stumbled onto something she shouldn't have. If it does relate back to Carl's murders, I need to learn more about my other suspects.

"What about Bubbles? Did she and Serenity get along?" I ask.

"I wouldn't know anything aboot that. As I mentioned before, Bubbles has only been here a few months, after she stopped working on the cruise ships. George and I thought about going on a cruise once, don't you know. Just a quick one, around the Caribbean, but the thought of all those gambling machines and food buffets...well, it just wasn't for us. We went camping on Prince Edward Island instead. But Bubbles, well, she might be more suited for all that fancy living. You know, Paul has been spending a lot of time with Bubbles lately. Maybe he would know something. Paul? Paul, can you come talk to your grandma for a minute? That's a good boy!"

Ritchie and Paul have been holding Curt afloat in the swimming pool; Ritchie has Curt's arms, Paul his legs. On being summoned by Jinny, Paul carefully released his grip on Curt's legs. Curt starts kicking his legs in panic until Paul gives him a quick thumbs up and climbs out of the pool.

In the background, I hear Ritchie cooing, "Relax, buddy. You can do this."

"What's up, Mémé?" A dripping wet Paul approaches us.

"Paul, do you know if Bubbles and Serenity are friendly?" Jinny asks.

"Serenity? Is that, like, a person? I thought it was a movie with Matthew McConaughey."

"A movie? No, no." Jinny shakes her head. "She's the art teacher here. Lives on the other side of the lake. I'm sure you've seen her. She has long white hair and always wears long chiffon skirts."

Paul shrugs. "I don't know who you're talking about."

"Never mind, go back to swimming," Jinny tells him, turning back to face me. "If Bubbles had mentioned her, Paul would remember. He's really taken quite the shine to her, don't you know. She thinks he has a lot of talent! Which we always knew. Of course, his father wants him to study something practical, maybe take over his dentistry practice. But it never hurts to have a little hobby on the side, eh?"

Jinny leans out from under the umbrella and promptly retreats into the shade, squeezing her eyes shut. She picks up her tote bag and rifles through it, sighing in frustration.

"Looking for something?" I ask her.

"George bought me the nicest pair of sunglasses for my birthday. Dior, don't you know. I said they were too fancy for me, but George insisted. But I can't for the life of me figure out what I did with them. I don't have the heart to tell George they've gone missing. I could have sworn I had them sitting right there on the table in the foyer, but when I went to grab them yesterday, they were gone. It's not like me to lose things. Paul, you haven't seen my sunglasses around, have you?"

Paul, sitting on the edge of the pool with his legs in the water, says he hasn't.

A thought occurs to me. "Has anything else gone missing in your house lately?"

Jinny's eyebrows disappear under the brim of her hat. "Why do you ask?"

"I seem to have misplaced a few things in my house. I was wondering if maybe the cleaners were moving things around. Or something."

She frowns. "Now that you mention it, I've been having trouble tracking down my old computer. I was showing Paul some pictures that I haven't moved over to my iPad. Afterward, when I went to put it away, I couldn't remember where I'd left it. But maybe I'm not so forgetful after all. That would make sense. I'll have to ask Maria about it. She probably put it away in the wrong spot and that's why I can't find it."

Hearing a splash, I see that Paul has rejoined Curt and Ritchie in the swimming pool. I'm amazed to see Curt floating on his own, a huge smile on his little face.

I, on the other hand, can feel myself drowning in confusion.

It now appears that Helen, Gina, Jinny and I have all had things taken from our homes and Molly had equipment go missing from her office.

Are the apparent thefts related to Carl's murder? And if so, how?

Twenty-One

From the outside, the Calusa Police Department doesn't look like much. Nestled in the leafy north quadrant of an upscale strip mall, it looks like someone forgot to install any windows as they were laying the bricks. Painted green in the center and white along the outer walls, there's a large star badge with the emblem of the local police painted to the right of the glass double doors.

"You sure you don't want me to come in with you?" Richie asks, leaning over the steering wheel of his rental car for a better look at the building.

"That's alright, dear. I know you promised Curt a game of chess after swimming. You should be more worried about losing to your son. I'll be fine," I say confidently, though inside I am a bit apprehensive.

"If you say so, lady. Call me when you want me to come pick you up."

My seatbelt is still on as I stare at the building. Somehow, it feels odd to be outside of Egret's Loft. I don't know why. I've lived there less than a month and there have probably been more crimes committed at Egret's Loft in the past few weeks than in any other part of town. Still, I suppose it has something to do with the devil you know.

"Lady?" Ritchie asks, curious why I'm hesitating.

"Sorry, dear. I was just thinking about what to make for dinner," I lie. "I'll see you in a little while."

Carefully climbing out of the large Suburban, I make my way toward the building.

Helen had called while I was at the swimming pool. She claimed she was using her one phone call on me. She said she wanted to speak to me in person. She wouldn't say over the phone what she wanted to talk about, only that it was urgent, and I needed to come right away. Also, she asked if I could swing by her house and pick up her manicure kit. She said the stress of everything was taking its toll on her cuticles.

Pushing through the double doors, I see several nice, upholstered chairs and wooden side tables with magazines facing a large wall with another set of doors and a glass partition. Behind the glass, a uniformed officer, who looks young enough to still be in high school, greets me and asks how he can be of service. I ask for Detective Fletcher and take a seat.

"Hello, Mrs. Delarouse," the detective says after opening the door from the inner office space. "I guess you're here to see Helen."

Slightly hurt by his impersonal greeting, I follow him through the door and into an open-plan police station with roughly a dozen desks. Only a handful of them are occupied. I'm surprised to find the interior well-lit with soft bulbs—none of those garish fluorescents—and sparkling clean.

"Thank you for your text about Serenity," I say. "How's she doing?"

He nods. "The doctors say she's going to pull through. They found cardiac glycosides and digitoxigenin in her blood. At least, I think that's what they said. I have no idea what any of those words mean, but it sounds bad."

Before I can respond, Detective Baptiste comes out of a door marked "Ladies' Locker Room" and sees me talking to her partner. She grins. "So, Pete. You finally relented and brought your little friend in for questioning."

"That's Senior Detective," he corrects her in his most authoritative voice. "And no. She is not here for questioning. Helen Richards requested to speak with her."

A look of horror crosses Detective Baptiste's face. "You're seriously going to let the prisoner talk, in private, to her accomplice? You can't be serious!"

"Accomplice?" I'm caught somewhere between amusement, anger, and panic. "Pete, you really think I had something to do with this?"

"That's Detective Fletcher to you," he now corrects *me*, though I am relieved when he sends me a wink behind his partner's back. "Mrs. Delarouse, you will be allowed to speak with the accused in an interrogation room. Since you're not an attorney, the rules of privilege do not apply. Do you understand?"

"Yes, I do," I tell him. He's making me aware that he, and most likely his overeager partner, will be listening in on the entire conversation.

"We have advised Helen...I mean, the accused, that the district attorney has offered her a deal. If she pleads guilty to manslaughter, he's agreed to ask the judge for a greatly reduced sentence. It's the best deal she's going to get. As her friend, you might want to try and talk her into taking the deal."

I beam with pride. Detective Fletcher really has come such a long way since I first met him. I want to ask him if he's pretending to be another character in his latest novel, but I don't want to embarrass him in front of his annoying junior detective.

"Thank you, Detective Fletcher. That was a very concise and professional explanation." I at least want him to know I notice how official he now sounds.

His blush inches all the way down the collar of his

starched white shirt. "Yes, well, if you want to take a seat in interrogation room one, I'll bring in the accused."

Detective Fletcher goes through another door marked "Cells" on the other side of the room. His partner walks to another door, opens it, and then indicates that is where I should wait. Detective Baptiste doesn't move out of my way, so I have to shimmy around her to get into the room. She seems bent on intimidating me. I wonder if she knows how transparent she's being.

"You're going to make a fine detective, dear," I tell her. "It's not easy, but if you have a little confidence in yourself and stop trying so hard, you're going to do really, really well. I know it."

Detective Baptiste's exquisitely proportioned jaw falls open, exposing perfect, white teeth. She looks like she wants to be combative with me but doesn't know whether to feel flattered by my belief in her or angered by the insinuation that she's not a good detective yet.

She's spared a decision by Helen's arrival.

"Madeline! Thank you so much for coming, sugar!" Then turning to the detectives, she adds, "You may leave now. Thank you."

Detective Fletcher closes the door from the outside, shaking his head. Helen clearly still thinks she should be pampered, even when she's in jail charged with murder. I admire her aplomb but doubt it's making her many friends.

We're alone now in a stereotypical interrogation room.

There's a table in the middle with a couple of chairs on either side and a mirror made of one-way glass lining the side wall. I consider waving at Detective Fletcher but decide that would seem a bit childish.

Helen surprises me by grabbing onto me and hugging me tight. Then, with her hands still on the outside of my arms, she asks, "Did you bring my manicure kit?"

"Of course. I hope I grabbed the right thing," I say.

"This is it! Bless your heart, you've saved my life," she pulls a nail file out of the bag and starts dragging the emery board across her long, shapely nails.

The door flies open, Detective Baptiste walks in, grabs the cosmetic bag and the file out of Helen's hand, and storms out of the room.

Thunder clouds descend on Helen's face. "You better give your heart to Jesus, missy, 'cause your butt is mine!"

"Helen, she's just doing her job," I try to reason with her, while also scooting my chair a little further away to get a safe distance from her temper.

"But I need to fix my nails!" she whines. "I'm gonna call my lawyer. This kind of treatment is plain inhumane! Don't they care that I just lost my husband?"

"Helen, you're suspected of *murdering* your husband. Don't you think you have slightly bigger problems than a hangnail?"

"No," she argues. "They can run all over hell's half acre

lookin' for clues. They won't find anythin'. 'Cause I didn't *do* anythin'. Why should I be worried?"

"Helen, they're planning to prosecute you," I say, though even I know the only evidence they have is circumstantial. "The DA is offering a plea deal if you admit to manslaughter."

"No!" Helen says, crossing her arms in front of her large, fake breasts.

"No?"

"Heck no! Why on earth would I be admittin' to anythin'? I didn't kill Carl!" she insists. "They can offer all the deals they want, but it'll go as well for them as tryin' to put a steerin' wheel on a mule."

I look directly at the mirror and tilt my head. As if to say to the detectives, *see, I tried*. Then, facing Helen again, I whisper, "I want to help you. I really do, but I need you to be straight with me. What's your name?"

She blinks. "My name is Helen. What kinda stupid question is that?"

"Helen, I know," I bluff. "Before you married Jimmy Sanders, you didn't exist. What kind of trouble are you in?"

"No whispering in there," Detective Baptiste's voice booms from the speakers in the wall. "Speak up."

Helen's eyes bore into me. I hit a nerve. I know I did. I just can't tell how it relates to whether or not Helen is a murderer.

"I'm not saying you're right," she says, her tone neutral. "But if you were, I promise you, it's got nothin' to do with Carl. You're chasin' your little squirrel up the wrong tree, sugar."

"Helen, you said Carl was your eighth husband. Which means Jimmy had to have been your third. What happened to the other two?"

The corners of her eyebrows fold down toward her nose, and she purses her lips into a thin line. "If you know what's best for you, sugar, you'll take my lead and let those sleeping dogs off their collars."

"Alright." I hold up my hands in surrender. "Can I ask you about Serenity? Was there any bad blood between the two of you?"

"Serenity?" Helen seems confused by the change in the conversation's direction. "If you ask me, she's crazier than a soup sandwich. I don't have much use for her, but we've never gotten into any scuffles, if that's what you're askin'. Why *are* you askin' about her?"

"Didn't the detectives tell you?" I glare at the one-way mirror. "She was poisoned yesterday morning."

"Poisoned? You don't say! Who did it?"

"Ummm..." I stall. "I think some people think *you* did."

She slams her hands on the table. "Me? I had nothin' to do with it! Why would I go doin' a thing like that? Or is it just that I'm now goin' to be accused of every crime inside the county lines?"

The Dead Men's Wife

"No one's saying you did anything." Then realizing my error, I correct the statement. "Aside from killing Carl, obviously. Since that's why you're here. But look, you asked for me to come. What do you need?"

The muscles in her face relax, at least as much as they can with all that Botox. "I need you to get in touch with someone for me. I don't have a number, but her name is Jolene Jeffers."

"Jolene?" I say. "You mean your sister?"

"My what?" she says, quickly adding, "How did you know she was my sister? We've been outta touch for years!"

"She's here!" I exclaim. "I mean, not here at the police station. But she's at your place in Egret's Loft."

Helen leans back in her chair. "You don't say?"

"Your niece, Savannah, is here too. I haven't spoken to them, but they introduced themselves to my son, Ritchie. You haven't been in touch with her yet?"

"I'm sure she's workin' herself around to it. But could you do me a favor?"

I hesitate, unsure about committing to anything before I know what it is. She is, after all, suspected of murder.

Sensing my indecision, Helen adds, "Don't worry your pretty little head, sugar. I'm not goin' to ask you to do anythin' illegal."

Suddenly ashamed of my reluctance, I nod. "Of course you wouldn't, dear. What can I do?"

"Tell Jolene, after all these years, we really need to sit down and have a good ole heart to heart about *Bob*."

"What about Bob?" I ask.

"He was—" she hesitates, "—our daddy. The chain that bound us forever. You tell her what I said, will you? I hate to admit it, but if anyone on God's green earth can help me outta this, it'll be Jolene."

Twenty-Two

"Jolene, I'm so pleased you could make it!" I give her a big smile before ushering her into the foyer of my house later that evening. "I know it was very last minute."

"It's real nice of you, invitin' us over for dinner." Jolene's drawl, while still achingly feminine, sounds rougher than Helen's—like a gemstone that hasn't had its edges polished yet. She swallows me in a big hug. "We don't know a soul in these here parts."

"Well, now you know me." I do my best to make her feel welcome while extricating myself from her embrace. "My son's made us a veritable feast. I hope you brought your appetite!"

"Oh, yes! I'm so hungry I could eat the north end of a south-bound polecat," she says.

Aside from their height, their colorful expressions, and a general air of being fiercely independent, I never would have guessed that Helen and Jolene are sisters.

Jolene's black hair, with hints of silver roots along the scalp, springs up in tight corkscrew curls, Helen's blond hair falls in soft waves. Helen's eyes are light blue, Jolene's a warm brown with flecks of green. And where Helen has a more voluptuous shape, Jolene's body is lean and sleek—like a greyhound in human form.

Between Helen's copious use of Botox and Jolene's apparent desire to age gracefully, it's virtually impossible to know which is the elder sister.

"And who is this beautiful young lady?" I turn my attention to the lanky twenty-something woman standing behind Jolene. Her skin is the color of skim milk, and she has bright green eyes, shining like emeralds. Her hair is long and a brilliant orange-red, like flame. I'd imagine that, seeing her in a windstorm, you'd be forgiven for thinking her head was on fire.

"This is my daughter, Savannah." Jolene beams. "Say hello, Vannah."

"It's a real pleasure to meet you, ma'am," Savannah says politely. Her chin aims high, but her eyes remain locked on her high-top Vans sneakers.

"The pleasure is all mine. Please, come on in." I shepherd the two women into the kitchen, introducing them to Ritchie and Curt.

"Mmmm. Something smells absolutely divine," Jolene gushes, resting her hand on Ritchie's arm.

Ritchie glances at me questioningly. I shake my head. I don't think she's flirting with my gay son. I just get the impression she's a very tactile person. The apple doesn't fall far, I suppose.

Ritchie clears his throat. "I wasn't sure if there were any vegans in the group, so I played it safe. I made vegetable curry and beef biryani—not too spicy. Both will be ready in a few minutes."

"Thank you, Ritchie," I say. "In the meantime, how about a glass of wine?"

Jolene scrunches her nose. "I don't suppose you have any beer. Where we live in Alabama, it's generally the safer option."

"Of course! Savannah, would you like one, as well?" I ask.

"No, thank you, ma'am. I'll just have a glass of water, if it's not too much bother," she says, peeking at me through thick, dark eyelashes.

As I round up their drink orders, I catch sight of Curt, rooted to the spot just outside the kitchen, staring at Savannah with a mixture of fear and fascination.

"Curt, dear, are you alright?" I ask.

Upon seeing Curt staring at her, Savannah gives him a bashful smile and kneels down. "Hi there, little fella. Is somethin' wrong?"

"Your...your hair," Curt stammers.

"What's wrong with my hair?" she asks.

"It's like orpiment!"

"Orpi-what?" Jolene looks confused.

I forgot to warn them about Curt. And it doesn't look like I'll get the chance now.

"It's a sulfide mineral usually found in hydrothermal vents," he explains. "The Chinese used it in their alchemic quest to create gold. They also used it in medicine—which really wasn't wise considering orpiment contains arsenic, which, if allowed to oxidize, can lead to poisoning."

I'm about to break the ensuing silence when Savannah begins to laugh. "Well, aren't you just smarter than a whip!"

Curt frowns. "I would hope so. Whips aren't sentient and are lacking in any form of intellectual capacity."

"Curt," I interrupt. "Don't you need to wash your hands before dinner?"

He finally looks away from Savannah. "You're absolutely right. In my distracted state, I completely forgot about my hygiene. Thank you, Grandmother."

As Curt runs off to sanitize himself, Jolene chuckles softly. "You've got quite the little spitfire on your hands there. I'm guessin' Helen gets quite the kick out of him."

"Actually—" I think about it, "—I'm not sure that Helen's met Curt yet."

"Really?" Jolene frowns. "Helen takes to kids like a duck

to water. You say she hasn't met your young fella? But I was told you're Helen's closest friend here at Egret's Loft."

Before I can stop myself, surprise compels me to blurt out. "Who told you that?" Then, feeling a stab of pity, I add, "Not that it's inaccurate, I just haven't known Helen very long. I only moved in about a month ago."

"Is that so?" Jolene pushes a dark curl off her forehead. "You did just go to see her earlier at the police station, am I right?"

"Yes, she wanted to see me," I confirm, wondering how Jolene could possibly know about that. "In fact, she was asking me to track you down. Have you been out of touch for a while?"

Jolene squints her eyes, assessing my motivations. It was forward of me to ask about their relationship. Then again, I can't imagine my kids ever becoming so distant they have to ask a relative stranger for help finding each other.

I'm convinced both Helen and her sister Jolene are hiding something from me. Judging from the look Jolene is giving me, she's wise to my suspicions.

"Dinner is served!" Ritchie calls out as he carries two steaming serving bowls to the dining room table.

The four adults and Curt take our seats at the table and exchange light chitchat as we serve ourselves. Across the table, I catch Jolene watching me. When our eyes meet, she smiles warmly, then glances down at her plate.

"Bon appétit," Ritchie says, sitting back to capture everyone's reaction to their first bite. I roll my eyes at him to show him I know what he's doing. He just smiles back.

"Oh my goodness," Jolene says after her first mouthful of biryani.

Concern clouds Ritchie's face. "Is it alright?"

"Alright?" Jolene asks. "Why, if you were to put a bite of that on top of your head, your tongue would beat your brains out trying to get to it."

Curt furrows his brow. "That's a physical impossibility! There's no way—"

"It's just an expression, buddy," Ritchie says. "Thank you for that, Jolene. I think that's the nicest thing anyone has ever said about my cooking. I might have to put that on a tea towel at home!"

"I'll have one made for you for Christmas," I tell him, before turning my attention back to Jolene. "It was so nice of you to come all this way to be here for your sister. I am curious though. Helen said the two of you haven't spoken in years. How did you know she was in trouble?"

Jolene stops the fork midway to her mouth. The table goes silent, except for the sound of Curt's fork scratching against his plate.

"She sent me a text," she finally replies. "I didn't respond to it right away. I was busier than a one-legged cat in a sandbox getting everything ready to come down here. So, she probably thought I'd changed my number."

Something about her explanation has all my senses on high alert. First of all, Helen didn't mention anything about texting Jolene. In fact, she'd said she didn't even have a phone number for her sister. I suppose Helen could have thought the number she had was wrong because Jolene never replied, but there's something else troubling me. If the sisters hadn't communicated for years, how did Jolene know the security code to get into Helen's house?

Realizing it would be rude to continue interrogating my dinner guest about the inconsistencies of her story, I simply say, "well, it's lucky you still had the same phone number. But then, most people do now, don't they? Back in my day, your number changed every time you moved to a new area code, or you'd be charged for calling long distance."

"You used to have to pay more to call other area codes?" Savannah asks sincerely.

"I knew I had you too late." Jolene laughs a little too loudly and winks at her daughter. "If I'd had you in my twenties, or even thirties, you might know there was a whole wide world before smartphones and the internet."

Savannah rolls her eyes, but both women seem more relaxed than they had just moments earlier.

"How old are you, Savannah?" Ritchie asks. "That's alright to ask, right? I mean, you're still young."

She smiles, color flooding her cheeks. "Yeah, it's fine. I'll be twenty-two next month."

Ritchie sighs. "Ah...great age. Are you in school?"

"I just graduated from the University of Alabama," she says, adding, "I studied creative writing."

"Good for you! I've heard that's a great program." Ritchie raises his glass, and we all follow suit. "So how long has it been since you've seen your aunt?"

Savannah flashes Jolene a questioning look.

Jolene answers, "It's gotta be going on about eight years now. It'll be nice for the two of them to get reacquainted."

"It'll be nice for you, as well," I say. "That's a long time not to see your sister. Oh, before I forget, she said, after all these years, she wanted to have a long talk about Bob."

"Who's Bob?" Ritchie asks, taking a sip of wine.

Jolene pushes some vegetables around her plate. "Bob? Right. He was...one of Helen's boyfriends when we were younger."

I practically choke on my biryani. "Boyfriend? Helen told me Bob was your father!"

Jolene freezes momentarily, then begins to laugh. "Oh! *That* Bob! We always just called him Dad. I thought she might have been talking about a different Bob."

Ritchie and I exchange looks across the table. I'd known something felt off, now it's clear Ritchie thinks so too.

"Hey, lady, have you had any updates on Serenity?" Ritchie makes the only tactful move and changes the subject.

"She's the resident art teacher. She was poisoned yesterday," I explain to our guests.

"Poisoned?" Jolene exclaims. "Good Lord! Is she alright?"

"The doctors say she'll be fine," I assure her. "Detective Fletcher said they found some things called cardiac glycosides and digitoxigenin in her system. But they don't know where they came from."

"Nerium oleander," Curt says, wiping some spices off his mouth with a napkin.

"What's that, buddy?" Ritchie asks.

"Both of those substances can be found in oleander plants. Like the ones next door."

Next door. At Natasha's house. I almost touched the flowers myself.

Thoughts whirl in my head. Does Natasha know Serenity? What reason would she have for poisoning the art teacher? And what, if anything, does it have to do with Carl suffocating on a champagne cork on his wedding day?

The only thing I do know is, the more answers I seek, the more questions I have.

Twenty-Three

Panic grips my chest and I'm finding it hard to breathe. "You're in the hospital? Is everything alright?"

Ritchie and I are huddled on the sofa in my living room early the next morning. Our coffees sit forgotten on the kitchen counter, as we stare at Eliza on the screen of my iPad. In the background, we can hear someone paging a doctor on the overhead speakers. Eliza looks frazzled, like she hasn't slept all night.

"Everything's going to be fine. I had to bring Emmy in," she says.

"What happened?" Ritchie demands.

"Ugh," Eliza moans. "She ate the battery from a greeting card. You know, the kind you can record voice messages on.

Tom's parents sent it to him for his birthday. Anyway, the doctors removed the battery endoscopically, it's all good, but they want to keep her here for a while to check her over. I swear, that kid will put anything in her mouth. She'd probably swallow a hand grenade if it would fit inside her mouth."

"Do you keep hand grenades at your house?" I ask.

"Yeah, Mom. Right next to our collection of AK47s," Eliza deadpans. When Ritchie and I glance at each other, she adds, "Kidding! Jeez. Of course, we don't have grenades in the house!"

With my daughter, you never really know.

"Anyway, I'm sorry I'm not there with you guys," she says. "But I do have some more information on Bubbles."

"What about Natasha?" I want to know. "Did you find out anything else about her?"

"Wait a minute." Eliza shakes her head as if to clear away a sudden mental fog. "Now we're thinking it's Natasha? I thought you said we thought Bubbles killed Carl!"

"Bubbles is definitely still a suspect," I assure her. "But right now, we want to know why Natasha might have poisoned Serenity with her plants."

"Somebody was poisoned? Ritchie, why didn't you tell me? Seriously? Can I not have one day where nobody's getting killed at Egret's Loft and my child eats only what she's supposed to?"

"Serenity isn't dead," Ritchie corrects his sister's understandable assumption. "Stop being such a drama queen."

Eliza glares at Ritchie.

I can practically feel the heat of her stare on my hands holding the iPad. "She's going to be fine, and, thanks to Curt, we now know she was poisoned with oleander—which Natasha has planted in her front yard."

Eliza chews on this latest information. "That seems brazen. If she was planning to poison people with her plants, you'd think she wouldn't put them where everyone can see."

"She has a point," Ritchie agrees.

"Don't sound so surprised," Eliza quips.

"Enough you two," I say before my kids start to bicker. They love each other dearly, but I've never seen a more competitive pair in my life. "If you can find out anything more about Natasha, let us know. But for now, what information do you have on Bubbles?"

"Her real name is Tiffany Hancock. She kept her maiden name when she got married, which probably makes things easier now that she's getting divorced," Eliza tells us. "From all accounts, it sounds like her husband was a bit of a loser."

"That's not a very nice thing to say!" I scold her.

"Well, he's not a very nice guy," she replies. "Womanizer. Alcoholic. Gambler. It sounds like Bubbles was willing to tolerate the first two character flaws, but when he lost his job, then blew through their entire savings and racked up hundreds of thousands in debt betting on slow horses, she'd had enough. She was about to file for divorce, but he beat her to it. He'd moved in with his latest mistress, saddling Bubbles with a mortgage she couldn't afford and half his debt."

"Poor thing," I commiserate. Bubbles may not have been very kind to me, but you never want to see anyone suffer. "That hardly seems fair she should have to pay for half his gambling debts!"

"Fair or not," Eliza continues, "she suddenly found herself in a world of financial hurt. That's when her nice Uncle Carl stepped in and offered to help her out."

"You mean by giving her the job and a place to stay in Egret's Loft?" Ritchie asks.

"And more. He was loaning her money until she got on her feet," Eliza tells us. "He actually seemed to be really trying to help her."

"How do you know all this?" I ask.

"That's not important," she retorts. "What is interesting—"

"Eliza Daphne Delarouse!" I interrupt.

Ritchie's head whips around to face me. Eliza's shoulders buckle forward. "Seriously, Mom? You're bringing out the middle name?"

"How do you know so much about Carl and Bubbles?" I demand.

"Fine, if you *really* want to know. But you're not going to like it," Eliza says, taking glances in all directions before leaning in closer to the screen. "There's a guy I know. A hacker. He might have *happened* to stumble upon Bubbles's email password and phone logs."

"Eliza!"

"Well, she did say you weren't going to like it," Ritchie reminds me.

"But that's an invasion of her privacy!" I exclaim. "Not to mention illegal!"

Eliza puts a finger over her mouth and makes a shushing sound. "You want to not scream about me breaking the law when I'm in a public place? Jeez, I do this kind of thing for work all the time."

"At the IRS?" Ritchie smirks. We all know she doesn't work there. Eliza's always been terrible at math. She could never expect us to honestly believe she's an accountant.

"Exactly," she says, her poker face in place.

Ritchie snorts. "Thank goodness for the Patriot Act, right?"

"Look, I don't need this abuse," Eliza complains. "Do you want to know about Bubbles or not?"

Torn between moral righteousness and my desire to know more about Bubbles, I'm ashamed to say my curiosity wins out. After all, Eliza already read the emails. Telling her to unread them would be like trying to have someone put back an endangered flower after it's already been plucked from its stem.

"I don't approve of your methods—" it somehow feels appropriate to lecture her a bit before capitulating, "—but the damage is already done. What did you find out?"

"Objection noted." Eliza rolls her eyes. It used to drive me nuts when she did that as a child. I even threatened that, one day, they might get stuck like that. When, years later, she realized that was a lie, she started doing it again—only much, much more. "Bottom line is," Eliza continues, "Bubbles is broke and needs Carl's money to avoid going bankrupt."

"Were they close?" I ask, remembering the tears on Bubbles's face the night Carl was murdered. Not long after, though, she'd been corralling all the guests in a very businesslike manner. Which prompts me to add, "Or do you think she was just using him for his money?"

Eliza's face softens. "Actually, she and Carl had been emailing for years. A bit sporadically until recently, but whenever Bubbles wanted advice, she turned to Carl. He was the one who suggested leaving her husband. He told her she could do better."

"That would be pretty heartless, then," Ritchie thinks aloud.

"What do you mean?" I ask.

"Well, if he was helping her out with advice, not to mention money, it would be pretty heartless of her to kill him just to keep from going bankrupt," he says. "Kind of like biting the hand that was feeding her."

"Only if that hand was going to *keep* feeding her," Eliza interjects.

Just yesterday morning, Molly told me that Bubbles was trying to convince her uncle not to tie the knot.

I nod, understanding where this is going. "Bubbles wasn't too happy about Carl and Helen getting married, was she?"

"Not at all," Eliza confirms. "She insisted Helen was only after him for his money. That she was a black widow. Things of that nature. Eventually, Carl had enough. He told Bubbles that he was getting married, and if she was going to make his life difficult, then maybe it'd be for the best if she left Egret's Loft."

"Oh wow!" Ritchie exclaims. "He told her to get lost?"

"That's why she planned such an extravagant wedding," I realize. "She was trying to show Carl she was supporting his choice so she could stay in his good graces."

I'm guessing Helen was right to suspect Bubbles of playing that offensive song at the reception. For the sake of a relationship with her uncle, she'd outdone herself with the attention she lavished on his wedding. But that niggling dislike of Helen—and the potential monetary interference she represented—needed to be sated with a little passive aggression.

Or perhaps even something far, far worse if she found out she was being cut out of Carl's inheritance.

"Did you see anything in the emails about Carl changing his will?" Ritchie seems to read my mind. "Did Bubbles know?"

Eliza shakes her head. "If she knew, they never talked about it. At least not over email."

"Thank you, Eliza. I'm still not pleased with how you came by this information." I take one more opportunity to chastise her. "But it is helpful."

"Yeah, yeah." She rolls her eyes again. "Emmy will be waking up soon, so I better let you go. Do you have any exciting plans for the day?"

"We promised Curt we would take him to the Museum of Osteology in Orlando for the day," I tell Eliza.

"Skeletons? Really?" She shakes her head. "You're taking a six-year-old to Orlando—the home of Disney World, Epcot, and Universal—but he wants to go see a bunch of old bones?"

"What can I say? My boy's an overachiever," Ritchie brags. "We have to be back early, though, because Mom has a big party tonight!"

Eliza's eyebrows shoot up. "A party?"

"Just a little get-together for everyone who lives on our street." I deliberately refrain from expressing my excitement. The chance of Bubbles and Natasha—my two main suspects—being in attendance tonight is quite high. But I don't want to say that to my kids.

There's no need for them to worry, right? It's not like anything bad is going to happen.

Twenty-Four

The thick, dusky air comes alive with the elegant strains of Pachelbel's "Canon in D," played by a string quartet nestled under a leafy canopy in Andy Romano's backyard.

I'm worried I might be underdressed in a silk wrap dress with kitten heels when I see the opulent scene our host has created. Aside from the fairy lights that adorn the palm trees, the only light comes from dozens of candles in antique brass lanterns perched on an equal number of standing tables spread across the lawn.

Bow-tied serving staff dance through the crowd, carrying a savory collection of bruschetta, caprese skewers, arancini, and stuffed mushrooms. Young women—in matching, sleek black dresses—saunter from guest to guest, offering from a selection of Italian reds, whites, and bubbly.

The fashion business has been very good to Andy indeed.

"I wasn't expecting anything this swanky!" A husky female voice confides, nearly causing me to spill my recently acquired glass of Prosecco.

I whirl around. "Gina! Why do you always insist on sneaking up on me?"

"I don't sneak," Gina insists. "And, quite frankly, for someone who's always trying to unmask murderers, you really should be more aware of your surroundings."

She has a point. Which means I need to change the subject.

"Andy has really outdone himself with this party," I say. "It's fancier than my wedding. And I thought that was sophisticated." For the amount Clint and I had paid for it all those years ago, it better have been. "Where's Leon?"

"He went home for a Sam Adams. Not a big fan of the Italian beers, my Leon. But he'll be back soon." She leans in conspiratorially. "Apparently, they'll be serving tiramisu and cannoli later. With the fireworks."

"Fireworks?"

"Oh, yeah!" Her eyes grow wider. "Didn't you hear he hired a barge? It's out in the bay. Packed with fireworks that will go off right over our heads!"

"You've got to be kidding me!" I've been to block parties

before. Usually, it's one guy on a barbecue, while everyone else drinks beer or cheap wine. This feels more like the opening of opera season in Florence.

"Wait and see!" she tells me, before flagging down one of the wait staff and transferring stuffed mushrooms onto a small, porcelain plate.

As she eats, I survey the crowd. Several people couldn't make it—Serenity because she's in the hospital, Helen because she's in jail, and Carl because he's dead. But everyone else I know on the street turned up for the event, with the exception of my neighbor, Phyllis. Though she could still be here and just doesn't want to be seen. Like a ninja.

Even Roy, whose loathing for Andy could suck all the oxygen out of a room, is putting in an appearance. He's out by Andy's boat, slurping Madri from a bottle, while talking to a heavily perspiring Dr. Rosen. Stan Polotski stands a few feet away, looking awkward and uncomfortable.

To their left, Marjorie Higginbottom chats up a new couple I don't recognize. The man is older, with an egg-shaped head and large, round glasses. The woman hanging on his arm is much younger, thinner, and is wearing more jewelry than I own. They all look a bit tense.

Across the lawn, Jinny and George are deep in conversation with Bubbles. Though, to my surprise, Jinny mostly just listens while Bubbles seems to do all the talking. It probably has something to do with how Paul is coming along in his private lessons. I wonder if the money Bubbles earns from those classes is enough to tide her over until Carl's money comes through.

"How's the investigation coming?" Gina says, drawing my attention away from watching the arrival of Jolene and Savannah—who look about as out of place as I feel.

I give Gina what I think is my most innocent expression. "What investigation?"

Her free hand takes up position on her hip. "That might work on your kids, but it won't work on me, hun. I haven't seen you since Holly was arrested, but I'd be willing to bet money you're up to something."

"Her name is Helen, not Holly. And no, I'm not up to anything," I assure her. "I'm just here to enjoy myself."

"Is that so?" She eyes me warily. "I don't suppose you'd be interested to know what I just overheard, then."

My heart picks up pace. "Why? What did you hear?" Belatedly, I realize I fell into her trap. She was baiting me.

"I knew it!" she exclaims. "You *have* been investigating. I guess that means you don't think Holly killed Carl. Come on. Spill it. Hurry, before Leon gets back!"

I tell her everything I know—about Bubbles's need for Carl's inheritance, Helen's former husbands, and her reticence to speak about her past, and about Helen's sister, Jolene, who seems to have some secrets of her own.

"And then there's the business with Natasha," I say.

"Your Russian neighbor? Did you know she spoke fluent Spanish?" Gina asks.

"I did not. Why do you mention it?"

Gina waves it off with her hand. "No reason, really. I was just surprised. She's over there talking to Selma—"

"You mean Selena?" I interrupt.

"That's the one. Anyway, I think they were saying something about used car salesmen. Which seems weird, right? I could be wrong. It's been a long time since I took Spanish in college."

"Do you think it had anything to do with Carl?" I wonder aloud. Selling cars is what made him all his money.

"No idea," she admits. "Why are you so interested in Nadia all of a sudden? I told you she was a weird one, didn't I? After that business with the mailbox."

"Her name is Natasha. And yes, you did," I grant her. "But I'm interested in her flowers."

"Flowers?" She looks confused.

"Yeah. Turns out Serenity was poisoned. Possibly with the oleander Natasha planted right after she moved in."

"Oleander?" Gina repeats. "Is that what those little yellow flowers are?"

Before I can respond, Andy appears with two glasses in his hands. In his starched linen pants and white Panama shirt, his style is chic and effortless, precisely the way a famous fashion designer should present themself. He also smells really good, I can't help but notice.

"Would either of you like a fresh glass of Prosecco?" he asks.

After we both heartily agree, he asks us if we're enjoying the party.

"It's definitely something. And the food is delicious," Gina gushes. "Thanks so much for inviting us, Antonio."

"Andy," he corrects her, his smile faltering slightly.

I glare at her. He's our host. If she can't get his name right, don't say his name at all.

"And you, Madeline?" He turns his intense eyes in my direction. "Are you having a nice time?"

"It's a wonderful party, truly…" I consider how much more to say.

He raises one perfectly groomed eyebrow. "But?"

"I don't mean to sound ungrateful," I begin, "it's just hard to want to feel like celebrating with Carl dead and Helen in jail for his murder."

He nods, his eyes cast down sympathetically. "Ah yes, poor Helen. She must be suffering greatly."

Something about his tone surprises me. "Oh, I didn't realize you knew Helen very well."

"But yes. I have known Helen for years," he says. "Her previous husband, Donald, was a good friend of mine. It was he who suggested I purchase a home at Egret's Loft."

"Where were you living at the time?" I ask, trying to imagine Helen living in Italy.

"I had a little place in New Mexico. Santa Fe," he specifies. "Donald was my neighbor. In fact, I was with him the night he met Helen."

Gina takes a long look at Andy. "Humph. She saw you and Donald together...and she chose Donald?"

Andy's melodic laugh rings out. "Alas, it is true. She would not have me. She has better taste, I suppose."

I find that hard to believe. Apparently, so does Gina.

"Come on, Antonio. Don't sell yourself short!" she says.

Anger flares behind Andy's dark eyes, and he leans forward, ever so slightly. "Andy. How many times must I tell you? My. Name. Is. Andy."

Gina takes a small step back, not even realizing what she did wrong. At that moment, a member of the serving staff is walking behind her with two fresh bottles of Prosecco. She bumps into the waiter and both unopened bottles of bubbly slip from his hands. One shatters as it hits the ground. The other punctures slightly, spewing alcohol at everyone in our general vicinity.

"Don't worry! I've got it," I cry out, grabbing the hissing bottle and then hurrying around to the side of the house where I'd spotted his garbage can when I arrived.

Throwing open the lid, I drop the bottle into the trash, shaking off the excess liquid from my suddenly sticky hands. I'm about to close the lid when I spot them—a bunch of cans.

He really should recycle those, I think to myself. Then, I notice the labels. All the cans are from Budweiser beer.

Feeling slightly dirty about going through someone else's trash, I can't resist the urge to take another look. I see a bunch of plastic wrappers from things like hot dogs and Twinkies.

It doesn't make any sense. Andy said he only drinks wine. So, why does he have so many empty beer cans? And judging by the food he had prepared for this evening, it seems surprising his culinary tastes would sink so low as to eat store bought Oscar Mayer franks.

I'm considering the oddity of the situation, when something across the street catches my eye. It's dark and the streetlamps barely illuminate the driveway across the street and to the right—at Carl's house—but I can see a shape moving in the gloom. Whoever it is, my first thought is that they're sneaking out of a dead man's house.

They step further into the driveway. I can barely make out the outline of a tall person. From their body language, I can tell they've seen me in the beam of Andy's outdoor solar lights. They take a step in my direction.

Just then, an explosion shatters the relative peace of the neighborhood.

I scream.

Twenty-Five

Fireworks erupt overhead, shattering the shelter of darkness.

It was only fireworks, you silly old thing, I think. The events of the past few days and weeks have me jumping at shadows.

Then, in the burst of a barium green peony shell, I see Dr. Frank Rosen staring back at me from across the street. His large ears shift higher on his bald head, like a dog when it's trying to interpret a new sound.

Breathing deeply to slow my heart rate and, assuming there must be a valid reason the good doctor is loitering outside Carl's house, I take a step in his direction. At first, he seems to be moving toward me as well.

"Is everything alright, Dr. Rosen?" I call out.

Abruptly, he makes a sharp right turn and walks quickly down the side of Carl's house, toward the lake. He seems to be carrying something under his left arm as he runs away.

"Dr. Rosen?" I pitch my voice louder to bridge the growing distance between us.

"Madeline, what's going on?" Gina's husband, Leon, rolls up beside me in his wheelchair.

"I don't know. But I think Dr. Rosen just broke into Carl's house," I explain. "When he spotted me, he ran that way."

Leon's eyes follow the direction my finger is pointing, then he looks back at me and says, "Wait here."

As he's quickly wheeling off in pursuit of Dr. Rosen, Gina joins me in the street.

"Mandy? Are you okay?" she asks. "I thought I heard someone screaming."

I briefly sum up the events of the last few minutes, concluding with Leon chasing after the fleeing Dr. Rosen.

Gina's dark eyes widen in alarm. "Leon went after him? He better not get out of that wheelchair again! His knee's never going to heal!"

With that, Gina races off into the darkness to chase after Leon.

Finding myself alone on the empty street, fireworks blossoming above me, I make the only decision that makes any sense. I follow them.

The Dead Men's Wife

Moments later, I arrive at the edge of the lake. Leon's wheelchair is on its side, abandoned. Its former occupant is now rolling around on the ground with Dr. Rosen. They seem to be scrambling to take possession of some item that I can't quite make out. Gina stands above both men, yelling at them to stop. When neither of them listens, she leans down and starts tugging on Leon's arm.

"Gina, no!" Leon screams, as Dr. Rosen extricates himself and runs to the shoreline. Transferring the item from his left hand, Dr. Rosen pulls back his right arm and launches what appears to be a book high into the air and outwards into the lake. Its pages flutter before it lands with a splash, disrupting a raft of ducks who voice their displeasure with a chorus of loud quacks.

Once the mysterious item is safely entombed in the water, Dr. Rosen turns back to face us, raising his hands in the air as if he's surrendering to an opposing army.

"What in the heck was that all about?" Gina demands, helping her husband back into his wheelchair and glaring at Dr. Rosen. "If Leon's hurt his knee, I *will* report you to the state medical board!"

"I'm sorry, but your husband attacked me. I was simply defending myself," Dr. Rosen says, his eyeglasses slipping perilously low on the bridge of his nose following the scuffle.

"Leon came after you because I saw you coming out of Carl's house," I inform him.

Dr. Rosen looks at Gina and Leon before answering. "You must be mistaken. I was merely out for a stroll and happened to be in front of Carl's house when you spotted me." His demeanor is calm and composed and more than a little condescending.

"Then why did you run away?" I challenge him. "And what did you throw in the lake?"

"Oh, that?" He shrugs his shoulders, lifting his hands higher into the air. "That was just a branch I landed on when Leon tackled me. I didn't want anyone to trip over it."

"What a load of BS!" Gina fumes. "That wasn't a branch. It was some kind of book!"

The patter of approaching footsteps alerts us that our little group is about to grow.

"Goodness me, we heard screaming and rushed over," Jinny, in a pink sundress, announces after emerging onto the lakefront. "It gave us quite a fright, don't you know. Is everything okay?"

Bubbles, who seems unable to keep up with her older companion, wheezes noisily in an attempt to refill her lungs. Paul, seemingly unsure quite what to do, pats her back.

"No, everything is not okay," Gina declares. "Dr. Reuben broke into Carl's house, attacked my poor, handicapped Leon, and then threw a *book* in the lake!" She looks directly at Dr. Rosen when she puts the emphasis on the word "book," as if daring him to dispute it.

Dr. Rosen glances at Bubbles before replying. "There has clearly been some kind of misunderstanding here. Nothing to worry about. Why don't we all just go back to the party and enjoy the rest of the evening?"

"How big was the book?" Bubbles asks.

It seems like a weird question but, in hindsight, the book had looked rather large. Even from my brief glimpse of it, I'd noticed that it was much bigger than a paperback. In fact, it was even larger than a hardcover book. It was roughly the size of standard letter paper, almost like a textbook of some sort.

Bubbles is temporarily living in Carl's house while she goes through his things. I wonder if there is a specific book she has in mind.

Ignoring what she apparently believes is an irrelevant question, Gina isn't done venting her anger. "I bet you'd like us all to forget about it. Wouldn't you, Dr. Reuben? Well, that's not going to happen. I think we should call the police, let them sort this out."

His name is Dr. Rosen, I think but decide to bite my tongue.

"Fine." Dr. Rosen rises to the bait. "If you want to make fools of yourselves, I'm more than happy to witness your humiliation. Go ahead. Call them."

There's so much about the situation I don't understand, but one question reigns supreme in my mind. If Dr. Rosen was able to get into Carl's house, could he be responsible for the thefts in the neighborhood?

"How did you get into Carl's house?" I ask. "Did you know his code?"

Dr. Rosen, having finally lowered his arms, pushes his glasses higher on this thin nose. "This is a thoroughly pointless inquiry. As I never broke into Carl's house, there is no way I can logically respond to your questions."

Gina seems to pick up on my train of thought. "Right, if you could get into Carl's house, maybe you could get into mine! Did you steal my casserole dish?"

Dr. Rosen laughs nervously. "What are you accusing me of now?"

"There have been quite a few thefts around here lately," I explain. "Helen's diamond bracelet, Gina's dish, Molly's body fat machine, Jinny's sunglasses..."

"Don't forget about my old laptop!" Jinny adds. "That's gone missing too!"

"I also had a security camera disappear," I say. "My kids were very upset when they couldn't spy on me. They're the ones who set it up, you see. If you did take my camera, that really wasn't a very nice thing to do. Gina may be right about calling the police."

"Yeah. Call the cops!" Bubbles chimes in angrily.

"This is all balderdash!" Dr. Rosen complains loudly. "I don't know what you're talking about! I didn't take any of those things!"

The Dead Men's Wife

Gina pulls her cell phone out of her purse. "We're all agreed?"

Everyone—except Dr. Rosen—nods. Gina dials 911.

I approach Dr. Rosen and softly, so that no one else can hear, ask, "Are you sure you don't want to sort this out before the police get involved?"

"The only thing I *want* right now is to speak to my lawyer," Dr. Rosen intones.

Seeing Leon grimace in pain, I make my way over to him to see if Gina should include an ambulance in her emergency request. He insists he's fine.

Turning back to make sure Dr. Rosen isn't trying to run away again, I see Bubbles whisper something in his ear. Dr. Rosen jerks his head to look into her eyes, his already pasty face blanches white.

The whole scene is over in seconds. This isn't the first time I've seen Bubbles seemingly challenge Dr. Rosen. There was some kind of threat beneath the surface of a comment she made to him at the memorial service. If my aging memory serves, it had something to do with Carl having once attended medical school.

Had she found something out about Dr. Rosen's past? From what Eliza told me, Bubbles clearly needs money. Maybe she was blackmailing the doctor? Or maybe she was his partner in larcenous crime and she's warning him not to rat her out.

Either way—much like the thefts themselves, Serenity's

poisoning, and the inconsistencies in Jolene's story—I can't for the life of me figure out what is has to do with Carl's wedding day death.

Twenty-Six

"It's very safe, I assure you. All I would need is a high-voltage power supply, radiation shielding, a Geiger counter and an x-ray tube," Curt pleads. "What do you say, Grandmother? Will you let me build an x-ray machine in your garage?"

"That's enough, buddy," Richie warns his son from the front seat of his rented SUV.

"But you're underestimating the cost-effectiveness and practicality of having one!" Curt argues. "According to the CDC, three million older adults, like Grandmother, present to the emergency room for fall-related injuries every year. Of course, that's only a fraction of the thirty-six million falls reported each year that don't require emergency—"

"As long as there's still room in the garage for my golf cart, dear," I cut off Curt, mid-speech. He's not happy about being interrupted, but that's outweighed by his excitement about getting permission to build a medical device in my garage.

"Really, lady?" Ritchie complains. "You wouldn't even let me build a birdhouse in our backyard at his age!"

With a feeble wave of my hand, I brush off his decades-old disappointment. If only they would both stop talking for a few minutes as I try to acclimate my eyes to the painful sunlight. Following Dr. Rosen's police-escorted departure the night before, the whole neighborhood had retreated to Andy's house for Prosecco, tiramisu, and gossip. It would seem I had one too many Proseccos, because my head is throbbing.

What were you thinking? I ask myself. *You're too old to be having a hangover!*

Ritchie whistles. "Look at all those people."

As we approach the Golf Club, I look up from under the visor of my large sun hat and see a long line of active elders forming outside the entrance. There must be at least fifty people waiting to get inside.

Every resident of Egret's Loft had received a hand-delivered letter from the board earlier this morning. The letters were intended to alert residents to a potential string of thefts that had been carried out in the past week and to let them know that Detective Samantha Baptiste would, this morning only, be manning a reporting station at the club if anyone wanted to report missing items.

At Ritchie's insistence, we'd come to report my stolen security camera. I think it had been driving him and his sister crazy, not being able to spy on me. It's the main reason Ritchie is here now. Another murder's been committed, and he's lost eyes on his mother.

The thought makes me smile. He is a good son.

"Do you think all of them were burgled?" Ritchie asks as we walk up and take our position at the end of the line.

"Either that or they're here for a big bingo game," I tease.

Outside of the car's air conditioning for less than a minute, my temples begin to sweat under the heat of the late morning sun. Ritchie notices me wiping a drop of it away.

"It's really not smart to keep all of you out in the heat like this," Ritchie says. "I'm going to go speak to someone about moving this line inside the building. Come on, buddy."

He takes Curt's hand, and the two walk past the line and into the club through the massive double doors. Seconds after they go inside, Detective Fletcher emerges, holding the arm of a ninety-year-old woman. I watch as he escorts her to her golf cart. When he turns around, I wave to get his attention.

"Good morning, detective," I call out as he approaches. The sound of my own voice echoes inside my skull. "This is some crowd. Has it been this busy all morning?"

"You have no idea," he says wearily. "It feels like every single resident of Egret's Loft has turned up. About half of them want to report missing items."

"And the other half?"

"Just want to be part of the excitement." He sighs while vigorously rubbing his fingers against his temples. "I don't think it's even possible to steal from this many people in the time frame we're looking at. My guess, a lot of these people didn't have anything taken, they're just ol... forgetful."

"You can say old. I won't be offended," I assure him. "And you're probably right. It took me ten minutes this morning to find my reading glasses, which had been on my head the whole time."

He smiles and points at my head. "If you're here to report a missing sun hat, I can save you some time."

"Very funny." I playfully swat at him with my handbag. The movement makes my head hurt even more. "How's the investigation going? Has Dr. Rosen admitted to anything?"

Detective Fletcher shakes his head. "Naw, nothing yet. He's one cool customer, I'll tell you that. But anything that gets reported missing now will go on a search warrant. If we find any of the stuff in his house, he's toast."

"Was this reporting station your idea?"

"Umm," he adjusts his collar. "Yes and no."

"Yes *and* no?" I ask.

"Well, Sammy was the one who suggested we come

here and take people's reports. But she only thought about it after I said it would be good to know what had been taken from everyone."

I pat his arm. "Don't worry. The next good idea will be all yours."

The line in front of us begins to move. Ritchie must be having some success. Knowing him, he's lecturing someone inside about the potential hazards of having old people standing outside on a hot November day.

Or, it occurs to me, Curt could be the talking. I pity the poor soul who comes up against either of them.

"My grandson told me he saw police boats out on the lake this morning," I tell Detective Fletcher as we inch forward in line. "I assume you were searching for something. What did you find?"

"The usual. Golf balls, food wrappers, things like that." His face begins to scrunch up. "But there was also some weird stuff. The guys found a prosthetic leg. I mean, who throws their fake leg into a lake?"

As fascinating a question as that may be, there are more important ones that need to be answered. Detective Fletcher is getting better, but sometimes he still completely misses the obvious.

"I mean, did you find out what Dr. Rosen threw in the lake last night?" I prompt.

"Oh, right." He stands up straighter, as if responding to a teacher who just asked him why he didn't do his homework. "The only book we found was an old yearbook."

"A yearbook?"

"Yeah, you know...they're like books that come out at the end of the school year with everyone's pictures and stuff."

"I know what a yearbook is, detective. I'm not *that* old." I glare at him. "I meant, why would Dr. Rosen have stolen Carl's yearbook? That doesn't make any sense. Was there anything out of the ordinary about it?"

He shrugs his shoulders. "Don't know. We haven't been able to do much with it yet. We need to dry it out first."

"How long will that take?"

"A couple more hours."

We both breathe a sigh of relief as we enter the Golf Club's air-conditioned lobby. Fortunately, the lights inside are dim, so my eyes don't feel quite so sensitive. As they adjust, I see Ritchie and Curt across the room. They're setting up folding chairs for people to sit on while they wait.

"I'm just curious." I speak slowly, plotting out my strategy. "Would it be possible to come take a look at the yearbook this afternoon?"

He looks at me with raised eyebrows.

"I know I'm not a detective, like you." I practically curtsy. "But it never hurts to have an extra pair of eyes, right? Maybe I'll see something you don't. Not because you would miss anything obvious, you understand. But I live here, and something might occur to me, looking at it, that you would be unaware of."

His eyes burn holes into my aching head as he makes his decision. Finally, he grunts and tilts his head to one side. "Sure, why not?"

"And since I'm going to be at the police station anyway—"

He cuts me off. "You're killing me, Madeline."

"It's nothing much. I just need to have a quick word with Helen," I explain.

"You know she's only supposed to be talking to her lawyer right now," he argues. "With that Karma woman being poisoned, the judge decided to hold off on granting bail until we know more."

So, the judge wants to know how that fits in with Carl's murder too?

I put the palms of my hands together in prayer and gaze at him through my eyelashes. "Please? It'll only take a few minutes."

"I don't know…" he hedges.

"I'll help you plot out your next novel," I promise. It's not really bribery. At least, I don't think it is.

Apparently, he doesn't mind it either. "Alright. But only for a couple of minutes. And it has to be when Sammy's not around."

"Deal," I tell him, smiling inside but also wishing I'd taken more aspirin earlier.

Ritchie and Curt approach us and offer me a chair, which I gratefully accept. I'll need to rest if I want to get a reprieve from this hangover before going to see Helen. I have some important questions to ask—about her sister and her life before Egret's Loft.

And this time, I'm not taking "no comment" for an answer.

Twenty-Seven

"Thanks for getting here so quickly." Detective Fletcher glances down at his watch. "Sammy's gone on her lunch break, which means we have about twenty minutes."

Luckily, the drive to the police station had only taken a few minutes from my house. Ritchie dropped me off after the detective called this afternoon with the all-clear.

"Can I see the yearbook?" I ask, not wanting to waste any time.

"Yeah, I've got it right over here." Detective Fletcher walks over to one of the desks in the station.

Aside from a laptop computer, the only things on his desk are a notebook and pens, an empty Snickers wrapper, and a photo frame.

Craning my neck to get a better look, I see the frame

contains a picture of a pretty brunette in her late forties. It occurs to me that Detective Fletcher has never mentioned anything about his personal life. He doesn't wear a wedding ring, though Clint used to say many police officers don't. Who's the woman in the detective's life?

"Here we go." Detective Fletcher captures my attention as he pulls a plastic evidence bag out of the top drawer of his desk. "I haven't sealed it yet, so you can take a peek. But you'll need to wear these."

He hands me a pair of gloves and I slip them on quickly.

"Have you had a chance to look at it yet?" I ask.

He nods. "Yup. Just a quick one. But I did find something interesting. Turn to page sixty-three."

He hands me the yearbook, and I flip to the referenced page. Staring back at me is a younger version of Dr. Rosen. I'm confused. Does the book belong to the doctor? If so, why did he throw it in the lake?

"Now, flip over to page one-twenty-three." A triumphant smile curves the outer corners of the detective's lips.

Obeying, I gingerly turn the starchy pages. It's a collection of candid snapshots of some of the students. I spot Dr. Rosen in one of the photographs, standing over what appears to be a dead body on a table. There's another man in the picture with Dr. Rosen, but the image is blurrier.

I lean my head away from the page, trying to make out

more detail, while my hand blindly scavenges my handbag for a pair of reading glasses. Finally finding them, I slip the temples over my ears and lean in close.

"Is that...?" I begin, certain I must be mistaken.

"That's right!" Detective Fletcher exclaims. "It's Carl Hancock!"

At the memorial service, Bubbles had mentioned something about finding out her uncle went to medical school. Dr. Rosen had been part of that conversation. In fact, he'd looked a little uncomfortable when Bubbles brought it up. Why didn't he say they went to school together?

"Look at the writing too." Detective Fletcher points to some runny ink. "It's hard to make out after being in the water, but can you read what it says?"

I'm now so close to the page I can feel the heat of my breath bouncing back on my face. "It looks like it says, 'If you don't tell, I won't tell. Brothers forever, Frank.'"

Detective Fletcher leans back, seeming satisfied.

"So." I attempt to piece together the puzzle aloud. "If Frank signed the yearbook, that means it belonged to Carl. It would appear that Dr. Rosen did break into his old friend's house, after all. Looking for this. But why? And what weren't they supposed to tell?"

The detective frowns. "How would I know? I just found the inscription and wanted to point it out." He consults the watch on his wrist. "We're running out of time. If you want to talk to Helen, you have to do it now."

My thoughts still chasing a meaning in the yearbook dilemma, I feel suddenly unprepared to face Helen. But I can't turn down the opportunity. "Take me to her."

Detective Fletcher leads me through a steel door on the rear wall of the police station. Behind it, I see a row of three cells that look like cages. Helen sits in one of them.

"Madeline!" She jumps up from her cot. "I can't tell you how tickled I am to see you!"

"You have five minutes," Detective Fletcher warns, then closes the door on his way out.

I try to organize my thoughts, focus on the questions I prepared, but it's no use, and I'm losing precious time trying to remember them. "Hi, Helen. We don't have much time, but there are some things I need to know. Okay?"

"I suppose." She seems skeptical.

My mind goes for the lowest hanging fruit. "Do you know anything about a secret between Carl and Dr. Rosen?"

The ghost of a tiny wrinkle appears between her brows. "No."

Dead end. Moving on to the oleander connection. "Before she moved into Egret's Loft, had you ever met my new neighbor, Natasha?"

"The Russki?" Helen looks perplexed. "I'm sure I never laid eyes on her before in my life."

As I'm listening to her answers, it occurs to me that Helen looks quite pretty without any makeup. I want to tell her that, but I'll have to remember to bring it up later. There's no time now.

"Andy Romano. You knew him before you married your last husband?" As I say it, I realize Carl was, technically, her last husband. I need to be more specific. "Donald, I mean."

Her lips curl into a catlike grin. "Oh, did I ever!"

Her response gives me pause. "Did you now?"

She looks at me like I've just asked if the Earth is flat. "That man's as fine as frog hair split four ways. Don't tell me you haven't noticed!"

Color rushes to my cheeks. "He is...attractive, isn't he?"

She chuckles. "You've got two eyes. You tell me."

"Did you..." I begin.

She crosses her arms over her large breasts. "Did I what?"

"You know." I realize I'm being vague, but I can't help myself. When I was growing up, you didn't really talk about this sort of thing. "Were you...you know?"

Helen sighs. "Sugar, would you quit goin' around your butt to get to your elbow? You want to know if he and I were ever...intimate."

I imagine my whole face is red at this point. "Yes."

"Sadly, no," she admits. "Not that it wasn't on offer, mind you. He was sweet on me. And the way those Italians dress? Why, their pants are so tight you can see their religion." She makes a noise anyone else might make before a nice meal. "You know something? Right before I married

Donald and we moved here, Andy asked me to run away with him."

"Really?"

"Really!" she confirms. "Showed up here right before Carl and me got married too. Asked me again if I'd run away with him."

Thinking of Carl and Andy, side by side—one in a Speedo, the other a fine Italian suit—I can't help but ask, "Were you tempted?"

"Not even for a second." She seems to take pride in the assertion. "I learned my lesson early on. Men who are *that* pretty, well, they're meant to look at, not to marry."

"Oh yeah? Which husband taught you that?" I ask.

Helen purses her lips. "It doesn't matter."

She'd been so forthcoming about the last six husbands, but the first two remain a mystery. It's impossible not to wonder why. "Was it one of your first two husbands? You haven't mentioned anything about them."

"It was such a long time ago, I don't remember." She looks me right in the eye as she says it, even though we both know she's lying.

I step closer to the bars of her cell. "Why don't you want to talk about them? What happened?"

The door to the jail opens and Detective Fletcher leans in, pointing to his watch. "Time to wrap this up," he says and closes the door.

My eyes plead with Helen. Her shoulders slump.

"Look sugar," she finally replies. "I honestly can't tell you what happened with my first two husbands." When I open my mouth to retort, she stops me. "I really can't. You're just gonna have to trust me on that."

All of this is going back more than forty years, yet her reticence to speak about it makes me suspect there may be some connection to what happened to Carl.

"You can't tell me *anything*?" I push.

Helen's face is neutral as she stares back at me with squinted eyes. "There's nothing *I* can tell you. But, if you *really* want to know, ask Jolene. She can decide whether to tell you or not."

"Jolene?" I'm still at a loss as to how she fits into the larger picture. Something about their relationship has been bothering me. Short on time, I decide to try and shock some answers out of Helen. "She's not really your sister, is she?"

Rather than confirm or deny, Helen calmly asks, "Why would you say that?"

She's called my bluff, but her lack of surprise at the question makes me think I might have hit the mark. "Bob. Your father? She didn't seem to know that was his name," I zero in on one of the many inconsistencies in their stories. "She thought you were talking about an ex-boyfriend."

Helen hangs her head and swings it from side to side. "Sometimes, I swear, that girl's only got one oar in the water. But look, just talk to her. She's solid, and we've known each other for years."

The jail door flies open on a frantic looking Detective Fletcher. "You need to leave! Now! Sammy's on her way back!"

I turn to Helen for one final question. "If you and Jolene are so close, does she know your real name?"

"Sugar, there ain't nothing about me that girl doesn't know," Helen confirms. "But it's on you to convince her to spill the beans."

"Madeline!" Detective Fletcher whispers harshly, his whole body fidgeting. "You're really putting me in a bad spot here. Hurry up! I have an Uber waiting for you outside."

"A what?"

"An Uber. You know, it's a ride-hailing service where people drive their own cars."

I frown at him. "You ordered me a car that I have to drive myself?"

"No, *you* don't drive the car. The driver drives *their* own car." With his hand on my back, he propels me forward as he explains.

"Who are these drivers? And why would they want strangers in their cars?"

"I don't know," he practically whimpers. "Just think of it like a really fancy taxi, okay?"

Still confused, I make my way as quickly as possible

through the station. Detective Fletcher did help me out, after all, letting me in to talk to Helen. I certainly don't want to create any kind of problems for him. Though there is one thing I need before I get into the fancy taxicab.

"If we're passing a ladies' room on the way out, I might as well go while I have the chance."

Twenty-Eight

Walking in my front door, I'm still trying to work out how Detective Fletcher arranged my ride home.

He didn't give the female driver any money when he practically shoved me in the back seat. He didn't even tell her where I wanted to go. She already knew. And then she refused to take my money when we got here, saying the ride was already paid for!

"Ritchie? Have you ever heard of something called Uber?" I ask loudly as I slip out of my sandals and into my house shoes.

"Hey, lady! Back so soon?" he asks, ignoring my question.

"The detective put me in this car that he called—" I've

been talking as I walk toward the kitchen table, but I now see Ritchie has company. "Oh! Hello, Paul. I didn't know you were here."

Jinny's teenage grandson is sitting next to Ritchie. Full glasses of lemonade sit, untouched, in front of them on the table. Paul looks like he's about to jump out of his seat. Ritchie lays a fatherly hand on his arm.

"While you were gone, Paul stopped by for a little chat," Ritchie informs me.

Looking around the room, I don't see my grandson anywhere. "Where's Curt?"

Ritchie points to the veranda. "He's been out there since you left, drawing up schematics for the x-ray machine you told him he could build in the garage."

I ignore the touch of resentment in his voice. He really needs to get over that birdhouse. The neighbors had a cat; I didn't want him or his sister to find little cardinal corpses littered across the back lawn when they were toddlers.

"Well, you both carry on with your conversation. I may go lie down for a bit and rest my eyes."

The truth is, I'm exhausted. The hangover had already sapped most of my energy. Anything I had remaining in the tank got used up waiting in line to report my stolen security camera and visiting Helen in jail.

"Not so fast, lady." The tone of Ritchie's voice makes me wonder if I've done something wrong again. I'm thinking *this better not be more about that birdhouse*, when he continues. "Paul has something he wants to say to you. Go ahead, Paul."

Paul's eyes are fixated on the lemonade sitting in front of him. "I'm really sorry, ma'am."

My exhaustion immediately dissipates. "Sorry? For what?"

"It was me," he practically whispers. "I'm the one who took your security camera."

My brain feels like a machine gun operated by someone who's blindfolded—firing off questions as fast as bullets, with none of them finding their targets.

How did he get into my house? Was I home when he did? Why would he want a security camera? Is he responsible for *all* the recent thefts?

If Paul is responsible for the thefts, that must also mean that Dr. Rosen is innocent. Yet he does appear to have broken into Carl's house for that yearbook. Were his actions completely unrelated to the thefts? And what does any of it have to do with Carl's murder?

As I move shakily closer to the table, Ritchie jumps up and offers me his seat. I slide in next to Paul. Ritchie remains standing behind me.

"Thank you for letting me know, Paul. That was a very brave thing to do, coming to tell me," I try to reassure him.

He finally drags his eyes off the glass to look up at me.

"I feel really bad about it. Like, you seem like a really nice lady."

"I'm sure my son would sometimes disagree," I tease to lighten some of the tension radiating off Paul. "Does your grandmother know you're here?"

His eyes widen in alarm. "She doesn't have to know, does she?"

"That depends," I tell him. "Am I the only person you took something from?"

He breaks eye contact. "No, ma'am."

Even though he's admitted to stealing from me, I can't help feeling sorry for the kid. Jinny, and I'm sure his father back in Canada, are not going to be happy about this.

I pat the young man's arm. "Alright. I appreciate your honesty, Paul. Let's just focus on the camera for now. Do you want to tell me why you took it?"

"I didn't want to." He's practically in tears. "But she told me she, like, needed the money. And she said if I helped her, she would help me."

I look over at Ritchie. He tilts his head toward Paul as if to indicate that I should keep listening.

"Who's *she*, Paul? Did someone here ask you to steal from me?" I think I already know the answer, but I don't want to put words in his mouth.

"She's been so cool with me. I don't want to, like, narc on her," he laments.

It's obvious who he's referring to, and he's clearly

tortured about saying her name, so I take pity. "It's Bubbles, right? She's the one who asked you to steal for her?"

He nods, his tears chasing each other down his cheeks.

"Did she ask you, specifically, to take my security camera?"

"No," he whimpers. "She just said to, like, go into different houses and take anything electronic or, like, jewelry and stuff. Anything that wouldn't be too hard to sell."

That would explain the randomness of some of the stolen items—an expensive casserole dish, an old laptop, designer sunglasses.

"How did you get in? Did Bubbles give you the codes to our houses?"

He closes his eyes and lets out a deep breath. "Yeah. She said she got them from her uncle's computer, after he died."

The fitness trainer, Molly, had told me only the board had all the access codes to people's homes. Carl was on the board, so that made sense, and all the thefts seem to have occurred after Carl died, within the past week.

Except for one.

Helen had things stolen long before Paul turned up to stay with his grandparents. Which must mean Bubbles was the one who stole from Helen, probably with the code she'd somehow gotten from Carl. That must be why Helen was the only victim before Carl's death. Her code was the only one Bubbles had access to.

But something about the timeline is troubling me, my camera went missing the morning after Paul arrived at Egret's Loft.

"When did Bubbles ask you to start stealing for her?" I ask.

"The day I got here. After the singing class," he specifies. "She said I was a good singer, and I told her that I, like, really want to be on Broadway. My dad wants me to be a dentist, like him. He won't pay for me to go to New York and audition or anything."

"That's how she said she would help you?" I guess.

"Uh huh. She said she would, like, sponsor me to go and pay my rent until I got settled."

"But first—" I carry his story forward, "—she needed you to help her get money to tide her over for a while."

The phone in my purse alerts me that I've received a new text. I ignore it.

"Yeah," Paul continues. "She said she'd be loaded soon but, like, she had to wait for her uncle's inheritance to come through." He's less tense now that he's coming clean about everything. "She told me he'd been helping her out with money when he was alive, but now that he was dead, like, his new 'gold-digging wife' wouldn't give her anything."

He'd used air quotes to emphasize gold-digging wife, which probably means it was a direct quote from Bubbles.

The same woman who planned such a lavish wedding for her uncle was secretly plotting against his new bride.

I'm now convinced Bubbles asked the DJ to play the song that had distressed Helen so much at her own wedding. The question is, did Bubbles only care about her uncle's money? And if so, how far would she have been willing to go to get it?

It appears it's become too quiet for Paul, because he rushes to fill the silence. "She said we wouldn't be hurting anyone. Like, everyone here is rich. They wouldn't miss a dish or a camera or an old laptop. It was just, like, stuff. And they could always buy more. She said she was going to replace everything we took after she got her uncle's money!"

But that would only happen *if* she got Carl's money. With Helen in the picture, that certainty had dwindled.

"I've never stolen anything before in my life! If my dad finds out..." Paul begins to ramble. I silence him by putting my index finger to my lips. I need to think.

Detective Fletcher will need to know about all of this, but I don't want to make things difficult for Paul. He needs to learn a lesson from all of this, but in my mind, the guilty party here is Bubbles. She's the one who enticed a minor to break the law for her own benefit.

As I'm considering what to do, I hear another text come through on my phone. It's rare for me to get two texts in a row.

Unless something's wrong.

I think of Emmy in the hospital after eating a battery.

"One second," I say to Paul as I fish my phone out of the bottom of my bag.

There's a flood of relief when I see the texts are not from Eliza, but the feeling doesn't last long. One of the messages is from Detective Fletcher. The other is from Leon. Both share the same horrible message.

Gina has been poisoned!

Twenty-Nine

My left hand feels numb, and I'm convinced it's begun to prune. Leon has been clutching it tightly for the better part of two hours in his own sweaty hand.

Looking at his face, he seems calm. His hand, however, tells a different story.

When a doctor emerges from behind the swinging double doors of the emergency room, Leon releases my hand and launches himself out of his wheelchair.

If Gina was here, she would tell him to sit back down and take it easy on his knees until they're healed. But she's somewhere behind the swinging doors, fighting for her life.

"Doctor, is she going to be alright?" Leon pleads for information. His skin, normally a rich shade of mocha, now looks a lot more like milky tea.

The doctor approaches, lowering his surgical mask. "Your wife is recovering nicely, Mr. Wilson. We had to get the poison out of her system, but she's resting comfortably now. I can take you back to see her—" the doctor glances at me, "—but I think it's best if only one of you goes. There's a detective in there with her already."

"Go," I tell Leon.

He doesn't hesitate. He sinks back down into this wheelchair, probably afraid his wife will yell at him, and follows the doctor through the double doors.

I sit back down, relieved, but alone. I'd sent Ritchie home over an hour ago with Curt—not because I was concerned that Curt would be traumatized by anything he might see at the hospital, but because he wouldn't leave the staff alone with his questions. By the time he asked if he could inspect one of the hospital's x-ray machines, the nurses had had enough. I promised Ritchie I'd text him as soon as I knew anything.

As I begin to type, I hear a familiar voice.

"Mom!"

I look up just in time to see Eliza flying across the cheap linoleum floor of the waiting room toward me.

"I got here as fast as I could!" she pants. "Have you heard anything?"

Standing and spreading my arms wide, I grip her fiercely in a tight hug. Her hair smells like jasmine, a nice change from the antiseptic odor of the hospital. "The doctor just came out. Gina's going to be fine."

"Thank goodness!" Eliza's words tickle the hairs hanging close to my cheeks. "I still can't believe it. How are you holding up?"

I've never told Eliza how close I feel to Gina, despite the relatively short amount of time we've been friends. But somehow, she knows. Eliza always knows.

"I'm doing a lot better knowing she's going to pull through." I fight to hold back my tears of relief.

"I bet you do." She squeezes me tighter before releasing the embrace. We're both seated when she asks, "So, who do you think poisoned her?"

Faces flash before my eyes. Bubbles. Dr. Rosen. Natasha. They're all connected to the bigger picture somehow. I just can't figure out how all the pieces fit.

"I honestly don't know," I admit. "I have to assume Gina and Serenity were poisoned by the same person. But I have no idea how they're linked. And if Serenity was poisoned by flowers from Natasha's yard, why would my new neighbor want to kill either of them?"

Eliza leans back in her chair and glances carefully in each direction. "I don't have any insight into that. But I did find out something interesting about Natasha."

She has my attention. "Really? What?"

"So, you know that, even though Natasha's husband just died, he'd been a vegetable for the better part of a decade."

I nod. "Nikolai, right? He was in a bad car accident. Ritchie told me."

"Sure. After I told him," she grumbles. Their sibling rivalry never truly rests. "Anyway, based on what I found going through old court records, Natasha blamed Carl for her husband's death!"

"Wh-What?!" I stammer, considering all of the implications of this new information. "Was Carl involved in the accident?"

"No, nothing like that," she says. "Apparently, Carl sold Natasha's husband a vintage Pantera—"

"A what?"

Eliza swats the air like my question is an annoying insect. "A fancy Italian muscle car built in the seventies. They're classics now. But that's not really important."

"Sorry. Go on," I encourage her to continue.

"Carl sold one to Natasha's husband, Nikolai, saying it was in tip-top shape. He said he'd had it all checked out by his mechanics. Except he hadn't. Or if he did, they missed the fact that the car's brake discs were corroded. I mean, really corroded. Nikolai got into the accident literally as he was driving it home from the dealership."

"How horrible," I sympathize.

"He was going a little too fast along Pine Tree Drive... you know, the same street Justin Bieber was arrested for drag racing on."

"Justin who? Is he a friend of Nikolai's?"

"Never mind." Eliza rolls her eyes. "Back to Nikolai. He was speeding on Pine Tree Drive and the brakes failed. He couldn't stop. Ran into someone's mailbox, and the whole thing flew through the windshield, nearly killing him, and turning him into a vegetable."

"A mailbox?" I exclaim.

Gina had told me that Natasha seemed paranoid and frantic when her own mailbox had been destroyed recently. Gina said she'd tried to explain it was just the result of Phyllis's poor driving, but Natasha was having none of it—insisting someone was out to get her. It suddenly makes sense why her response seemed like an overreaction. It must have felt very personal.

"Yeah, a mailbox. Keep up, Mom!" Eliza rolls her eyes. Again. "So, Natasha sued Carl, but she lost. Not because she didn't have the evidence. She did. But before Carl's attorneys could do their own inspection on the car, it suddenly disappeared. Probably at the bottom of Biscayne Bay. His lawyers argued that, without independent verification, Natasha could be fabricating evidence to suit her own ends."

"That's awful! You think Carl destroyed the car just so he wouldn't have to pay Natasha?"

"That's not something anyone would be able to prove," Eliza states firmly, "but I do think that's what happened. I think Carl was worried about his reputation if people started to think he was selling busted-up luxury cars. No one would buy from him again. So, he buried it."

"Poor Natasha," I say, though I'm simultaneously wondering if the grieving widow is also a murderer.

It's starting to feel far too coincidental that she moved to Egret's Loft, where Carl lived, so soon after her husband succumbed to his decade-old injuries. And she'd been at the clubhouse the night Carl was murdered. I'd seen her standing out by the front doors when I went to the ladies' room. She could have easily waltzed inside, killed Carl with a champagne cork, and then slipped away into the night.

It's impossible not to consider that she's also responsible for poisoning Serenity and possibly Gina now, as well. Though I can't think of any possible reason why she would have wanted to hurt either of them.

Natasha had a connection to Carl prior to moving to Egret's Loft, that much Eliza has proven. Did she also have something against Serenity and Gina? It seems unlikely. Unless she connected Gina somehow to the destruction of her mailbox.

"Mom, look." Eliza nudges me with her elbow, interrupting my thoughts. Looking up, I see Detective Fletcher standing by the double doors into the emergency room. He shakes hands with the doctor and begins crossing the waiting room, heading for the exit.

Eliza and I both chase after him.

"Detective Fletcher!" I call out just as his feet step onto

the sensors that activate the sliding doors. He turns around, smiling when he sees it's me. The smile turns into a frown when he sees Eliza beside me. He sucks in his slightly pooching belly and rises to his full height.

"Madeline, I'm sorry about your friend. But it looks like she's gonna pull through just fine." His voice is laced with sympathy and hope.

"Do you know who might have done this to her?" Eliza asks, even though the detective has yet to acknowledge her presence.

He looks at her briefly but turns back to me before responding. "The doctor says she was poisoned with oleander, but Gina has no idea how or when she ingested it."

"Oleander again." I'd suspected as much, but now it's confirmed. "I suppose you'll want to know the names of anyone at Egret's Loft who, I think, might have had grudges against both of them."

"Thanks, but that won't be necessary," Detective Fletcher stops me.

Eliza lets out a deep grunt. "Look, I know you've got something against me because I haven't always shared information with you. But don't be such an arrogant jerk! My mom really might be able to help. Gina was her friend. At least let her try!"

"That's enough, dear." I rest my hand on Eliza's arm. She's only trying to argue on my behalf, I know. But if the detective didn't like her before, he certainly won't now that she's called him an arrogant jerk.

"It won't be necessary," Detective Fletcher speaks slowly and with deliberation, "because nobody poisoned Serenity."

Eliza makes a sound that can only be described as a chortle. "Right. Okay. So what are you trying to say? That Serenity poisoned herself?"

"Actually, yes. She did." He smiles. "Who looks like the arrogant jerk now?"

"Will you two stop acting like spoiled children and explain what's going on?" I demand. "How did Serenity poison *herself*?"

Detective Fletcher shoots a glance at Eliza, seeming to revel in the fact that he knows more than she does, for once, before speaking. "The doctor said it was an accident. Serenity picked some flowers out of one of the neighbor's yards, thinking it was St. John's wort. She said she'd been feeling a little depressed after Carl was murdered, and she thought making tea with the flowers would put her in a better mood."

If what he's saying is true, Natasha had nothing to do with Serenity getting sick. If anyone is to blame, it's Serenity herself for picking plants that didn't belong to her.

That's one less homicidal connection to make, but it still doesn't mean that Natasha's in the clear. Knowing

Gina, I find it highly unlikely *she* would poison herself accidentally.

"How is Serenity doing?" I mentally add up the length of time since she'd collapsed in the painting class. "It must have been bad, if she's been in here for three days!"

"Oh, she's not here anymore. She checked out two days ago." Detective Fletcher consults the little spiral notebook he always keeps in his shirt pocket. "She went to some luxury detoxification and yoga retreat in Miami. She left the address, in case we needed to get a hold of her, but, get this, asked that we not disturb her 'spiritual reawakening' unless it was really important."

He seems dismayed when I don't react to his attempt at humor, but I have more important things on my mind. "If Serenity was released the day after she was poisoned, do you think Gina will be out tomorrow?"

He frowns. "Probably. Why?"

"Assuming someone intentionally poisoned her," I think aloud, "they're not going to be so happy if she goes back tomorrow, safe as houses."

"You think they may try again," Eliza accurately interprets my concern.

Since we don't know who tried to poison Gina, we have no idea how they might respond when they realize their murderous efforts were unsuccessful. Which means Gina could be in more danger than ever if we can't get some answers...and fast.

Thirty

"What do you mean I can't go home?" Gina explodes. "I'm sure as heck not staying here! You know what they fed me for breakfast? Powdered eggs and a pudding cup! I'm sure I don't know what hell is like, but I'm starting to think I may have already died and went there!"

It's early Sunday morning. Detective Fletcher and I have been trying to convince Gina to stay in the hospital for a few more days but it's not going as well as we had hoped.

"Hear them out, sweetheart," Leon cajoles. "They're only trying to do what's best."

"What's best? I'll tell you what's best—sleeping in my own bed and eating my own food," Gina argues. "I'm from New York! You think I'm afraid of some coward poisoning me with plants? Someone too chicken to even look me in the eye when they're trying to kill me?"

"We know you're not afraid," I assure her. "We just want to find out who wants you dead. Until we do that, you really can't trust anyone!"

"Except the three of you?" She points to Detective Fletcher, Leon, and me. "The ones really trying to kill me by keeping me here in this hospital."

Leon throws his hands up. He's been married to Gina for over forty years and has learned to accept defeat. I, on the other hand, am not so easily swayed.

"We're narrowing down the suspects, but we're not there yet." I turn to Detective Fletcher, silently asking for his support. In turn, he nods his agreement and gestures that I should continue. I oblige. "I've been thinking about this all night, trying to figure out who would have wanted both you and Carl dead. You gave Dr. Rosen a pretty thorough tongue lashing the other night out at the lake. Which might have given him motive, but he was arrested right away. I don't see how he would have had the opportunity."

Gina rolls her hand at the wrist. "Keep going, girl. You've already eliminated one suspect from the list. At this rate, I could be out of here by lunchtime."

"Next we have Natasha," I continue, ignoring her. "She planted the flowers you were poisoned with. And she flipped out at you when you asked about her mailbox.

Which makes sense now. She might have thought *you* were trying to send her a message."

"She flipped out because I was trying to send her a message in a mailbox?" Gina sounds dubious. "Isn't that how most people send letters?"

"Who sends letters anymore?" Detective Fletcher chimes in. "Everyone I know uses email."

"You young people." Leon shakes his head at the detective. "You have no idea what it's like to live without the internet. In my day, you used to have to get our information from a newspaper! We didn't have no blogs or Twitter or that other one where it's all just videos of people dancing."

Detective Fletcher, who's in his early fifties, scratches his bald head. He seems torn between admitting to his age or running with the assumption that he's a much younger man.

I try to herd everyone back to the point. "Not that you were sending her a letter. She might have thought that you talking about her broken mailbox *was* the message!"

"Why would me making small talk about a woman's mailbox make her want to kill me?" Gina clucks her tongue. "That just doesn't make any sense, hun."

I explain what Eliza told me the night before about how Natasha's husband died from injuries causes by bad brakes and a mailbox, and how she blamed the whole incident on Carl.

"How did you find out about that?" Detective Fletcher's back is up. He's already mad, anticipating my answer.

"Eliza found out about it from the court records," I tell him.

I can practically hear the kettle of his head whistling from all the sudden heat. "Madeline, you and me need to have a chat about your daughter meddling in my investigation!"

Gina sits up in bed, the effort making her grimace. "Would you cut it out, detective? We're trying to find out who poisoned me. If you don't want to play nice and help, well, there's the door!"

Detective Fletcher, whose jaw is now grazing the collar of his button-down shirt, looks around the room as if we've all gone mad. He has a valid point. He's the only one of us in the room who actually has a police badge, which should give him automatic authority. But he also knows, without us, he might never have solved the previous murders at Egret's Loft.

As he flounders for a response, another thought occurs to me. "Gina, when we were at the party Friday night, didn't you say you overheard Natasha and Selena talking about used car salesmen?"

"I think that's what they were talking about. But I can't be a hundred percent on that," she explains. "They were talking in Spanish. For all I know, they could have been talking about the weather."

"Did they know you overheard part of their conversation?" Leon seems undeterred by Gina's skepticism.

"Maybe. How would I know? And why would that matter?"

I nod at Leon, who continues with the thought. "Because, if Natasha thought you heard her, then she may have realized you were on to her. That she had a motive to kill Carl."

"Precisely!" I exclaim.

"Now hold up a minute," Detective Fletcher interjects, putting his hands on his hips in a way that draws all our eyes to the badge on his hip. "There's no way of knowing for sure that the same person who poisoned Gina also killed Carl. They might not be the same person."

Now it's our turn to look at him like he's gone mad.

Leon finds his voice first. "You think there's more than one murdering psychopath at Egret's Loft?"

"I think there could be." When we begin to grumble, he throws his hands up in the air to silence us. "Hear me out. It's not like this is the first time people have died before their time in your little retirement village. Just last month you had another homicidal lunatic killing people. So, yeah, why shouldn't there be more? You people seem to attract the crazy!"

"Well, that's not a very nice thing to say," I chastise him, even though I know there is logic to what he's saying. But there's also something more. "Is this about Helen?"

His whole forehead lowers, creating shadows around his eyes. "What's that supposed to mean?"

"It means that you want to be right about Helen." I confront him. "You arrested her, and you want to be right. You want to think she did it. But she couldn't have poisoned Gina, now, could she? She was in your jail. You *are* her alibi!"

"Just because she didn't poison Gina, doesn't mean she didn't kill Carl. That's what I'm saying. Maybe she has, like, an accomplice or something," he argues, though with less conviction than before.

"An accomplice?" Leon guffaws. "You're saying now that there are two people who want my wife dead?"

"I don't know!" Detective Fletcher rubs his temples with his forefingers. "Maybe it's like you said, Natasha wanted revenge, so she teamed up with the black widow. Or what about Bubbles?" He shifts his focus to me, excitement in his voice. "You thought she was guilty, being the beneficiary of the will and all."

It suddenly occurs to me that, in all the excitement, I'd neglected to give him some crucial information about Bubbles. "Oh, I forgot to tell you. Bubbles is responsible for all the thefts at Egret's Loft."

"She's the one took my casserole dish?" Gina snarls.

Anger drips from Detective Fletcher's voice when he asks, "And how did you find out about that? Were you ever going to share that information with me?"

My head begins to hurt. "It wasn't Eliza, if that's what you're getting so bent out of shape about. You need to let this competition with her go, dear. You have different jobs. She's not a threat to you, and she's my daughter, so you have to be nicer," I lecture him. "As to your question, Paul, Jinny and George's grandson, admitted to my son, Ritchie, that he was the one burglarizing people's houses, but Bubbles asked him to do it because she was short on money. I was going to tell you, but my friend almost died. My mind was on other things."

"It was Paul then? Not Bubbles?" he clarifies.

"Paul's just a kid." I jump to his defense. "She convinced him to do her dirty work by pretending to be his friend. It's not his fault. Not really."

"I knew something wasn't right about that woman, on account of how she planned that wedding," Gina says. "But as fun as this is, I just want to go home. Are we getting any closer to making that happen?"

"I don't think you can come home, sweetheart." Leon takes his wife's hand in his. "I can't risk losing you. Especially if there could be two people out there wanting you six feet under."

Tears of frustration well up in Gina's eyes. "That's sweet you're worried, baby. But I can't stay here another day! Can't we just tell everyone I'm already dead, and I'll hide in the house until you find the murderer?"

Detective Fletcher and I lock eyes. "Funny you should say that," he says.

"We had a feeling you wouldn't agree to stay here," I tell her. "So, we came up with a plan B. It involves you pretending to be dead, us taking a picture of you looking like you're dead, and you staying at my house until all of this is over. What do you say?"

Leon asks the first question. "Why would she stay at your house?"

"Because," Detective Fletcher cuts in, "if anyone suspects she's still alive, they might come snooping at your house. That's where they'd expect her to go."

Gina's eyes are shining with the prospect of some real-life cloak and dagger. "How are you going to make me look dead for the picture?"

I reach into my bag and pull out two Ziploc containers full of the Mary Kay makeup I bought from Selena last week.

I smile at Gina. "If this stuff isn't enough to kill you, I don't know what will."

Thirty-One

All I want to do, by the time I get home from the hospital, is sleep.

It had taken longer than any of us expected to make Gina look convincingly dead, but by the time we finished, even Gina couldn't believe she was still alive.

After that, Leon had contacted the Egret's Loft board to inform them of his wife's passing, and Detective Fletcher had given the hospital staff strict instructions to direct any questions about Gina straight to the police.

Our plan was officially in motion.

"You all settled now?" I ask Gina, who's resting comfortably in one of the guest bedrooms. "Is there anything you need?"

"Naw, I'm good." She rubs her stomach, satisfied. "That son of yours can really cook."

Ritchie had picked us up from the hospital, stowing Gina in the back of the SUV for the short journey back to Egret's Loft. We'd snuck her into the house through the garage, so no one saw her.

So far, so good. If only I didn't feel so exhausted. But I suppose investigating a murder, faking your friend's death, and then hosting four people in your house would be enough to wear anyone out. Unfortunately, I can't afford the luxury of relaxation just yet.

"I need to pop out for a little while, but Ritchie and Eliza are here if you need anything," I assure her.

"Where are you heading off to at this hour?" she asks, even though it's just past four o'clock in the afternoon.

"I need to speak with Jolene. See if she can help me make sense of some of this mess, so I can clear Helen's name."

"You still think Holly's innocent?"

"Helen," I correct her. "You know, you're going to get yourself in trouble someday. People don't like being called by the wrong name."

"Yeah, yeah." She waves off my concern. "I'm just tired. I think I need to rest my eyes."

"You do that. I'll be back in a while."

Coming out of the guest room, I see Ritchie and Eliza huddled on the couch watching a film. Curt's sitting at the kitchen table with a pencil in his hand and his tongue sticking out in concentration. He's drawing some design—

probably for his x-ray machine—on graph paper. Nobody pays me any attention, so I step out the front door and into the late afternoon sunshine.

The sky matches the color of a robin's egg, and there's a light breeze rolling in from the west. I close my eyes, enjoying the warmth filtering through my skin to my tired old bones. When I open my eyes, I realize I'm not alone.

"Madeline," Natasha says from her position at the end of my driveway. She clutches a bouquet of yellow flowers in her hand. "I heard about your friend and wanted to express my condolences."

I can't take my eyes off the yellow petals. "Are those for me?"

"Yes." She extends her arms out but doesn't move any closer. "I thought they might cheer you up. I picked myself."

"That's a very lovely gesture, dear. Though I admit to being a little confused. You wanted to cheer me up with a bouquet of the same kind of flowers that killed my friend?"

Her face, already the color of skim milk, loses more of its pigmentation. "*Izvinite*?" She slips into her native Russian and then realizes I don't understand. "Pardon me?"

"That's oleander? In your hand. Isn't it?"

She glances down at the flowers as if only just realizing they're in her hand. "No, these are hibiscus. I grow many plants. But my oleander flowers did not kill your friend."

"She *was* poisoned with oleander. The doctor

confirmed it." I watch her face for any signs of deception but find none. She could just be good at hiding her true feelings. Being Russian, she probably would've had a lot of practice. "You didn't poison my friend, Gina. Did you?"

I pull my phone out of my handbag and show her my screensaver. It's the picture of Gina all made up to look deceased. Ritchie had made it my screensaver, because he said it was taking me too long to find it in my photos.

"Me?" She takes a step back, away from the accusatory picture, the flowers now hanging down next to her thighs. "Why would I do this thing? I did not know her!"

"Maybe not," I grant her. "But she overheard you talking about used car salesmen at Andy's party on Friday night. Were you telling Selena about Carl? About how he sold your husband a car with bad brakes?"

"But...but how do you know this?" she stammers. "No one is supposed to know!"

"You told Selena, didn't you?"

"No. That is not right," she insists, the veins in her slender neck protruding. "Selena talks to me about Carl trying to sell her a car. I say nothing about Nikolai. I just agree that used car salesmen are not to be trusted."

"But you did blame Carl, didn't you? For Nikolai's death."

"I do not need to blame. Carl was guilty. He made my husband into vegetable. He is reason my Nikolai is dead."

"That's not how the courts saw it. You lost your lawsuit against him," I point out.

She laughs, but there is no humor in the sound. "That is because he lied. He said the car disappear before he can inspect. This is not true. He made car disappear to protect himself."

"I know what it's like to lose your husband. I miss my Clint every single day." I try to hold back the tears I can feel forming in the corners of my eyes. "I can't even imagine what I would have done if I thought someone killed him and was getting away with it."

She nods her head so vehemently I would swear the hair pins holding up her chignon are going to fly right out of her head. "Nikolai, *moya lyubov*. We married in Russia when I was young girl and very much in love. In sixty years, we never fight. Except when he drink too much of the vodka.

"When he got into accident, I pray he come back to me. I pray so hard for many years, but my prayers do nothing. Then, he dies. And I'm alone in strange country."

I want to tell her that even your own country feels strange when you've lost the one person that gave everything meaning. I want to tell her I really do understand. But first, I need to find out if she's a murderer.

Clint always used to tell me that most criminals want to admit to what they've done—whether out of guilt, or because they want to brag about how clever they are. Sometimes, he'd say, all you need to do to get a confession is ask the question. So that's what I do.

"Is that why you killed Carl? Because you wanted revenge?"

"I not going to lie. I wanted this man, who took my Nikolai from me, to suffer," she tearfully admits. Despite her obvious pain, her eyes stay focused on me, and her spine remains straight in defiance. "I move here to Egret's Loft because I plan to kill him."

"So, you did kill Carl?" I can't believe Clint's straightforward approach actually worked! "I saw you at the wedding reception when the party was almost over. Is that when you did it?"

"No, this is not correct."

"But you just said you killed him."

"No, I say I *plan* to kill him. Planning and doing are not the same."

I'm confused, and my ankles are starting to swell from standing out here in the early evening heat. "You're telling me you wanted to kill him, but someone else beat you to it?"

"No, this is not correct either." She sighs in frustration as she searches for the right words in a foreign language. "I could have killed Carl. That night. I went to reception with intention of stabbing Carl with cake knife."

"You were going to stab Carl with the wedding cake knife? But the blades on those are so dull."

She narrows her eyes. "That is point. Cut slower. Hurt more."

I shiver even as the setting sun bakes my skin. "So why didn't you do it?"

She shrugs her shoulders. "I choose not to."

I'm convinced ice would not melt in Natasha's presence. What I'm less convinced of is that her stone-cold determination failed her when she had the ability to exact her revenge.

"Did you get scared?" I wonder aloud.

She laughs. "Nikolai and I defected from Russia. You think skinny old man who drinks too much alcohol at wedding would scare me?"

"So why then? Why did you choose not to kill him when you had the chance?"

"If you must know, I choose not to kill him for his wife. She look so happy in wedding gown. If I take life of husband, she will be just like me. She will suffer. For her husband's mistake. That is not right thing to do."

"That's actually very big of you," I surprise myself by saying. "Under the circumstances, I might have wanted to kill Carl myself. But someone—" I almost say *tried to*, but catch myself in time, "—*did* kill Gina. Using your flowers as poison. Has anyone, aside from me, asked you about them?"

She takes a moment to think. "Several people at party on Friday talk about flowers they want to plant. I think I talk about my oleander."

"Do you happen to remember if Bubbles was part of that conversation?" I press.

Natasha squints her large brown eyes. "Big woman? Very loud? Likes to sing?"

"That's the one," I confirm.

"It was large group, but yes. She started conversation about flowers. I don't remember anything more." Natasha looks down at the bouquet in her hand and moves it around behind her back. "Forgive me. I came to give condolence, but it seems I only upset you. I'm very sorry. Good night."

Natasha pivots gracefully on the balls of her feet and glides off down the sidewalk, depositing the bouquet in her trash bin before entering her house.

I glance down the block toward Helen's house. Jolene's car isn't in the driveway, where she normally has it parked. That must mean she stepped out for a little while. I wonder if she went to the jail. No matter what their relationship truly is, it surprises me that after coming all this way to offer support, Jolene hasn't made more of an effort to see Helen.

Ah well, it's one more thing to ask Jolene about when she comes back. Speaking to her seems imperative if I want to solve this case, and the sooner we can have that conversation, the better. But what can I do? She's not home.

I might as well wait in my house. It's cooler inside, and my ankles hurt. Also, it probably wouldn't hurt to rest my eyes. But only for a few minutes. I'm far too busy and, in an expression that's gaining in poignancy, I can sleep when I'm dead.

Thirty-Two

"Lady! Wake up!" Ritchie's anxiety-laced voice startles me into opening my eyes.

"There's no need to shout, dear. I wasn't asleep. I was just resting my eyes for a minute," I tell him, trying not to sound annoyed.

"You've been *resting your eyes* for nearly three hours!" he loudly states. "And snoring. It's after eight o'clock."

"It can't be that late." It feels like only minutes have passed since I was outside talking to Natasha in the driveway. But looking out my bedroom window, I can see the sky has turned inky black. "Oh no, I need to go and see if Jolene is back at Helen's place!"

"Not yet, you won't. We have a little bit of an emergency here."

I sit up straight in bed. "Is Gina alright?"

Ritchie shakes his head. "She's fine. It's Detective Fletcher I'm worried about."

"Why would you be worried about him, dear?"

"Because he's out there with Curt," Ritchie hurriedly explains. "And Curt is trying to convince him to hand over his service pistol so Curt can practice taking it apart!"

Two distinct threads of concern cause my heart to beat faster. One. Curt can be very persuasive when he wants something and, usually, he's smart enough to find a way to get it. Two. Detective Fletcher has already accidentally dropped his gun in my house once, and he tends to get frustrated when he can't get on board with a train of thought.

Curt is going to eat him alive!

"Where's Eliza?" I demand, thinking my daughter would knock some sense into the both of them.

"She went home an hour ago. She has to be at work tomorrow morning." Ritchie is one breath away from a panic attack. "Please, lady! Detective Fletcher will listen to you!"

In my mind, I launch myself out of bed. In reality, Ritchie pulls me to my feet, and my body creaks and groans as I walk quickly into the living room. Curt is sitting on the sofa, sipping from the straw in his Yoo-hoo bottle. Detective Fletcher sits beside him with a puzzled look on his face and his police issue firearm in his hand.

"Detective Fletcher, put that gun away this instant!" I shout.

Startled by my sudden presence and the anger in my voice, the detective jumps before sliding the weapon back into its holster. Curt, watching his opportunity vanish, sinks back into the sofa, pouting.

"Curt, what's gotten into you?" I demand. "You're terrified of guns!"

"And with good reason," Curt responds. "Did you know that the Brady Center to Prevent Gun Violence estimates an average of twenty-two children are shot in the US every day? In fact, guns recently overtook motor vehicle crashes as the leading cause of death in children and teenagers."

"What's your point, buddy?" Ritchie asks. He's been afraid of guns since he was little, too, always running into the other room if Clint forgot to lock up his service weapon before coming into the house.

"I believe," Curt begins, "that your statistical odds of surviving potentially life-threatening situations go up when you have sufficient knowledge of how to avoid them."

"We know!" Ritchie and I say simultaneously.

"Then you'll understand why, after I conquered my fear of swimming earlier this week, I concluded that I should face all my fears, in order to have a better understanding of things that have the potential to harm me. Since humans have a track record of deception and pretending to be things they're not, I figured I'd have better success disarming someone's weapon than their mind," Curt explains, sitting up to his full height but still looking tiny next to the tall, beefy detective. "Since it has three internal safeties built in, I thought the policeman's Walther PPQ M2 would be the safest gun to try and disassemble."

We all take a moment to contemplate his logic.

"Detective." Detective Fletcher is the first to break the silence.

"Excuse me?" Curt tilts his head, and a furrow appears between his brows.

"You called me a policeman," the detective laments. "I'm not a policeman. I'm a detective."

It strikes me as bizarre that *that* is his biggest takeaway from Curt's speech. Poor thing, he'd been doing so much better with his confidence lately. All it took was a six-year-old unintentionally demoting him to set Detective Fletcher back.

"Hey, buddy, it's almost bedtime." Ritchie quickly changes the subject. "You want me to read you some Dr. Seuss? How about *One Fish, Two Fish*?"

Curt jumps off the sofa. "Can I look at the pictures while you read? I really like the pictures!"

"Of course, you can. Off you go." Ritchie sends Curt out of the living room, says goodnight, and leaves me alone with the detective.

"Your grandson..." Detective Fletcher begins.

"He's really something, isn't he?" I beam with pride.

"But that's not why you're here. Did something happen? Did you find out who poisoned Gina?"

"No, nothing yet," he says, still sounding distracted. "I just wanted to swing by to let you know we took Bubbles in for questioning. Sammy's been grilling her pretty hard."

I realize I haven't seen much of Detective Baptiste in the past few days. I think Detective Fletcher is trying to hide me from her. Or vice versa. "How are things with your new partner coming along?"

"Oh, you know. She's anxious to prove herself," he says.

I can tell he's holding something back. I remember when Clint had to work with new detectives. He always said they either wanted to be mentored so they could learn, or they wanted to be the best so they could become your boss.

From my interactions with Detective Baptiste, I think I knew on which side of that fence she fell.

"Is she being pushy and obnoxious?" I ask.

Detective Fletcher sighs deeply. "Oh my gosh, *so* pushy and obnoxious! I had to leave because she kept pushing Bubbles to find out how Helen helped her kill Carl. As if the two were working together. Sammy wouldn't stop. Not even after Bubbles admitted that she was the one who made the anonymous calls implicating Helen."

"Bubbles admitted to reporting Helen's conversation in the ladies' room? And the fight with Serenity?" I'd suspected that Bubbles had been responsible for the call. Clint would be so proud of me for figuring that out.

"Yep. She said she knew Helen killed her uncle and that she just wanted to help us along in our investigation." He tuts. "As if we need help with the investigation."

My mother, may she rest in peace, raised me to be polite, so I bite my tongue before moving on to firmer ground. "Has Bubbles admitted to anything other than the anonymous call?"

He nods. "She came clean about the thefts. She said, when he was alive, Carl had been helping her out with money. Once he died, all his assets were frozen and, apparently, her ex-husband ran up a lot of debt and she's a whisker away from having to file for bankruptcy."

"Is that so?" I play dumb, not wanting to aggravate him by telling him I already knew all of that from his self-prescribed nemesis, Eliza.

"Yeah. She said she was desperate, and when she found the codes to all the houses in Carl's things, she thought stealing might carry her through until she inherited. She convinced Paul to help her because he's younger and lighter on his feet."

"I hope you're not planning to punish Paul too much," I plead. "I think he's just desperate to live out his dream of being on Broadway and she told him she would help."

"That all depends on you," he says.

"On me? How so?"

"Well, homeowners like you. Anyone who had something stolen. If you choose not to press charges, then we've got nothing on him."

He's barely finished speaking when I jump in with, "I don't want to press charges!"

"Fair enough." He seems to find my desire to protect Paul amusing. "Anyway, she admits to that but swears up and down she had nothing to do with Carl's murder."

"Did you bring up Gina being poisoned?" I ask, leaving out Serenity's incident, since it's now clear that was her own fault.

"I did. Even showed her our little picture of Gina," he chuckles. "She fainted. I guess we did a pretty good job with that makeup after all."

"What did she say about that? I mean, after she woke up, poor dear." I can't prevent the little smile that creeps across my mouth.

"She said she barely knew Gina and would have no reason to hurt her. Then again, I'm not sure she'd be too willing to implicate herself if she did try to kill your friend."

"True," I say, but my mind has already moved on. "Did she happen to say anything about Dr. Rosen when you questioned her?"

He looks at me from out the sides of his eyes. "Now how do you know that?"

"Just a hunch," I say truthfully, though I was suspicious of the way she brought up Carl's medical training in front of Dr. Rosen, as if she wanted to watch him squirm. "What did she say?"

"You're going to have to teach me how to do that *hunch* thing. That could come in handy." His eyes tell me that he actually believes it's possible for me to teach him intuition.

"Later, perhaps. What did Bubbles say about Dr. Rosen?" I repeat the question.

"Right. She saw what was in the yearbook, the inscription about telling no one, and decided to see if it registered with Dr. Rosen. Apparently, it did, because he asked her how much she wanted to keep it quiet."

"Blackmail, of course!" It should have occurred to me sooner that Bubbles would be trying to get her hands on quick cash however she could. That explains the exchange I saw between them at the memorial service.

"Apparently, though, her price was too high for him. Which is why he took matters into his own hands and broke in to dispose of the incriminating evidence himself."

"But what did the evidence incriminate him of exactly?"

Detective Fletcher shrugs. "She didn't know. She didn't really care. She just wanted money."

I take a moment to think about this latest development. "If Carl was threatening the doctor with the same information, by extension, Dr. Rosen would have a reason to want him dead too."

Detective Fletcher scratches his bald head. "I hadn't

thought about it like that. But I suppose you're right. Great, just what we need. Another suspect!"

I clear my throat. "Given that you now have multiple suspects, don't you think it's time to let Helen out of jail?"

"Oh, yeah." He slaps his hands against the outsides of his thighs. "I've got to go back to the police station to do just that. The judge said, since she couldn't have poisoned Gina, or Serenity for that matter, we have to let her go. She'll be back home later tonight."

As Detective Fletcher stands and prepares to leave, I'm tempted to ask about the picture of the woman on his desk. But, for now, we have a bigger mystery to solve, if we want to make sure whoever targeted Gina the first time doesn't get a second chance to kill her.

Thirty-Three

"Well, bless your heart for bringing breakfast," Helen purrs after opening her front door and accepting my offering of french toast. "I'm so hungry, my belly thinks my throat's been cut."

After Detective Fletcher left the night before, I tried coming by Helen's house to speak to Jolene, but she and Savannah were still out. Any hope I'd had of speaking to Jolene in private this morning disappeared when Helen opened the door.

"It's nice to have you back home," I tell her. "I hope I didn't wake you up. It's still pretty early."

"Not at all, sugar." She reaches up and touches her unkempt hair. "Just don't tell anyone you're seein' me before I put my face on. Come on in!"

Helen ushers me into her entryway. A small glass table sits at the center of the room, boasting a large bouquet of fragrant orchids that weren't there the last time I came over for breakfast.

"This smells plumb delicious," Helen says, sniffing at the tin foil covering the french toast. "What do you say I fix us up some coffee and we dig in?"

"None for me, thanks. I ate at home," I tell her while scanning the interior rooms. "I was actually hoping to speak to Jolene."

Helen glances at me, then back down at the plate. Her stomach grumbles. "Well now, I reckon you might want some privacy while you're speakin' to Jolene. And I'm sure I wouldn't mind a little privacy while I eat this here breakfast. Let me just rustle her up for you, sugar."

She opens a door off the entryway and indicates that I should wait in her office. I walk in, expecting a desk, some chairs, and a computer. Instead, I find a couple of large velvet settees and several pieces of artwork depicting bright pink neon lips in various stages of being licked by red neon tongues.

Why anyone would want a large electrical sculpture of a mouth on their wall is beyond me. To have several of them, on the other hand, just means you have far too much money to be throwing around. Still, I can't tear my eyes away from the unsettling artwork until Jolene, thankfully, enters the room. She catches me looking at the lips.

"Do you know just one of those things would pay for a whole semester of Savannah's grad school?" She shakes her head. "Rich people. Haven't got the sense God gave a goose."

I don't disagree, but then again, since I live at Egret's Loft, too, she probably considers me to be in the same category.

I laugh to myself. She couldn't be more wrong. I'm still trying to squeeze the expense from all that Mary Kay makeup into this month's budget. After using it to make Gina look dead, it's probably too late to try and return it.

"It must be nice to have Helen home," I say, testing the waters.

"Sure is, though the police waited until the middle of the night to let her go. Pure uncivilized to be interrupting a person's sleep like that," she moans. "But I guess I can't complain. When we got back, I slept like a baby. Helen's got those memory foam mattresses. Pure heaven."

I cringe a little inside. Given Helen's track record with men, I'm not sure you'd want the mattress to remember anything.

Realizing that I'm being sidetracked by my own thoughts, I decide to be direct.

"I don't mean to be rude, dear," I warn her, so she knows I'm about to be slightly impolite. "But my friend is in danger. Do you mind if I cut to the chase?"

"Be my guest." She gestures for me to proceed.

"What is your relationship with Helen? I think *Bob* made it clear you're not sisters."

She frowns. "Bob?"

"Exactly my point. You don't remember your own father's name?"

"You got me." She holds her hands up in surrender. "And you're right. Helen's not my sister. Not by blood anyhow."

"Then how do you know her?"

She rubs her neck with one hand and lets out a long breath. "I really shouldn't be tellin' you any of this. But what the heck? I'm retired anyway." She's been talking out loud, seemingly to herself, up to this point. Now she looks me square in the eye. "Up until a couple years ago, I was a US Marshal. I met Helen when I was assigned her case, goin' on forty years ago now."

"Her case?" I try to understand until, suddenly, it clicks. That's why there's no record of her prior to a certain age! "Helen's in the Witness Protection Program!"

"You really are slicker than owl poop." She means it as praise, I think. "When I first met Helen, she was Doreen Deluca from New Jersey. Her husband, Bobby, had been a lieutenant in the mob, working for the Rossi crime family. They caught him stealing and, before he could rub his shiny new nickels together, they'd put a bullet in his head."

"Oh my gosh!" No wonder Helen couldn't talk about her past. "Was the mob planning to kill Helen as well?"

"Oh, sweetie, they tried. She was in the room when Bobby got shot. They shot her, too, only she survived. I swear, that girl's tougher than a two-dollar steak. She woke up in the hospital, screamin' for protection, sayin' she'd give up the big boss, Antonio Rossi, if we could keep her safe. She said he'd always been real sweet on her, so he told her a lot of things. She reckoned he might even have told his goons not to *really* kill her, so the two of them could be together."

"What happened? Did you prosecute this...Antonio Rossi?" My curiosity has me now fully invested in her story.

"That was the plan. But we never made it that far. Before we could take him in, somebody did us a favor. Cut off his head and threw his body in the Hudson River."

"Did you ever find his head?" It's probably not relevant, but I still want to know.

"Naw, we never did. If you'd ever seen him, you might think the killer did us a kindness." She senses my confusion and adds, "Let's just say, if I had a dog as ugly as Antonio, I'd have shaved his butt and made him walk backward."

That image won't be leaving my mind anytime soon. "Did you catch whoever killed him?"

Jolene shakes her head. "We always figured it was his little brother, Giovanni, ordered the hit to protect the family. But with Antonio gone, we had no case. Still, we'd already made the deal with Doreen to become Helen, a librarian from Louisiana. And it's been no cakewalk, believe you me."

"What do you mean?"

"She kept me runnin' like a headless chicken! I had to move her four times! Each time her latest husband died—drownin' or blowin' up or fallin' into a wood chipper, I'd have to race in to clean up the mess and get her outta there before her picture ended up in the local newspaper!"

"Did you ever get suspicious? Let's face facts, she has lost a lot of husbands in bizarre ways," I point out.

"Suspicious of Helen? Never! Now if you're askin' if I didn't wonder if that body in the Hudson may not have been Antonio…then, yeah, I guess you could say I was suspicious."

"Any specific reason you think the body might not have been his?" I ask.

"Nothin' official. Nothin' I coulda gone to my boss with," she says. "But Helen and me became real close, almost like sisters. She was practically a second mom to Savannah when she was little. Which has been good for my little girl, havin' no daddy and all. Anyway, Helen and me talked all the time. And every time she was fixin' to get married again, weird things would start happenin' right before the weddin'."

"What do you mean, weird things?"

The left side of her face bunches up in contemplation. "Nothin' sinister. Just, like, she'd get flowers with weird stalkery poems or expensive lingerie. This one time, the local bakery came by with her favorite kind of cake, all decorated with hearts. She thought her fiancé at the time—I guess that might've been Herbie—had sent it. But he said it wasn't him."

"But what made you think that Antonio might have sent those things? Isn't that a bit of a stretch?"

"Not if you knew anythin' about Antonio. He was always one for big, grand gestures. Like, the kind of guy who'd buy a new boat when he got the other one wet. Not to mention, he thought Helen hung the moon. Add those things up and throw in the fact that the mystery stalker kept findin' her every time she moved…I don't know. It just got us thinkin', maybe Antonio wasn't dead after all. Well, that, and the tattoo."

"Tattoo?"

"Yeah, Antonio had this tattoo on his neck, just below his left ear. A wolf with Romulus and Remus—you know, the founders of Rome. Antonio was born in Jersey, but real heavy into his Italian ancestry. Anyway, somethin' didn't sit right with me about the body. Like, even with the head missin', I thought you should have still been able to see part of the tattoo—the wolf's legs or somethin'."

An image of the scarring on Andy's neck comes to mind. I'd initially thought it was a burn mark, but could it be a scar from tattoo removal?

As soon as I've had this thought, others start sliding

into place. Helen said he'd asked her to run away with him right before she married Carl. And then there's Gina. He'd been so angry when she'd called him Antonio. Could he have poisoned her because he thought she was onto his secret identity?

"I know this is probably going to sound crazy," I admit. "Do you think Andy from down the street could be Antonio? I mean, he would have had a lot of work done. But if he was the head of a big crime family, he would have been able to afford it, right?"

"The handsome one what threw that party the other night? No way." She's completely unconvinced. "If there was a plastic surgeon *that* good, you'd better believe I'd be bookin' in for an appointment. And all that wine and fancy food? Hu-uh. I mean, I don't think you'd catch Andy dead eatin' hot dogs and drinkin' Budweiser."

She's laughing at her own inside joke, but the reference makes my skin crawl. I'd found those two items in Andy's garbage can on the night of his party. "Why do you mention hot dogs and Budweiser?"

"Antonio drank Bud like it was water, and the organized crime squad nicknamed him Wiener, because he'd eat, like, ten hot dogs a day." She sticks her tongue out in disgust.

Lost in thought, I barely notice.

If Clint was still alive, he would tell me that the thoughts running through my head are purely circumstantial. You can't make a case against a mobster based on a neck scar, an angry conversation over someone's name, and a man's secret proclivity for beer and frankfurters.

On the other hand, if he *is* a big-time mobster, what horrors would face anyone who *did* flush out his real identity? Gina just happens to be really bad with names, but he may have still tried to kill her with a poisonous plant because she called him Antonio. Bad luck for her, the wrong name just happened to be the right name.

I take Jolene's hand in mine. "Can you keep an eye on Helen? Don't let her out of your sight for a few hours?"

Concern and doubt compete for space on her heart-shaped face. "Yeah, sure. Why? What's goin' on?"

I think of Helen, who lost her husband and was then accused of his murder. I think of Gina, who could have died after being poisoned with oleander.

I tell Jolene, "I've got to go see a man about a flower."

Thirty-Four

"Madeline, you're going to have to speak up. I can't hear a word you're saying." Detective Fletcher's voice is thick with frustration.

"I said, I think Andy Romano might be our killer!" I whisper back, equally annoyed.

From my hiding place near Andy's trash cans, I can see the owner of the house preparing his boat for a late-morning excursion on the water.

My knees are starting to lock up from crouching here while I'd waited for the detective to call me back. Fortunately, I'd remembered how to put my iPhone on silent.

"Andy? Who the heck is Andy?" Detective Fletcher demands.

"The Italian guy who had the party on Friday. Except I

think his name is really Antonio Rossi, an ex-crime boss from New Jersey!"

"You think our killer is Andy, who's really Antonio?" I hear Detective Fletcher's palm hitting his forehead. "Last night, you told me Dr. Rosen was our guy. We just brought him in for more questioning."

"I may have been a little off base with that," I acknowledge. "It could still be him, but I'm starting to think Andy is a much more likely candidate."

"Do I even want to ask why you now think this Andy or Antonio, or whatever the heck his name is, killed Carl?"

I peek around the smelly bins to make sure Andy is still by the boat, too far away to hear what I'm about to say. Satisfied that he's out of earshot, I slink back into the shadows.

"For starters," I begin, "I think he faked his own death forty years ago to avoid going to jail, but he's been so obsessed with Helen—whose real name, by the way, was Doreen before she went into the Witness Protection Program—anyway, he couldn't let her go. So, he had plastic surgery to change his face, then followed her here, and took out the competition, namely Carl. Then, he tried to kill Gina, because she called him Antonio, which we now know is his real name."

"Wait, *who* was in the Witness Protection Program?"

I sigh. Wishing, not for the first time, that the detective would be able to keep up. "Helen! She was married to a mobster when she was younger. They killed him and shot her. But that doesn't matter. She was going to testify against Antonio, but then his headless body turned up in the Hudson. Only it might not have been his body, because there was no sign of his tattoo."

I pause to take a breath. The back of my throat feels scratchy from all the whispering. I hear typing on the other end of the line.

"What are you doing?" I ask.

"Looking up symptoms of dementia," he calmly replies.

"Would you please take this a little more seriously?"

"Oh, I'm taking this as serious as a heart attack. Confusion? Check. Difficulty expressing thoughts? Check."

"Just because I'm old doesn't mean I'm senile," I hiss. It upsets me to sound so hostile toward him, but it's not easy to express displeasure sotto voce.

"Well, would you listen to yourself?" He's trying very hard not to start shouting. "I mean you're talking about the mob and witness protection and headless bodies and plastic surgery! I mean, you have to admit, it sounds a little crazy."

"Does it, though?" I persist. "What if all of Helen's previous husbands *were* murdered? Your partner certainly thinks they were. Only Helen didn't kill them! Antonio Rossi, pretending to be Andy Romano, did! You'd not only be solving Carl's murder, you'd also be solving at least six other murders across the country. Imagine the publicity," I appeal to his baser nature. "Imagine what it could do for your book sales!"

The seconds tick by as I wait for him to respond. Leaning out from behind the garbage cans, I expect to see Andy, but he's no longer on the dock. He might be aboard the boat. Or he could have gone back inside his house. Either way, the longer I'm here, the more likely he is to discover me.

"Alright," Detective Fletcher finally concedes. "I'll look into it, alright? As soon as we get done questioning Dr. Rosen, I'll come to you. Will you be at home?"

"Right now, I'm hiding behind Andy's trash cans. Just seeing what I can see. But I'll be heading home soon."

"Madeline! What is wrong with you?" He's screaming now. "You think this guy might be former mafia, and you're sneaking around with his recyclables trying to spy on him? Would you please just get yourself home and let me take care of the police work?"

His loud voice carries so well down the cell phone line I have to hold the phone away from my head to keep my eardrums from exploding. I want to yell back that I'd love for him to do his job, so I don't have to worry about more of my friends being murdered, but I keep my mouth shut. It's actually quite touching that he cares so much about my safety.

"Yes, yes. I'm leaving now, detective."

"Thank you," he grudgingly says. I don't think he likes fighting with me either.

"No, thank you for caring. See you soon."

I'm smiling as I hang up the phone. He might not be the best detective, not yet, but he really is a good man.

Now, I just have to follow his advice and sneak out of here. I can see the street from my perch at the side of the house. There's no one out at this time of day. Everyone's probably inside preparing for their early lunches.

Stepping out from between the bins, I hear a loud crunch and freeze. I must have stepped on some broken glass. Luckily, there doesn't appear to be anyone around to hear it. I take one last long glance into Andy's yard, but there's still no sign of him.

Turning around, I come face to face with Andy.

He must have snuck around the front of the house while I was searching for him in the back.

His lips are parted in a smile, revealing his sparkling white teeth. An undercurrent of amusement is reflected in the creases around his eyes.

"My dear lady, what a surprise to find you here." His husky voice comes across calm and measured.

I need to come up with an excuse for being here. And fast. My biggest difficulty is going to be convincing him of my lie. I am, quite possibly, the world's worst liar. "Yes, sorry to be sneaking around out here. I...um...I...would you believe I think I lost my earring here on Friday night when I brought that bottle out to the trash?"

It's not technically a lie. I'm not telling him that's what happened. I'm merely asking him if he could *believe* that's why I'm here.

"That is most unfortunate indeed," he laments. "Here, let me see if I can help you find it."

"Oh...that really won't be necessary," I try to argue.

"I insist," he says before leaning forward, forcing me to take a step back between the trash cans, toward the house. My back is literally up against the wall.

"My mother lost an earring once when I was young. I remember because she was so upset about it. Emeralds and diamonds, I think. A very elegant and expensive piece," he reminisces. "Funny how, when you think of a loved one, even years after they are gone, you can still remember all their quirks and idiosyncrasies. Do you know what I mean?"

I nod, unable to speak. He's being extremely polite, yet, for some reason, that terrifies me even more.

"I remember my mother loved to talk," he continues, his eyes still searching the ground for my fictitious earring. "It drove my father to distraction; he was always telling her to be quiet. So, she started to whisper...or so she thought. But her whisper was louder than my voice is now," he chuckles. "It was embarrassing. She'd think she was passing on a secret to someone standing beside her, when, in reality, everyone within a two-block radius could hear every word."

Sweat begins to roll down my back. I don't know where this is going, but I'm guessing it's nowhere I want to be.

He glances up and locks eyes with me. "Did you know that whispers travel? People are not always as quiet, or as clever, as they think they are."

In one step, he closes the distance between us, his muscular body driving me further against the wall as he presses his left hand firmly over my mouth to stop me from screaming.

I consider biting him, but my dentist says the enamel on my teeth is weak. I'd probably just break a tooth.

"Eventually," he goes on, "my mother whispered one too many secrets. That earring, the one she 'lost,' my father fed it to her. Along with the ear she'd been wearing it on. You see, my father wanted to teach her a lesson. So, he cut off her ear and made her eat it. He said, if she wasn't going to listen, he'd at least make sure she couldn't talk for a while."

I can't speak, but I can hear the whimper that originates from underneath his strong, sandalwood scented fingers. It's coming from deep inside me.

"And now, Madeline—" I can feel his breath rustling my hair as he speaks, "—it's time for me to teach *you* a lesson."

He reaches behind his back, pulling out a long bar of

some sort. I didn't even see him carrying it. My eyes follow its trajectory as he swings it high in the air. *Oh no,* my mind registers, *I think it's a golf club.*

My body tenses and I struggle to push him off me, but he's too strong. I can only watch in wide-eyed disbelief as the club races toward my head.

For a moment, I feel blinding pain. Then, I feel nothing at all.

Thirty-Five

My body sways gently back and forth, almost as if I am in an adult-sized version of one of those rocking cribs Eliza purchased when Tory was born. The pungent scent of salt and brine assaults my nose, and there's a buzzing in my ear that sounds like a swarm of flies is angrily circling my head.

Opening my eyes, I find myself gazing up at an azure sky, the hot orb of the sun sitting high in its center.

Dismayed, I realize I forgot to put on any sunblock when I raced out the door to find Jolene earlier this morning. But it quickly occurs to me, melanoma isn't my biggest concern. Looking to my left, I see the polished white perfection of a fiberglass hull. I'm on Andy's boat, and I have no idea where he's taking me!

Using my elbows to ease my torso up off the deck, my

vision begins to spin, and I have to lower my aching head back onto the ground.

"I thought you'd be out for a while." The silhouette of Andy's head temporarily blocks out the sun. "But it's good you're awake. This way, we can have a little chat before…"

He doesn't finish the sentence, and I don't ask him to. Instead, he reaches behind my neck and uses the collar of my button-down shirt to haul me into a seated position on one of the boat's built-in benches. He sits down in the captain's chair beside me.

Seeing water on all sides, fear begins to grow inside me, putting pressure on my insides as it makes more room for itself. Only I don't know what terrifies me more—drowning in the vast waters of the Gulf of Mexico or enduring whatever nightmare Andy has in store for me.

There are houses lining the shore on both sides of me, which means we haven't yet made it out past the cut. We're too far away for anyone to hear me scream, but with a little flotation assistance, I might be able to reach the shore in an emergency.

"If it's not too much trouble, can I have a life preserver?" I ask Andy. "I don't know how to swim."

His lips curl upward toward the sides of his nose, like a boa constrictor preparing to encircle its prey. "Trust me, you won't need one where you're going."

His voice now sounds less cultured, more Jersey. He doesn't have to pretend with me anymore.

"And where is it we're going, Andy? Or, should I say, Antonio?"

Taking his hands off the steering wheel, they slowly come together in a mockery of applause. "Bravo. I admire your deduction, even if it does make for a rather uncomfortable situation for me. For forty years, I've been hiding in plain sight. I mean, think about it. Who would ever suspect that the head of the notorious Rossi crime family would be masquerading as a famous clothing designer?"

"Why would they? Everybody thought you were dead," I remind him. "Whose body was that in the Hudson anyway?"

"My brother Giovanni," he says, his voice calmer than the sea on a windless day. "He was the one who suggested I should find a...decoy. He clearly didn't think it through beforehand. If he had, he would have realized we were the same height and weight, not to mention, his DNA would also match the family's DNA, should the cops bother to check."

"You killed your own brother?" My stomach feels queasy—whether from seasickness or repulsion, it's impossible to say.

"He was weak. Too weak to fight for what he really wanted. Just like all those sniveling fools who tricked Doreen into marrying them. They never wanted her as badly as I did. If they had, they wouldn't be dead."

It takes me a minute to remember that Doreen was

Helen's name when she first met Antonio Rossi, before she entered witness protection.

"You *did* kill her husbands, then?" My first thought is, I can't wait to tell Detective Fletcher that I was right. My second thought brings me back to the reality of my current predicament.

I'll probably never get the chance.

"Of course, I did! Except the first one. I didn't know her then. I think he had some freak accident in a tanning bed. But all the others were me!" His eyebrows tilt down toward his nose like lightning bolts. "None of those jerks deserved my Doreen! None of them would have done for her what I've done! Month after month of plastic surgery. Years of tracking her down, again and again, after every time she moved. That kind of dedication can only be called one thing—love."

"I can think of another word for it—obsession." I probably shouldn't be antagonizing him. But the way I see it, if he was willing to kill his own brother, what hope do I have? My best, and only, plan should be escaping. Until I come up with a viable escape route, though, I need to keep him talking. "It must have hurt when Helen chose to marry both Donald and Carl over you."

"It wasn't Doreen's fault," Andy angrily defends her. "I never had the chance to explain who I was or what I'd already done for her! She would have definitely picked me, if I had. I tried to get past it after she married Donald. For years, I tried to just be her friend, but it was no use. Deep down, it made me sick to think about her with a man who didn't deserve her!"

"So, you killed Donald, but that didn't help, did it? She was still choosing other men over you." I attempt a casual glance over the side of the boat. It's a short drop to the water, but a long swim to shore. But I'll have to do something soon. We're approaching the cut, and then it's the open waters of the Gulf of Mexico. *Just keep talking*, I tell myself. "And then she agreed to marry Carl. That must have driven you crazy!"

Andy's knuckles turn white on the wheel. "He thought he was in for a big celebration. Well, I gave him one alright. I nabbed one of those mouth props from my dentist to hold Carl's mouth open. I put that in and then uncorked that champagne bottle right into the back of his throat. How's that for a celebration?"

A dentist's mouth prop. That explains the bruising around Carl's mouth. I'd completely forgotten about that. But there's still one thing I don't understand about the crime scene.

"What about my hair clip?" I ask. "How did it end up in Carl's hand?"

Andy sighs. "Ah, yes. He must have grabbed it out of my pocket before I managed to get him taped to the chair."

"But how did it end up in your pocket? I put it in Helen's hair myself."

"Doreen was so angry when that song came on the speakers, do you remember?" When I nod, he continues. "I was there, you see. Waiting for my chance to get Carl alone. When Doreen tugged at her hair, the clip fell onto the ground. She didn't notice, but I did. I picked it up off the floor when no one was looking."

I'm still confused. "You wanted a memento from Helen's marriage to another man?"

"Her name is Doreen," he corrects me. "And no, I just wanted something that had been close to her."

The way he says it gives me the feeling that he has a collection of creepy souvenirs, random things Helen has lost over the years, stashed in a safe in his basement.

But by correcting me about Helen's name he reminds me of something else. "And my friend, Gina? You poisoned her because she kept calling you Antonio?"

He frowns and looks at me questioningly. "I was wondering about that. Did she know that was my real name?"

I shake my head. "Not a clue."

He makes a tutting sound with his mouth. "That's a shame. I didn't really want to kill her. It was a spur of the moment thing. I'd heard you mentioning that the hippie chick was poisoned with oleander. When you guys were across the street with Doc Rosen, I got some from Natasha's front yard and put in the tiramisu that I sent home with your friend. She shouldn't have called me Antonio. She'd still be alive. But it's better to be safe than sorry. For me, anyway."

I consider telling him that Gina's still alive but decide against it. It might make him more careful about making sure he's done the job right with me. Instead, I need to find a way to distract him so I can get off this boat before we make it to the gulf waters.

I can't swim, and I have no flotation device, but drowning seems like a better way to go than whatever scenario Andy has in mind.

"You know, you might still get your chance with Helen." I'm still thinking through my strategy as I speak, knowing if I attempt to outright lie, the jig is up. He'll see right through me.

He turns his head to look at me. "What do you mean? Did she say something?"

I purse my lips. "You might say that."

"Did she say we have a connection? Does she want to go out with me?"

His enthusiasm might be endearing. If he weren't a serial killer.

I think back to my conversation with Helen at the jail. "She said something about you being a hairy frog…"

"A what?"

"Sorry, I'm sure I have that wrong. It was a good thing. Trust me. You know how hard it is to understand some of her Southern expressions!"

He takes this into consideration and seems to find it valid. "True. She really invested herself in her new personality. What else did she say?"

My brows knit in concentration. "Umm...well, she definitely noticed your tight pants! Oh! I asked her if she was tempted to run away with you, and she said men as pretty as you are meant to be looked at."

Sure, I'm bending the truth slightly, but I *am* using Helen's own words.

He blushes. "No one's ever called me *pretty* before."

"You should ask her out!" I encourage him. "Why wait? You can send her a text now!"

"You really think she would say yes?"

"I do!"

He grins. "Alright. Hang on a second, I left my phone in the cabin."

As soon as I hear the sliding doors open to the cabin, I make my move. My hips are too wobbly to trust climbing over the side, but there are steps at the back of the boat. If I can make it to those, at least I'll be off this death trap.

I'm standing on the lowest step, my right toe hovering above the water, when I hear a cry behind me. "What do you think you're doing?"

Hearing Andy's angry voice behind me, I put my weight forward over my suspended foot and fall forward into the water. Water stings the inside of my nose. I open my mouth to cough, and water floods in. I swing my arms and kick my feet, all to no avail. I'm drowning!

I'm praying not to die. I'm praying that my kids and grandkids know how much I love them. I'm praying that Clint will be waiting for me on the other side of death. Then I hear a sound, muffled and obstructed by water. Is that Clint, calling out to me?

I tilt my head so one ear is just above the surface of the water, and I hear it again. An angry voice saying, "Stand up, you old fool!"

Trying to keep my mouth above the tide, I can only choke out, "Can't. Drowning."

"Oh, for crying out loud!" Andy says as his fist closes around the collar of my shirt, and he hauls me to my feet. Miraculously, my feet find purchase. I'm standing in water up to my shoulders, but I can breathe! I'm not going to drown! "You weren't kidding. You really can't swim. This water's barely deep enough to drown a cat."

"Is it all this shallow?" I ask between huge gulps of air.

"Yeah," he confirms. "Pretty much all the way to the cut."

Hearing that, and knowing now that I won't drown, I set off as quickly as my legs can move through the water, toward the shoreline. I don't make it very far before he grabs my shirt again and drags me back onto the boat.

"You've got some stones, old lady. Jumping in the water when you can't swim. I really wish I didn't have to kill you."

There's only one thing left I can think of to do. "Do you know Molly, the fitness instructor?"

He frowns. "Sure. Why?"

She had told me that people who worked with her in the gym are given respect by all the other active elders at Egret's Loft. Maybe Andy's heard the same myth. With any luck, he believes it. "Because I'm one of her students!" I proudly announce.

He's looking right at me, but I can't read the expression on his face. "Whoopdeedoo!" He finally says. "Is that supposed to mean something to me? What, is she training you to carry home your own shopping bags?"

When he starts to laugh at me, something shifts in my chest. At first, I think I might be having a heart attack. Then I realize, it's not a myocardial infarction…it's anger!

This man almost killed my new best friend, *and* he's treating me like I've lost my edge! Like I'm a harmless active elder! I can't be having that now, can I?

"Not exactly," I say, though he probably can't hear me above the sound of his own laughter.

I put my right hand just below his left armpit, like Molly taught me. Then I turn around, so my back is to him, bend forward at the hip, and flip him right over my shoulder and onto the fiberglass bottom of the boat.

"She trained me to do that, you old windbag!"

Thirty-Six

"I'm about as lost as last year's Easter eggs," Helen says bewildered. "Antonio Rossi is still alive? And he's been killin' all my husbands?"

"I'm sorry, Helen, but yes," I repeat myself for the third time. It's taking a while for the information to sink in with her.

Gina sighs in frustration. I glare at her to keep her mouth shut.

Since the sun set half an hour ago, a good portion of the day's heat has dissipated from the air. I'd been sitting on the back patio with Ritchie, Gina, and Leon, going through the day's events, when Helen came knocking, Jolene and Savannah in tow.

After their initial surprise at finding Gina alive and well, they'd wanted all the details of my harrowing ordeal, relishing in the fact that, when I flipped Andy onto his back on the deck of his own boat, he'd bumped his head on the edge of a bench. Last I heard, he still hasn't regained consciousness.

"This is great news!" Jolene squeezes Helen's arm. "You're not cursed after all. You never have to worry about your husbands bein' murdered from now on!"

"Oh heck no!" Helen exclaims. "No more husbands for me."

"Eight is enough?" Ritchie smirks. He loved watching reruns of that old sitcom when he was younger. I'm guessing he's been waiting for the perfect opportunity to throw in the reference since he found out the tally of Helen's dead husbands.

I kick him under the patio table.

"My marryin' days are done," Helen states, oblivious to Ritchie's pun. "The way I see it, I've been married for twenty-eight years...just not in a row, and to different guys. The *only* man I'd even be tempted to get hitched to in the future is the plastic surgeon that worked on Antonio. That man's an artist! Antonio didn't happen to drop his name, did he, sugar?"

I shake my head, not trusting myself to speak.

"If he ever wakes up, I can ask him," Detective Fletcher's voice comes from behind me. Turning around, I see him standing on the other side of the patio's screen door.

"Please, come join us," I urge him. "Would you like some sweet tea?"

"No, thank you. I...umm...I only have a few minutes." He seems jittery, on edge.

Gina doesn't seem to notice. "I've got a question. What was the deal with Dr. Rosen? If he didn't kill Carl, why did he break into his house to steal that yearbook?"

"Apparently, back when they were in school, Carl and Dr. Rosen played a practical joke on their teacher," Detective Fletcher explains. "Something involving one of the cadavers they were carving up for their anatomy class. A bit of harmless fun, he said. But it startled the teacher, who had a heart attack and died. They were worried they'd get in trouble, so they covered up the prank and prayed no one would find out."

I nod, understanding. "Then Bubbles came along, threatening him about the thing he and Carl swore never to talk about. He had no way of knowing she was clueless about what that secret was."

"Exactly. He said it'd happened so long ago, he didn't even know what she was talking about at first. But when he remembered, he started worrying about the damage it could do to his reputation," Detective Fletcher confirms, glancing at his watch. "He knew the code to Carl's house—they'd been friends for years—so he went in and stole the evidence out from under Bubbles's nose."

Gina laughs. "He must have nearly peed himself when

Mandy caught him in the act and sent Leon chasing after him in his wheelchair!"

I don't even bother to remind her that my name is Madeline. What would be the point? Calling someone the wrong name had nearly gotten her killed, and even that didn't cure her of the problem. What good would me nagging her about it do?

"Are you sure you wouldn't like some tea, detective?" I change the subject.

"I really can't stay. I just came to drop something off." He reaches in the right inside pocket of his jacket and pulls out a jewelry box. Extending his hand, he offers me the box.

Now that the case has been solved, he's finally able to return my hair clip! The one Clint gave me to wear to the policeman's ball. I'm so excited to have my prized possession returned, it doesn't even occur to me that the box seems rather small for a hair clip. I open the box and suck in a deep breath.

"Pete?" I use his first name. "I...really don't know what to say. You're a very nice man, don't get me wrong. But..."

Ritchie leans over beside me, and his eyebrows shoot up when he sees what's inside. "Lady, is there something you haven't been telling me?"

A confused look on his face, Detective Fletcher steps closer to look at the contents of the box. He sees the diamond solitaire ring twinkling under the patio lights. His tanned face floods with embarrassment, and he reaches out and grabs the box back.

"No. Umm. That's the wrong box." He rummages in the inside left pocket of his jacket and takes out another, larger, velvet-covered box. "This is yours. I'm just returning your hair clip. That's all!"

"Hold on now, sugar!" Helen croons. "Is that an *engagement* ring?"

Detective Fletcher turns an even deeper shade of red, and I take pity, asking, "Is the ring intended for the lovely woman in the picture on your desk?"

He nods, a trickle of sweat running down the side of his face. "Her name is Nancy. She's the reason I have to go. We're meeting for dinner."

"Nancy?" Helen sounds like she's tasting the name as she says it. She twists her own wedding ring on her finger. The one Carl gave her on the day he met his end. "You're asking her tonight?"

Detective Fletcher bounces his head up and down. The veins in his neck betray his rapidly beating heart. He doesn't know if she'll say yes. Feeling suddenly maternal toward him, I want to ask him all about her. How did you meet? How long have you been seeing each other? When did you know she was the one? But right now, none of that matters.

Clint asked me to marry him a month after we first met. When it's right, you know.

"She'd be very lucky to have you," is all I say. I'm hoping she says yes.

Gina clears her throat, an uncharacteristically serious expression on her face. "Now the case is solved, we won't be seeing you around as much. I want you to know, I really appreciate all you did for me when I was poisoned," she says. Are those tears in her eyes? "If you don't mind, I think we'd all like to know how it goes for you tonight."

For the first time since he arrived, Detective Fletcher looks relaxed. He's even smiling. A playful smile, like he's about to explain the punchline of a joke we haven't understood. "You bet I will. But I don't know who you think you're kidding. This isn't goodbye. The way things go at this place, something tells me I'll be seeing all of you again very soon."

Those of us seated at the table groan in unison, annoyed that he'd bring up the prospect of another murder at Egret's Loft.

But we're even more annoyed that, deep down, we know he's probably right.

END OF THE DEAD MEN'S WIFE
Egret's Loft Murder Mystery Series
Book 2

Did you enjoy your time at Egret's Loft?

Keep reading for a preview of **Serial Seniors**, the third book in my Egret's Loft Murder Mystery series!

And from the beaches of Florida to the coast of Ireland, continue your cozy mystery adventure with a preview of the first book in my Raven's Wing Murder Mystery series, **Strange Winds.**

Thank You!

If you enjoyed *The Dead Men's Wife*, I'd be incredibly grateful if you could leave a quick review.

Your feedback not only helps other readers discover the book but also supports my work in bringing you more cozy mysteries to enjoy. Reviews make a world of difference for authors, so thank you for considering sharing your thoughts!

Join me on social media for updates and info on new releases!

instagram.com/teharkinsbooks
facebook.com/teharkins.author

Acknowledgments

This book is dedicated to my wonderful mother for always encouraging me to follow my dreams.

I want to begin by thanking all the family members and friends who helped make these books possible—from reading drafts to helping me choose a cover design to giving me suggestions on how to promote this series. But most of all, I appreciate how you encouraged me to pursue my passion for writing. I feel so incredibly lucky to have all of you in my life.

I also want to thank my editor, Shannon Cave, for reading my novels with a critical, yet extremely supportive, eye. I value your input more than you know.

Another person to whom I am extremely grateful is my brilliant cover designer, Joe Montgomery. Before anyone even reads a word of my book, they have to be drawn in by the cover. Thank you so much for helping my books stand out from the crowd.

Finally, as always, my deepest gratitude goes to Steve. You generously put up with me constantly running through plot lines, fretting about deadlines, and pulling out my hair over technical difficulties. Thank you for being so amazing, sweetheart.

SERIAL SENIORS

An Egret's Loft Murder Mystery

T.E. HARKINS

BLURB

One killer podcast...

Following a series of murders months earlier, the elderly residents of Egret's Loft are finally breathing easy again as

First Look: Serial Seniors

they gear up for a community-sponsored family weekend. Madeline Delarouse has been looking forward to spending fun-filled days with her visiting grandchildren going to bouncy castles, petting zoos, and picnics. She never anticipated stumbling upon another dead body...at the bottom of the River Club swimming pool.

Before the coroner can even determine the cause of death, Madeline's kids are plotting to move her out of the luxury retirement community. Madeline, however, has other plans. Alongside her wisecracking best friend, Gina, she decides to wade through the suspect pool herself to catch the killer. But who would have wanted to kill the neighborhood cookie lady? The chef with anger issues? The one-eyed NASA scientist? Or maybe even the overzealous cop?

But as they hunt for the murderer, a cocky podcast reporter thrusts Madeline into the media spotlight—accusing her of all the untimely deaths at Egret's Loft. Can Madeline get to the truth before the court of public opinion finds her guilty of being a serial-killing senior?

Grab your copy of *Serial Seniors (Book 3 of the Egret's Loft Murder Mystery Series)* today!

First Look: Serial Seniors

EXCERPT

CHAPTER 1

Deep breath in. Deep breath out.

The English muffin I had for breakfast sits like a bowling ball in my stomach. It seems to sway from side to side as my grandson and I walk, hands entwined, across the parking lot to the River Club. Equal parts excitement and terror war against each other inside me, and I can't help but reconsider this foolish plan to tackle my deepest fears head on.

"It follows sound logic, though—" my grandson, Curt, lets go of my hand briefly to scratch the tip of his nose, "—that mechanical factors should be assessed in order to determine the best use of positive fluid dynamics through the water."

"Of course, dear," I say, digging through the contents of my oversized beach bag. "Did we put your arm floaties in your bag?"

"Yes, Grandmother." Curt nods his little blond head. "I ran through a full checklist of necessary items before we left the house."

Curt is six years old, but he has an IQ of 185. He is adorable and brilliant and curious.

He's also afraid of his own shadow, spiders, large bodies

of water, and everything else that falls outside his cerebral comfort zone. So, when the daughter of one of my neighbors offered to give Curt swimming lessons, I thought his answer would be a resounding, *no, thank you.*

To my surprise, he'd agreed. But to make matters worse, he'd convinced me to take the lessons with him. At the end of last year, I'd nearly succumbed to my worst fear—drowning—in an attempt to avoid being murdered by a psychopathic serial killer. I survived, but now Curt has convinced me that, at nearly seventy years old, it's high time I learned how to swim.

Which is why, on this warm and sunny February morning, we're headed to the swimming pool at Egret's Loft, the upscale West Florida retirement community I moved into several months ago.

Curt had insisted on applying waterproof SPF 50 sunblock before we left my house, so there is nothing to do once we reach the sun loungers except set down our bags and stare, terrified, into the achingly blue, chlorinated abyss.

Out of the corner of my eye, I spot Curt rummaging around in his Iron Man backpack. I turn my head in time to see him snapping on a pair of too-large rubber gloves and pulling what looks like a remote control out of his bag.

"What do you have there?" I ask.

Curt's eyes sparkle as he retrieves a blister pack from

the front compartment of his bag. "This is a pool water photometer. By dipping it into the water and using the receptacle located at the front of the device to dissolve the various reagent tablets, I can accurately ascertain the levels of chlorine, bromine, and cyanuric acid in the pool water. It also measures pH and alkalinity, but those are somewhat superfluous, as I already have test strips that serve the same purpose."

Another thing that terrifies Curt is allowing anything dirty to touch his skin.

"Did your father buy you that?" I wonder aloud.

Curt shuffles his feet and stares down at the ground. "Yes."

I frown. "Did your father *know* he was buying you that?"

"Technically, no," Curt admits. "But if he didn't want me to use his Amazon account, then he should seriously consider making his passwords more of a challenge!"

"Curt—" I begin, but my grandson is spared my lecture by the arrival of Savannah Jeffers.

"I'm so sorry I'm late!" The beautiful twenty-two-year-old sets down the large piece of foam she's been carrying and swipes a lock of fiery red hair out of her green eyes. "The roads out there are busier than a moth in a mitten!"

"You're not late," I assure her, though technically she is. Knowing she has a tendency to show up tardy for everything, I purposefully didn't arrive on time either. "But, yes, the place has been packed since I got back from spending the holidays in DC. I've never seen so many golf carts!"

"Me neither! Back home in Alabama, folks like to drink a can of Bud after each hole," Savannah says in a soft, melodic Southern drawl. "Country clubs wound up having to ban golf carts, on account of too many folks driving 'em drunk. So, you don't see 'em around too often."

The color on Savannah's cheeks deepens after what is, for her, a lengthy monologue, and her eyes shift to the ground. Shy around most people, Savannah has been warming up to me slightly in recent days. But Curt, whose intelligence and mannerisms tend to put most people off, really brings Savannah out of her shell.

"Hey, little man," she calls out to my grandson, a smile gracing her naturally ruby lips. "You ready to swim?"

"Good morning, Savannah." From his perch at the side of the pool, Curt nods his head in the young woman's direction. "All the chemical levels appear to be acceptable, and, at eighty degrees, the water temperature is within recommended guidelines. So, yes. I suppose I am prepared to follow through with our lesson."

"Excellent!" she exclaims, pulling her sundress off over her thin frame to reveal a one-piece bathing suit underneath. "We're off like a herd of turtles! Everyone into the pool."

"Oh, no!" Curt and I cry out in unison. He looks to me to lead the opposition.

I oblige. "We're not ready just yet. We have to put on our arm floaties and—"

"Oh, you don't need floaties, Miss Madeline. I brought you this here kickboard to use." She holds up the large piece of foam, smiling. "You know, just until you're comfortable."

"Thank you. That's very kind." I return her smile. "But I still have to put on my swim cap. And Curt needs his goggles..."

"If I didn't know better, I'd think the two of you were tryin' to stall." Her emerald eyes narrow as she accurately assesses the situation. "How about I do a few laps while you settle yourselves? Five minutes?"

Suddenly wishing I was still home in bed, all I can do is nod my head.

A rush of blood temporarily deafens me, and my fingers shake as I tuck my shoulder-length, whitish-blond hair inside the plastic swim cap my son, Ritchie, purchased for me online. My lungs have also joined in on the bodily rebellion, curtailing my efforts to blow up Curt's inflatable Batman arm floats.

"The psi is still not optimal, Grandmother," Curt repeatedly tells me. It's his version of Goldilocks, with me unable to find the pressure per square inch that's *just* right. We're both stalling. And we both know it.

Finally, we can no longer postpone the inevitable.

With Curt clutching my finger so tightly it feels like my pinky finger might snap, we plant our feet on the first step of the pool, and I feel the water rise to my ankles. Savannah glides effortlessly through the pool to join us.

"I was thinkin' we could start with a game," she says. "What do you think?"

"Will it be in shallow water, so we can stand up if we need to?" I ask, while Curt simultaneously demands to know, "Is there a prize for whoever wins?"

Savannah giggles. "Yes, you'll be able to stand up. No, little man, I don't have any prizes for the winner. *But* you would walk away with braggin' rights."

Curt looks at me, then back at Savannah. "I suppose that will be sufficient."

"Great! The game is called red light, green light," Savannah explains. "You'll float on your bellies. Don't worry none, I'll get you into position. Then when I say, 'green light,' you start kickin' your legs like a sprayed cockroach. When I say, 'red light,' you stop. We'll keep on doin' it until we get to the other side of the pool. Got it?"

"The rules seem rather simplistic," Curt complains.

"Well, maybe they are. That doesn't mean it won't be fun!" Savannah picks up Curt and pulls him deeper into the water. "Miss Madeline, you grab the kickboard there, hold onto it in front of you, and then just kind of fall onto it."

Holding Curt under the armpits and keeping an eye on me, Savannah calls out, "Green light!"

Curt bites down on his lower lip, as he and I frantically begin kicking our legs.

Before long, the pool deck is thoroughly soaked, and our earlier fears are, at least partially, forgotten. Our laughter even draws out an Egret's Loft staff member, keen to capture our enjoyment on her cell phone's camera. The attractive young woman, who I would guess is roughly the same age as Savannah, has long black hair, parted down the middle and large, black-framed glasses that swallow a good third of her thin, alabaster face.

"Hey, Sydney!" Savannah calls out to the woman. "Are we disturbin' you?"

Sydney smiles. "Not at all! Just keep doing what you're doing. This is perfect for TikTok!"

"Tick, tock?" Curt looks up at Savannah, his small body tense during the red light. "Is this a timed competition?"

Savannah laughs softly. "No, little man. TikTok. It's a social media thing. People put up videos, and other people watch 'em."

For all his intelligence, Curt seems as oblivious about social media as I am. The thought brings me comfort until something else occurs to me.

"Oh no! Other people will be able to see me in my bathing suit?" I start to panic. While I have managed to retain my slender figure into my advanced years, I don't relish the thought of anyone seeing the way the skin on my arms and legs has begun to crepe. "Who would want to watch *us*?"

"Anyone interested in moving here!" Sydney chimes in. "We haven't met. I'm Sydney Walsh. I do PR for Egret's Loft."

"It's nice to meet you. I'm Madeline Delarouse. Are you new here?" I ask, wondering why I haven't seen her around before now. Having worked in marketing myself before retiring, I would have thought that having three people murdered in the community a few months ago would have been a bit of a public relations nightmare. Then again, a bunch of dead residents probably wouldn't be the kind of relations the community would want to make public.

"No, I've been here about a year," she explains. "But I took some time off in November to do some traveling. When did you move in?"

I nod. "That's why we haven't met before. I moved here in November, and I've been out of town, with family, for a few months over the holidays."

"Green light!" Savannah interrupts us by announcing.

Curt and I flail our legs for all we're worth. I can hear my little grandson roaring with laughter, and any tension I'd felt from my aquaphobia melts away.

My children and grandchildren will all be in town tomorrow for a special family weekend hosted by the staff

First Look: Serial Seniors

at Egret's Loft. It feels like the perfect opportunity to relax, kick back, and put murder out of our minds.

I couldn't possibly know, as Curt and I frolicked in the swimming pool, that, by this time tomorrow, another one of my new neighbors would be dead.

Grab your copy of *Serial Seniors (Book 3 of the Egret's Loft Murder Mystery Series)* today!

STRANGE WINDS

A RAVEN'S WING IRISH MURDER MYSTERY

T.E. HARKINS

BLURB

Find Audrey Murphy. She'll know what to do.

Those were my mama's final words to me. A cryptic message that led me from the beaches of Florida to a quaint, coastal village in the south of Ireland. All to track down a woman I've never heard of who, supposedly, has answers to questions I never even knew I had.

But as I sit outside the crumbling ruins of an ancient castle, working up the courage to go to Audrey's house, I see something. Or at least, I think I do. Out of the mist, a woman dressed in white materializes. She seems to need my help. Then, as quickly as she appeared, she vanishes. Like a ghost. Maybe my grief-stricken mind was just playing tricks on me.

Or maybe not...

Before long, the little village is buzzing with news of a brutal murder. And, as the only witness to the crime, I find myself squarely in the killer's crosshairs. Which means I'll have to get to the truth of what happened...or the next obituary in the local paper could just be my own.

Grab your copy of *Strange Winds (Book 1 of the Raven's Wing Irish Murder Mystery Series)* today!

EXCERPT

CHAPTER 1

Also By: Strange Winds

Why are you here?

The thought repeats over and over in my head. The last time I felt so trapped in a mental loop was when I heard Wham! on the radio a few months ago at Christmas. You can't go through a holiday season without hearing George Michael singing about how someone broke his heart at least a hundred times. The resulting earworm had eaten away at my brain well into the new year.

And now, sitting here in my rental car, late on a soggy March afternoon, staring at the crumbling ruins of an ancient Irish castle, my head is humming away. "Why are you here?" echoing to the beat of "You gave it away."

My journey began with a brief letter my mama left for me when she died. As a former US Marshal, hiding witnesses from violent felons, my mama must have thought about dying a lot. Otherwise, she wouldn't have left me a cryptic message about what I should do if she was no longer around:

If you're reading this, it means I'm dead. Find a woman named Audrey Murphy in the south of Ireland. She should still live somewhere in County Cork. She'll know what to do.

Those were the final words my mama left her only daughter. Not *I love you*. Not *I'll finally answer all the questions that I ignored, like who's your father*. Just instructions to travel from our new home in Florida to a country I know nothing about to seek out a woman I've never heard of.

As has been the case every few minutes since I lost her, I really wish I could talk to my mama.

To honor her wishes, and with the help of one of her friends, a kind and razor-sharp widow named Madeline Delarouse, I'd managed to track Audrey Murphy to a small village called Ballygoseir. She lives only a few miles from where I sit in front of this moss-ravaged castle on a cliff. The vacant eye of a steadfast stone window frame stares back at me like a bad omen.

Mist rolls in from the sea, thick and mysterious. As it wafts over the car, it leaves behind tiny liquid fingerprints on the windshield, making everything outside the warmth of my rented Ford Fiesta shift further out of focus.

Knowing I can't sit here all day, I'm mentally preparing to drive away, when out of the swirling, dense nothingness, a woman emerges. With translucent skin, golden hair the color of cornsilk, and clothed in a white gown, everything about the woman seems muted, ethereal. Her floor-length, chiffon-like dress seems to undulate, a combination of fabric and wind impersonating the waves of the ocean.

My heart beats faster, and my hand hovers over the rental car's gear shift.

The strange and unearthly woman seems to be heading straight for me. Her mouth opens in a terrible, ear-splitting scream.

Before I can decide whether to jump out and help her or speed away from the ghostly sight, the woman comes to an abrupt halt. Her fingers seem to pluck at imaginary strings in the air, reaching for something that only she can see. It's as if she's coaxing me to do something, though I don't know what she wants or needs.

Then, in the shake of a dog's tail, she vanishes.

Replaying the scene in my head, seconds later, I can't quite figure out whether she dissolved into the thick fog now devouring the castle ruins, or if she was yanked back by an unseen force, almost as if an invisible rope around her waist dragged her back into whatever nightmare she'd been trying to escape.

I don't know which scenario seems worse.

Shaking my head to reorder my thoughts, I try to convince myself I'd only been daydreaming. My mama always said I had a vivid imagination. That's why I'd gone into creative writing at the University of Alabama. And so, remaining inside the safety of my rental car, I persuade myself that the whole scenario was just a trick of the light at dusk, a long way from home. It's the atmosphere, nothing more, I tell myself.

I can't escape the overwhelming, if fanciful, feeling I'd been experiencing since the moment I'd left the airport in my rearview mirror—that this place has a kind of knowing. Driving down windy and narrow roads, with speed limits that border on the suicidal, past crumbling buildings and stone Celtic crosses, I carried with me the romantic notion that the land is carrying stories in its soil, with the present and the past locked in a struggle for dominance.

Was the woman really there? Or was she an echo reverberating across time to settle some long-forgotten score?

You need to pull yourself together, Savannah. I attempt to shake some sense into myself. *If the woman was real, she might need your help.*

Before giving myself the time to think better of it, I throw open the driver's side door and step out onto the gravel road. A thick blanketing of mossy weeds makes the ground slippery. Moisture seeps through the thin fabric of my Vans sneakers, sending shivers down the length of my arms.

"Hello?" I call out. "Is anybody out there?"

At first, the only response comes from the ocean, its thunderous waves crashing against the jagged stone of the cliff. I'm about to climb back into my car when I hear it. Loud and feral, the unseen woman howls a single word.

"*Help!*"

Grab your copy of *Strange Winds* (Book *1* of the Raven's Wing Irish Murder Mystery Series) today!